An Evening With W. O. Mitchell

❧

An Evening With
W. O. Mitchell

A Collection of the Author's Best-Loved Performance Pieces

SELECTED AND EDITED BY
BARBARA AND ORMOND MITCHELL

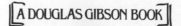

Canadian Cataloguing in Publication Data

Mitchell, W. O. (William Ormond), 1914 –
   An evening with W. O. Mitchell

ISBN 0-7710-6088-2

I. Title.

PS 8526.I9765E93   1997   C813'.54   C97-930190-4
PR9199.3.M54E93   1997

Typesetting by M&S, Toronto
Printed and bound in Canada

The events and characters in these stories are fictional. Any resemblance to actual persons or happenings is coincidental.

The publishers acknowledge the support of the Canada Council and the Ontario Arts Council for their publishing program.

A Douglas Gibson Book

McClelland & Stewart Inc.
The Canadian Publishers
481 University Avenue
Toronto, Ontario
M5G 2E9

1 2 3 4 5   01 00 99 98 97

*Thanks to my creative partners, Barbara Mitchell and
Ormond Skinner Mitchell. Also to my father, O. S.,
who died when I was seven and who was a
turn-of-the-century stand-up comedian.
I owe them all.*

O. S. Mitchell, 1898

Acknowledgements

Text credits: Chapter 31, "The Poetry of Life," appears courtesy of The Writers' Development Trust.

The material in Chapters 5, 7, 13, 20, 23, 24, 28 and 29, all attributed to the books in which they appeared in the individual chapter introductions, is reprinted by permission of Macmillan Canada.

Photo credits: pp. v, 1, 17, The Mitchell Family; 11, University of Calgary Special Collection; 28, 44, 56, 80, 92, 104, 117, 123, 126, 133, 157, 178, 194, 238, 261, Glenbow Archives (NA-2864-39504); 35, 73, 144, 182, 200, 224, 248, Peter Paterson; 51, 139, *The Windsor Star*; 86, 170, Michael Cullen; 205, The Banff Centre; 219, J. Coleman Fletcher; 252, *The Globe and Mail*, Toronto.

Contents

Preface ix

1. The Day I Spoke for Mister Lincoln 1
2. How to Fail at Public Speaking 11
3. Melvin Arbuckle's First Course in
   Shock Therapy 17
4. The Day I Sold Lingerie in a
   Prairie Whore House 28
5. Old Kacky and the Vanishing Point 35
6. Saint Sammy's Creation of the World 44
7. Jake Invents the Jumping Pound 51
8. Love's Wild Magic 56
9. Brian's Skates 73
10. Take One Giant Step 80
11. Of Tar Paper, Shiplap, and
    Shingles Made 86
12. The Shocking Truth About the
    Undefended Border 92
13. Take Me to Your Cannibal Chief 104
14. Hang Your Mink on a Hickory Limb 117
15. The Day I Caught Syphilis 123

16. Grandmother MacMurray   126

17. See the Pattern Forming   133

18. Interlude at La Guardia   139

19. The Napoleon Threat   144

20. Whites Herd Better   157

21. Santa Comes to Shelby   170

22. How Do Rabbits Get Started?   178

23. Aunt Pearl   182

24. Body Language   194

25. Stopping Smoking   200

26. Willie's Contract with Old Cloutie   205

27. Dear Mr. Manning . . .   219

28. King Motherwell   224

29. Never Settle for Anything Less   238

30. The Wind Wings On   248

31. "The Poetry of Life"   252

Preface

The art experience is not private; it is a bridging, or at least the illusion of bridging, between two creative partners, the artist and his audience. If the artist has found fragments from his past life, and then built from them an illusion in which every single bit is the truth, and the whole thing is a more dramatic, more meaningful lie, there will be triggered off for his partner explosions of recognition, which the reader mistakenly attributes solely to the artist. Actually, the recognition belongs to both of them, and the reader's contribution comes out of his own subconscious notebook during the art experience. It is quite possibly the most intimate relationship between two humans, barring none.

And yet, writing is an intensely private and lonely act. Writing is like playing a dart game with the lights out so that the writer has no way of knowing whether his darts are coming anywhere near the bull's-eye or are missing the board entirely. This is a cruel analogy, a nightmare which most writers, beginning or experienced, must relive over and over. For the writer, the lights come on long after his darts have been thrown. Even though his readers and reviewers may indicate that he has scored, the next time the writer plays the game he will again be alone and in the dark.

Early on I was lucky enough to find two creative partners who helped dilute that lonely darkness for me, who acted as caring, honest, and perceptive sounding-boards for draft after draft of my stories – Professor F. M. Salter, for the six years I spent writing *Who Has Seen the Wind*, and my wife, Merna, for almost everything I have ever written. *Almost* everything, for on occasion she refused to be "verbally flogged" by yet another draft of a scene.

Then, later on in my career, I discovered another way to help dilute the writer's darkness – reading performances. My one-man shows over the years have given me what all stage performers love – the immediate thrust of a live audience as it responds to story magic. Here, on stage, is no *illusion* of bridging between story-teller and audience. And I know immediately when the darts hit the centre, when we are really flying together.

The pieces in this anthology have formed the heart of my reading performances over the past thirty-five years. Some of them are in the tradition of the oral performance pieces performed on the reading circuit by Mark Twain, Bret Harte, and Stephen Leacock. Others are episodes selected from my fiction. I hope they give as much enjoyment in the reading as they have given me in their telling.

W. O. Mitchell
Calgary, Alberta
December 1996

1

The Day I Spoke for Mister Lincoln

"The Day I Spoke for Mister Lincoln" describes W. O.'s first major public performance as an "elocutionist" on May 30, 1930. He was sixteen years old, roughly the same age as he is shown here. This is one of seven pieces, based on childhood memories and written in the early 1960s, that launched his career as a performer and became the backbone of his reading repertoire over the next thirty-odd years. At the time W. O. described these pieces as "not fiction, but . . . also not exactly fact." Some of them, such as "Melvin Arbuckle's First Course in Shock Therapy," are reminiscential tall tales. Others, such as "Take One Giant Step" and "Of Tar Paper, Shiplap, and Shingles Made," are closer to the kind of nostalgic childhood memory pieces perfected by Dylan Thomas in "A Child's Christmas in Wales" and "A Visit to Grandpa's."

W. O.'s readings are dramatic performances – both aurally and visually. His shock of white hair, brown snuff-dusted moustache (and shirt *front), gravelly voice and ad libs have become trademarks of his story telling. He brings the house down with a well-timed pause, a grin, or a raised eyebrow. Over the years his snuff box and reading glasses have become stage props. His glasses, usually damaged and held together at the hinge or bridge with white adhesive tape, sometimes take on a perverse life of their own and refuse to behave. In the middle of a reading at the Banff Centre they clattered onto the lectern and bounced to the floor. As he retrieved them he explained, "I left my glasses in Prince Edward Island. This is my spare and one arm is gone. I get them at Woolworths. I get six at a time because I drop glasses all over North America."*

In "The Day I Spoke for Mister Lincoln," when describing Miss Finch's elocution lessons, he gives a seemingly impromptu performance of "The Fool." He pauses, looks up at his audience over his glasses and, holding up his original copy of "The Fool" given him in 1930, says, "Well, look – here's 'The Fool.' And here's Billy Mitchell performing it." He then steps aside from the podium and microphone and punches out "The Fool" in classic elocution style using the various facial and hand gestures he had been taught by Miss Finch.

"The Day I Spoke for Mister Lincoln" was first published in the Imperial Oil Review *(June 1962), and it was later worked into the novel* Ladybug, Ladybug . . . *(1988).*

Each year now for over thirty years, whenever Dominion Day rolls around, I am pulled by an inner current of old guilt. I am not too sure that I did not commit treason against Canada, my native land, on Decoration Day in Williams Park in St. Petersburg, Florida, three decades ago.

That was the year I studied to become an elocutionist – every Saturday morning. Had it been *every* day of the week, it would not have lasted. I know now that I have never had the flaming stubbornness necessary to the defence of Moscow and to becoming an elocutionist.

The first of three winters we were in St. Petersburg, my mother, without benefit of Mendelian Law, decided that musical and recitative talents were sex-linked characteristics. My grandfather on my father's side had been tone-deaf. My father, who had died when I was seven, was tone-deaf. I too was an evident monotone. But embedded in the pastor's elegy given at my grandfather's funeral in East Flamborough County, Ontario, September 18, 1906, was: "Some of the finer selections from the poets took on new meaning under his recitation." Add to this that my father was an elocutionist; that Mother believed both disasters and happy events came in threes; the inescapable corollary, then, was that I was elocutionally gifted.

I did put up some sort of resistance, but it was not proof against a scrapbook of my father's, filled with recital announcements: "Lawn Social at the Manse, Christie"; "A Peach Festival Under the Auspices of the Ladies' Aid of Balmoral Church"; "Young Men's Literary Society of Dundas Street Concert"; "Gore Street Methodist Church Social and Concert under the auspices of the Epworth League of Christian Endeavour." Nor could I deny that the *Dundas Banner* had said, "His humour is clean, wholesome, and refreshing," though it did occur to me that under such auspices there could hardly be any other kind of public humour in the first decade of the century. "He is an elocutionist of rare ability," the *Perth Expositor* said, "His splendid voice and attractive stage presence at once command your attention." I argued that this was hardly fair, for at thirteen I was a horn-rimmed spectacled wishbone of a child with the stage presence of an introverted chameleon.

My mother was not faint-hearted. She turned the scrapbook pages listing my father's recitations: "Caleb's Courtship and What Come of It," "Trouble in the Choir," "The Flag," "The Heelin' Man's Prayer," "Never Forget the Dear Ones," "The Romance of a Hammock," "When Father Rode the Goat," and, of course, "Casey at the Bat." Then she closed up the scrapbook and enrolled me in Madame Brocklebank's School of Dance, Drama, Music, and Elocution.

Against my will each Saturday morning I roller-skated to Madame Brocklebank's; fifteen blocks of cathartic grind and crack-clinks under the shrill lace of pepper trees, past the stubbed trunks of palms with funeral-wreath fronds, the arterial red of poinsettias, shoving on the skates with anger and indignation and rage. At ten blocks' distance I could hear Noreen Symington's cornet; at two blocks, some piano student protesting "The Robin's Return." The doors and windows of Madame Brocklebank's were always open – for advertising purposes, I think. In front of the school itself, you could generally hear "Tiptoe Through the Tulips," which seemed to be the only piece the school's tap-dancing students could tap-dance to – once they had conquered "East Side, West Side," that is. Within was artistic anarchy and my current notion of merry hell. In each of the cribs off a long hallway that went through and then out the back, a woman was closeted with a client. My assignation each Saturday was with a Miss Dora Finch, who waited for me in a doll's house under a pecan tree at the back.

Miss Finch came from Birmingham and anticipated Tennessee Williams by some twenty years. I suspect now that she was tuberculous, for she had the most lovely complexion I have ever known, transparent ivory and rose. Her features were beautifully chiselled and her profile reminded me of Queen Nefertiti in our Ancient History book. She moved as though wading through a lagoon and the illusion was heightened by the gauzy gown she wore. She did not get up from a chair; she bloomed from it. She did not sit down; she sank with all the grace of drifting dandelion down. She was my idea of a very spiritual woman – about 99 per cent spirit and one per cent flesh; as opposed to Madame Brocklebank, an ample woman with monocotyledonous bosom, who was about 99 per cent flesh, and one per cent spirit.

I was allowed one hour under Miss Finch each Saturday morning, during which she gave me gestures and facial expressions and postures to go with such pieces as "The Fool": ". . . look from the window . . . all you see was to be his one day – forest and furrow – lawn and lea.

And he goes and chucks them away . . . chucks them away to die in the dark . . . somebody saw him fall . . . part of him mud . . . part of him blood . . . the rest of him . . ." (LONG LONG PAUSE – PUT OUT LEFT HAND IN THE SPURNING GESTURE AND CLOSE EYES IN THE PAIN-TOO-GREAT-TO-BEAR-EXPRESSION – LOWER VOICE BUT DON'T FORGET THE CHEST CHAMBERS) ". . . not at all!"

When we were through I would leave her, passing the next one coming in to her, just as I had earlier passed the previous one coming out from her. Madame Brocklebank would be waiting for me, and just before I strapped on my skates I would give her the $2.00 charge. I have wondered in later years if the women who worked for her were not possibly the culls of white slavers.

After eight weeks of this I qualified for one of the twice-monthly recitals held at the School. These were incestuous affairs attended only by parents and close relatives of the students. Madame herself was the star artist: she came out at the beginning and reported on the progress of the school; again and again she lowered an introductory gangplank for each performer. And now we come to Noreen Symington.

I disliked and distrusted her as you would any girl who played the cornet, had you by two inches, and was built blockily enough that you suspected she could put you down, quite easily. At my first concert and every other school concert, she played the same selection, "The Eagle and the Rabbit." Madame Brocklebank would explain that the piece about to be played by Noreen Symington depicted ". . . the little rabbit startled from cover and going lipperty-lipperty-lip over the meadow. Then high in the cloudless blue, an eagle wheels and hangs and soars effortlessly. Far, far below he spies the rabbit and down he plummets, pounces on the rabbit, clutches it in his talons and bears the furry creature struggling helplessly – aloft – higher and higher in ever decreasing concentric circles . . . until he disappears . . ." Madame Brocklebank never did pursue that eagle to its logical destination.

Noreen then would march squatly, cornet mouth resting on her hip, to the centre of the stage. There she would stop and come about. You could hear the first inhale clear to Jacksonville as she raised the cornet to seat it on her mouth. This inflated her to almost double her already adequate size; her cheeks distended like two balloon fish attacked by enemies. I knew then and I know now that a woman playing a cornet is the most astonishing thing to be witnessed in the known world. A woman playing a harp is honestly funny too, but not incredibly so like a woman playing a cornet – or spitting.

My mother was not too impressed with these concerts. In her opinion I had been expensively loaded and it was time to truly discharge me publicly. This she did at the Canadian Club: "Giuseppe Goes to the Baseball Game"; The Shrine Club: "A Negro's Prayer"; and Captain Holly's Boys' Sunshine Club program to raise funds. The latter was my first outdoor concert, held on the Million Dollar Pier. I found myself in staggering competition with a seven-year-old boy, Palm Beach Tippy, who dived unfairly from a fifty-foot tower into gasoline ignited on Boca Ciega Bay. After all that "The Bald-Headed Man and the Boy and the Fly" could come only as an anti-climax.

By this time I recited in what I had come to consider my elocution suit – a double-breasted blue serge coat and cream flannel pants. And it was shortly after the Sunshine Club engagement that Miss Finch told me Noreen and I had been selected to take part in the Decoration Day program in Williams Park. I was to deliver Lincoln's Gettysburg Address and we had only a month to work on it.

Almost two weeks went by before I truly appreciated the enormity of what I was practising for. Before accepting the honour I should have remembered that I was a Canadian, owing allegiance to the King, the Beaver, and the Maple Leaf. How I had overlooked it, I do not know, for every time I turned around I knew I was amid alien corn. These people said "zee" for "zed," divan for chesterfield, napkin for serviette. They accused Canadians of saying "hoose, moose, and loose" for "house, mouse, and louse," denied our smashing victory in the War of 1812, insisted they had won the First World War. They celebrated Thanksgiving on the wrong day and in the wrong month. Their picture shows stayed open on Sundays, and the backs of their church pews were stocked with fans for fanning themselves sacrilegiously during the Scripture reading and the sermon.

My patriotic conscience ached for almost a week. Then I took it up with my mother. It was perfectly all right, she said. I said that Abraham Lincoln was not to my knowledge one of the Fathers of Canadian Federation. She had not heard me practising at all, she said, and if I really wanted to disgrace my country, I could get up there in front of a lot of Americans and make a botch of it, and that was just what would happen if I didn't hurry up and memorize the Gettysburg Address.

This exchange was only partly reassuring, for I knew that my mother, ordinarily incorruptible, would turn back at nothing to prove that one of four sons of her dead husband was an elocutionist.

I was still truly disturbed and put off memorizing another week, thus disappointing but not surprising Miss Finch, who gave me three more facial expressions and seven new gestures and told me to skate home and practise them before the mirror and memorize the speech by next Wednesday so I wouldn't let Madame Brocklebank's School of Drama, Dance, Music, and Elocution down. I wasn't too worried about the School. Canada was another matter.

During a Solid Geometry class the next Tuesday I hit upon a solution that would satisfy all allegiances. I spent the entire evening memorizing Lincoln's Gettysburg Address – but with thirty-nine very slight changes. Wherever Mr. Lincoln had said "we" or "us" or "our," I changed it to "you" or "your" so that the opening sentence started out: "Four score and seven years ago *your* forefathers brought forth . . ." And my adapted ending became: "With malice towards none, with chivalry for all, it is for *you* to resolve that this nation, under God . . ."

But I did not try it on my mother, let alone Miss Finch, for by the next morning, I knew that it would never do.

On Decoration Day afternoon, the Williams Park band shell was frighteningly crowded: one Tallahassee Senator who was to be master of ceremonies, forty-nine Daughters of the American Revolution, Mr. Sousa and all his band, Madame Schumann-Heink (who was combining a visit to St. Petersburg with her last concert appearance that night at the Congregational Church), Noreen Symington (who would of course play "The Eagle and the Rabbit" on her cornet), Babe Ruth (who would do nothing except be Babe Ruth and that would be the greatest contribution made on that stage that day).

I have left out one celebrity; he sat between me and Noreen, a turtle-old Confederate Civil War veteran, his field uniform faded grey, his forage cap tipped forward on his head. He was surrounded by a bitter aura of mothballs, but as well he smelled of ripe figs. It took me a moment to figure that out; then I saw the morning-glory mouth of a magnificent spittoon between his right foot and my left one. The Decoration Day Committee had considerately placed it there for him, and he needed it, though it was not doing him or the stage floor much good. The palsy, which jigged his feet and jumped his knees and trembled his hands and rippled through his shoulders, jerked his head with such crack-the-whip violence that it ruined his aim. I was, of course, wearing my cream flannel elocution pants.

I can remember Madame Schumann-Heink and Mr. Sousa doing the "Star-Spangled Banner" rather well together, but I recall little else except Noreen Symington and her hysterical trumpet. For the very first time I could accept that grunting, kicking rabbit that was being borne aloft in the eagle's triumphant talons. I also discovered that the palsy of the old man beside me was very highly contagious.

Noreen finished, bowed, knocked the saliva from her cornet mouth-piece, turned and marched back to her place. I saw then that the Senator was looking over to me and nodding. He was smiling, too, with the polite and pitying smile of one inviting another to step out onto a tight rope stretched over Niagara Falls. I deliberately pulled myself together, tightening chest and shoulder muscles to still the tremors, reminded myself of Noreen's nerveless approach to public performance, rose smartly and stepped firmly into the Confederate War veteran's spittoon.

To get a spittoon off your foot, you cannot tip your toe forward as a ballet dancer would, for doing so thrusts out your heel so that it hooks up under the flange of the spittoon collar. Turning *up* the toe stops the spittoon from coming off the other way.

This was established in a whispered conference with the Senator, who asked me if I didn't wish to forgo my part in the program. I was tempted to, but I said no, I guessed I'd just wear the Confederate spittoon and do Lincoln's Gettysburg Address the way my mother had promised I would. To this end I anvil-chorused my way to the front of the band shell.

The green benches were empty all over town and the shuffleboard courts deserted that day. Everyone white had been issued a fan as he came into Williams Park. The entire park had palsy now; the impatient breath of thousands of fans set every leaf on banyan and mango trees a-dance, stirred and trembled the hanging tendrils of Spanish moss. Also I had forgotten Lincoln's Gettysburg Address just as my mother and Miss Finch had predicted I would.

I managed the opening paragraph but from there on I left Mr. Lincoln, or he left me. I kept right on by myself, however, ad-libbing in a Lincolnesque way, then caught up to him and solid land for the last paragraph: ". . . shall have a new birth of freedom; and that government of the people, by the people, for the people, shall not perish from the earth."

The fans stopped; leaves and Spanish moss were stilled; then every Northerner in Williams Park, in or out of a wheelchair, cut loose with applause that would have made Palm Beach Tippy and his death-defying dive into flaming gasoline look like a piker.

After I had unlaced my shoe and my mother had helped me free my foot from the spittoon, she said she was very proud of me and my father if he were here today would have been proud of me too. I realized then that she thought I had delivered Lincoln's Gettysburg Address, and I did not disillusion her. I said that I still did not feel it had been right for a Canadian to have done the thing and she said she guessed that it was, for Lincoln belonged to the whole world.

She may not have known her Gettysburg Address, but she did know her Lincoln. In his time he had been a pretty fair elocutionist, too.

2

⚜

How to Fail at Public Speaking

In the late 1950s and early 1960s W. O.'s reputation as an "elocutionist" rapidly grew. Indeed, his fees from his reading performances became a substantial part of his free-lance writing income. While he has always loved to perform his stories for audiences, he at times encountered attitudes and behaviour on the reading circuit which were not endearing – particularly early on when he spoke mainly to local clubs and business associations. "How to Fail at Public Speaking" grew out of some of these experiences. It has been reported that, on one of these occasions, the master of ceremonies introduced him shortly before midnight and W. O. gave the shortest reading ever in his career: "I have now been waiting two hours to give my address to you . . . [LONG, LONG PAUSE – SCAN THE AUDIENCE WITH OVER-THE-TOP-OF-READING-GLASSES GLARE] . . . It is Box 519, High River, Alberta, and I am going there right now."

⊷⊶

Perhaps it was a good thing my mother thought that recitative talent was a sex-linked characteristic and sent me off each Saturday morning to study elocution under Miss Finch. Chance, and an undisciplined, even lazy nature have conspired to make me a writer. And writers, a rather limited segment of our society, seem to be the nation's greatest source of banquet speakers, both for luncheon clubs and for conventions.

The convention is a North American phenomenon – district conventions, Provincial conventions, Dominion, International, everyone has conventions: florists and librarians, meat packers and doctors and veterinarians and pathologists and sanitary engineers. All gather together annually for a convention – druggists and motel owners, teachers and licensed embalmers. Migratory birds do this in spring and in fall, but they don't select one of themselves to address the assembled throng. Just humans do this – I believe.

I'm not thinking so much of the esoteric professional address, delivered by a specialist to all his convention-gathered fellow specialists. Little can be said one way or another about this sort of address. If you're a pathologist asked to speak to an audience of bacteriologists, physiologists, pharmacologists and biochemists, there's no difficulty at all. You get up after the sauterne and Sussex game hen to speak about "Graft Versus Host Reaction in Immunologically Competent Recipients of Allogenic Spleen Cells" – perhaps – or even "The Apparent Intensification of the Xanthine Oxidase Activity of Rat Liver Homogenates by Aging – at 4 °C." This is a traditional and well defined and rigid area. But it is on its way out. The feeling that has been growing is that by the time of the banquet, the convention is over and now is the time to bring on the jesters and the minstrels, the tumblers and sword-swallowers.

Actual professional entertainers are now being used at these banquets, generally after all the business and the introduction of the head-table guests and the new officers for the coming year – after these and before the speaker himself. Like the stand-up comedian and knife-throwing act that preceded me at the Western Meat Packers' Convention for 1960. It's a form of insurance really, a sort of hedge in case the speaker isn't any good.

The space between the toast to the Queen and the speaker's address gets longer and longer. There are minutes from last year's annual banquet to be read, the accolades to the members of the con-vention panel responsible for the smooth running of this convention, and nineteen honorary lifetime memberships to be presented – and accepted. Actually in this regard the service club or dinner or lun-cheon speaker has the longest gangplank to cross before he leans forward into the public-address microphone. I recall a writing club dinner that involved the reading of every single placing poem in a recent poetry contest; then the three winners in the regional orator-ical contest gave their orations, all three about Cecil Rhodes, who reared up on his death bed to say: "So much to do – so little time in which to do it." These were followed by the little thirteen-year-old daughter of the club's secretary-treasurer, who played five sonatinas from Scarlotti's inexhaustible supply. I stood up with my notes at a quarter to midnight, and I understood why Cecil Rhodes had reared up on his death bed saying: "So much to do – so little time."

Speaking to service clubs and convention banquets is not gen-erally the speaker's idea to begin with. Such a talk generally takes two days anyway to prepare. Another couple of days is taken up by getting to the convention centre, delivering the talk, and returning home. In the end the better part of a working week seems to be needed. It has been the Canadian custom, though this seems to have changed in the past few years, to invite the speaker in a letter at the end of which he is told that, "we will of course pay all expenses." This is considered more than generous, and several times I have been tempted to invite the President of the Sanitary Engineers of Canada to come to my summer home north of the Okanagan, to do our septic tank, sinks, toilet, shower, hot and cold water; I would of course pay all his expenses.

I don't think that a banquet speaker seeks out engagements; it's just that word gets around. He may, after having refused so many times that his conscience bothers him, speak to the graduation exercises of the Okotoks High School, or the Rotary club of his home town, his father having been a charter member. This is the way it so often starts. Perhaps he is a foothills fox breeder and a member of the Azure District – or rather his wife is a member of the Azure District Farm Women's Union, who have been looking forward to hearing at their annual pancake breakfast, a Calgary Juvenile Court Judge noted for his inspirational addresses. He comes down with laryngitis, and our man's wife shoves him forward to pinch hit; this he does, commendably, his topic, "The Rewards and Hazards of Raising Pearl Faced Foxes," illustrated with fox pelts. What he does not know is that a niece visiting with an aunt, a member of the Azure District Farm Women's Union, from Foxhole, tells her husband, who has neglected to do anything about his turn to get a speaker for the Foxhole Activarians' next lunch. The thing proliferates from here, for every member of any audience belongs to more than the club or group being addressed; in the case of an extremely heterogeneous group like the YWCA Marriage Counselling and Coupling Club, the permutations and combinations are almost limitless.

A writer is not actually the sort of person for this sort of thing; I know that each time I accept an engagement, an old and inner feeling of guilt lifts within me. After-dinner speakers should really have risen to positions of prominence in the political or the financial world; they should not be simply *talkers*. Their position in the national hierarchy of finance should have especially equipped them to embed in their speeches a revelation or a message of great import, something to twitch a purse string, something that will make news or headlines the next morning or afternoon.

Now a writer is simply not in a position to do this for his audience – for himself. He is not a cabinet minister, provincial or federal, he is not even a member. If for instance he were Minister of Education he could say: "Next month – at the latest – I am pleased to announce that – it is our intention to reinstate – in a position of highest honour again – the study of English grammar in our high-school curricula." A deputy minister of Highways has no trouble finding newsworthy topics – Miss Violet Bowdry of Okotoks has been selected Miss Municipal Gravelled Roads of 1964.

Fifteen years ago I tried to remedy this great lack of impact. The occasion was the annual Turkey Supper given by the Gladys Ridge Homemakers, catered by the Burning Bush Auxiliary of the United Church. This time I decided that for once I would have a topic of such stunning news value it would make instant headlines from Victoria to Halifax. Just the announcement of the topic itself, whether or not I successfully developed it or not, would make headlines: MITCHELL'S ALTERNATING PLAN FOR THE PROPAGATION OF THE HUMAN RACE.

My plan was simplicity itself. It was based upon the axiomatic premise that child-bearing had been pretty well a woman's monopoly down through the centuries, but that men, given the necessary machinery or equipment, could do just as good a job of it. My modest proposal was that women of the world should, as they had been doing, have the first child. The men would have the second. At this point in my address I noticed upon the faces of a number of older, experienced-appearing women in my audience knowing looks, as they nudged the woman next. I could hear them whispering, "That'll be the end of that nonsense." But no – out of their natural generosity men would permit women to have the third child, *then* it would end.

I recall thinking at the time that the plan had no fault at all: three-child families throughout the world, the answer to the population explosion, yet a neat and tidy number of young in each home. I went on to give the men in my audience pre-natal hints, advice. The ladies of the Gladys Ridge Homemakers and the ladies of the Burning Bush Auxiliary who had catered for the annual Turkey Supper listened as I described the knee to chest exercises by which the men could restore the muscle tone to their once graceful figures. I described expectant father trousers, two versions or patterns: the one which featured elastic gussets at the sides and the other with an expanding forward panel that had a front tie. I begged them, those fathers who might later *find* themselves in an interesting condition, not to wear their top coats in the middle of a sweltering August afternoon when they had left the store or the office for a coffee break, this being a dead give-away.

The headlines I looked for the next day – weren't. I didn't make the *Winnipeg Free Press*, the *Toronto Star*, the Halifax *Chronicle-Herald*, the Vancouver *Sun* – needless to say. I didn't even make next Thursday's *High River Times*. But there was this: it has been roughly fifteen years since I have been asked to give an address within a fifty-mile radius of Gladys Ridge.

3

❦

Melvin Arbuckle's First Course in Shock Therapy

In this piece and in "The Day I Sold Lingerie in a Prairie Whore House" W. O. changed some names to protect the innocent. Khartoum is actually Weyburn. Some other autobiographical facts may have been slightly stretched in this memoir about how five bored boys on a hot August afternoon found some excitement. It is probably the most popular of W. O.'s performance pieces. An accomplished actor, he slips easily into the various voices of this piece, from Melvin's interrogative sentences to Peanut's English schoolboy accent. In his imitation of Melvin's Grandfather's "saliva trouble," he shakes his jowls as if "rattling dice" and dry-spits into the microphone. He appears to be ad-libbing most of the time and seems to lose his way in the first half of the piece. But it is all very carefully planned story-telling and the seemingly disparate pieces come together in the explosive climax.

This first-person reminiscential tall tale was first published in Maclean's *(October 1963) and it was later reworked into* How I Spent My Summer Holidays *(1981).*

Last year, like thousands of other former Khartoumians, I returned to Khartoum, Saskatchewan, to help her celebrate her Diamond Jubilee year. In the Elks' Bar, on the actual anniversary date, September 26, the Chamber of Commerce held a birthday get-together, and it was here that Roddy Montgomery, Khartoum's mayor, introduced me to a man whose face had elusive familiarity.

"One of Khartoum's most famous native sons," Roddy said with an anticipatory smile. "Psychiatrist on the West Coast. Portland."

I shook hands; I knew that I should remember him from the litmus years of my prairie childhood. As soon as he spoke I remembered: Miss Coldtart first, then *Pippa Passes* – then Melvin Arbuckle.

I was tolled back forty years: Melvin Arbuckle, only son of Khartoum's electrician, the boy who had successfully frustrated Miss Coldtart through all our Grade Four reading classes. Then, and today it seemed, he was unable to say a declarative sentence; he couldn't manage an exclamatory or imperative one either. A gentle-spoken and utterly stubborn woman with cream skin and dyed hair, Miss Coldtart called upon Melvin to read aloud every day of that school year, hoping against hope that one of his sentences would not turn up at the end like the sandal toes of an *Arabian Nights* sultan. The very last day of Grade Four she had him read *Pippa Passes* line for line after her. He did – interrogatively down to the last "God's in His Heaven? – All's right with the world?"

And forty years later it seemed quite fitting to me that Melvin was a psychiatrist, especially when I recalled Melvin's grandfather who lived with the Arbuckles, a long ropey octogenarian with buttermilk eyes and the sad and equine face of William S. Hart. I liked Melvin's grandfather. He claimed that he had been imprisoned by Louis Riel in Fort Garry when the Red River Rebellion started, that he was a close friend of Scott whom Riel executed in 1870. He said that he was the first man to enter Batoche after it fell, that he'd sat on the jury that condemned Riel to hang in '85. By arithmetic he could have been and done these things, but Melvin said his grandfather was an historical liar.

Melvin's grandfather had another distinction: saliva trouble. He would gather it, shake it back and forth from cheek to cheek, the way you might rattle dice in your hand before making a pass – then spit. He did this every twenty seconds. Also he wandered a great deal, wearing a pyramid-peaked hat of RCMP or boy scout issue, the thongs hanging down either cheek, a lumpy knapsack high between his shoulder-blades, a peeled and varnished willow-root cane in his hand. Since the Arbuckles' house stood an eighth of a mile apart from the eastern edge of Khartoum, it was remarkable that the old man never got lost on the empty prairie flung round three sides. Years of wilderness travel must have drawn him naturally towards habitation: Melvin's after-fours were ruined with the mortification of having to knock on front doors in our end of town, asking people if they'd seen anything of his lost grandfather. All his Saturdays were unforgivably spoiled too, for on these days Melvin's mother went down to the store to help his father, and Melvin had to stay home to see that his grandfather didn't get lost.

No one was ever able to get behind Melvin's grandfather; he sat always in a corner with two walls at his back; this was so in the house or in the Soo Beer Parlour. Melvin's mother had to cut her father's hair, for he refused to sit in Leon's barber chair out in the unprotected centre of the shop. If he met someone on the street and stopped to talk, he would circle uneasily until he had a building wall or a hedge or a fence at his back; sometimes he would have to settle for a tree. He had a very sensible reason for this: they were coming to get him one day, he said. It was never quite clear who was coming to get him one day, but I suspected revengeful friends of the man he called the half-breed renegade, Dumont. He may have been an historical liar, as Melvin said, but there was no doubting that he was afraid – afraid for his life.

I sincerely believed that someone was after him: nobody could have spent as much time as he did in the Arbuckle privy if somebody weren't after him. From mid-April, when the sun had got high and strong, to harvest he spent more time out there with four walls closing safe around him than he did in the house. I can hardly recall a visit to Melvin's place that there wasn't blue smoke threading from the diamond cutout in the backhouse door. Melvin's grandfather smoked natural-leaf Quebec tobacco that scratched with the pepper bitterness of burning willow root. He had the wildest smell of any man I had ever known, compounded of wine and iron tonic, beer, natural leaf, wood smoke, buckskin and horses. I didn't mind it at all.

He was a braggarty sort of old man, his words hurrying out after each other as though he were afraid that if he stopped he wouldn't be permitted to start up again – and also as though he knew that no one was paying attention to what he was saying anyway, so that he might just as well settle for getting it *said* as quickly as possible. Even Miss Coldtart would have found many of his expressions colourful: "she couldn't cook guts for a bear"; "spinnin' in the wind like the button on a backhouse door"; "so stubborn she was to drown'd you'd find her body upstream"; "when he was borned they set him on the porch to see if he barked or cried." Even though you felt he was about to embarrass you by spitting or lying, I found Melvin's grandfather interesting.

Yet I was glad that he was Melvin's grandfather and not mine. Even though he kept dragging his grandfather into conversation, Melvin was ashamed of him. He was always reminding us of his grandfather, not because he wanted to talk about him but just as though he were tossing the old man at our feet for a dare. I can't remember any of us taking him up on it. Perhaps now that he is a psychiatrist out on the West Coast, he has decided what compelled him to remind us continually of the grandfather he was ashamed of.

The summer that I have in mind was the year that Peanuts moved to Khartoum from Estevan, where his father was an engineer for a coal strip-mining company. Some sort of cousin of the Sweeneys, Peanuts had immigrated to Canada from England just the year before. He'd only had three months in Khartoum to pick up the nickname, Peanuts. He was not a peanuts sort of boy, quite blocky, very full red cheeks, hemp fair hair and wax blue eyes. At ten years of age, I suppose John Bull must have looked a great deal like Peanuts. His given name was actually Geoffrey.

He was quite practical, and could give all kinds of sensible reasons why a project could not work; this unwillingness to suspend disbelief tore illusion and spoiled pretend games. He had no sense of humour at all, for he seldom laughed at anything Fat said; English into the bargain, he should have been the most unpopular boy in Khartoum. However, he had piano-wire nerves which made up for his shortcomings. When we held our circus that July, he slipped snake after snake down the throat of his blouse, squirmed them past his belt and extricated them one by one from the legs of his stovepipe British woollen pants. They were only garter snakes, but a week later to settle a horticultural argument in Ashford's Grove, he ate a toadstool raw. Just because he didn't die was not proof that he was right and that we were wrong, for immediately after he pulled up and ate two bouquets of wild horseradish, with instantaneous emetic effect.

Now that I think back to a late August day that year, I can see that Peanuts has to share with Melvin's grandfather the credit or the responsibility for Melvin's being today a leading West Coast psychiatrist. It was a day that promised no excitement. The Khartoum Fair was past; Johnny J. Jones's circus had come and gone a month before, its posters already nostalgic and wind-tattered on shed and fence and barn walls. We couldn't duck or bottom it in the little Souris River, for it was filled with rusty bloodsuckers and violet-coloured algae that caused prairie itch. The bounty was off gopher tails for the rest of the year so there was no point in hunting them.

There was simply nothing to do but sprawl in the adequate shade of McGoogan's hedge, eating clover heads and caragana flowers. With bored languor we looked out over Sixth Street lifting and drifting in the shimmering heat. Without interest we saw the town wagon roll by, darkening the talcum-fine dust with spray; moments later the street was thirsty again, smoking under the desultory August wind.

Fin pulled out the thick glass from a flashlight, focused it to a glowing bead on his pant leg. A thin streamer of smoke was born and we idly watched a fusing spark eat through the cloth until its ant sting bit Fin's knee. He put the glass back into his pocket and said, "Let's go down to the new creamery and chew tar." Someone said, "Let's go look for beer bottles and lead instead"; someone else said, "How about fooling around in the loft of Fat's uncle's livery stable"; someone else said, "The hell with it."

About that time we all got to our feet, for an ice dray came down the street, piled high with frozen geometry. When the leather-chapped driver had chipped and hoisted a cake of ice over his shoulder and left for delivery, we went to the back of the dray. We knew we were welcome to the chips on the floor, and as we always did we popped into our mouths chunks too big for them. The trick was to suck in warm air around the ice until you could stand it no longer, then lower your head, eject and catch.

Someone said, "Let's go over and see Melvin stuck with his grandfather." Inhibited by ice and the cool drool of it, no one agreed or disagreed. We wandered up Sixth Street, past the McKinnon girls and Noreen Robins darting in and out of a skipping rope, chanting: "Charlie Chaplin – went to – France – teach the – ladies – how to – dance . . ." At the corner of Bison and Sixth we turned east and in two blocks reached the prairie. I think it was the tar-papered and deserted shack between the town's edge and the Arbuckles' house that gave us the idea of building a hut. By the time we had reached Melvin's, we had decided it might be more fun to dig a cave, which would be lovely and cool.

Melvin was quite agreeable to our building the cave in his backyard; there were plenty of boards for covering it over; if we all pitched in and started right away, we might even have it finished before his grandfather had wakened from his nap. Shovel and spade and fork plunged easily through the eighteen inches of topsoil; but the clay subsoil in this dry year was heart – and back – breaking. Rock-hard, it loosened under pick and bar in reluctant sugar lumps. Stinging with sweat, our shoulder sockets aching, we rested often, reclining at the lip of our shallow excavation. We idly wished: "If a fellow only had a fresno and team, he could really scoop her out . . ."

"If a fellow could soak her good . . . run her full of water – soften her up. Easy digging then."

"If a fellow could only blow her out . . ."

"How?"

"Search me."

"Stumping powder – dynamite . . ."

"Oh," Peanuts said, "yes – dynamite."

"Whumph and she'd blow our cave for us," Fin said.

"She sure would," Fat said.

Melvin said, "Only place I know where they got dynamite – CPR sheds."

"I have dynamite," Peanuts said. "I can get dynamite."

We looked at each other; we looked at Peanuts. Knowing Peanuts, I felt a little sick; Fat and Fin and Melvin didn't look so happy either. We had never even seen a stick of dynamite; it simply did not belong in our world. It had been quite *imaginary* dynamite that we had been tossing about in conversation.

Fat said, "We can't go swiping dynamite."

Fin said, "We don't know a thing about handling dynamite."

"I do," Peanuts said.

"Isn't our yard," Fat said. "We can't set off dynamite in Mel's yard." Peanuts got up purposefully. "Can we, Mel?"

"The cave's a hundred yards from the house," Peanuts said. "Nothing dangerously near it at all." He turned to Melvin. "Are you frightened?"

"Well – no," Melvin said.

"My father has a whole case of 60 per cent," Peanuts said. "From the mine. While I get it you have them do the hole."

"What hole?" Melvin said.

"For the dynamite – with the bar – straight down about four feet, I should say."

"The whole goddam case!" Fin said.

"Dead centre, the hole," Peanuts said and started for his house.

"He bringing back the whole case?" Fin said.

Fat got up. "I guess I better be getting on my way . . ." His voice fainted as he looked down at us and we looked up at him. "I guess I better – we better – start punching – down that hole," he finished up. "Like Peanuts said." It was not what Fat had started out to say at all.

Peanuts brought back only three sticks of dynamite, and until his return the hole went down rather slowly. He tossed the sticks on the ground by the woodpile and took over authority. He did twice his share of digging the dynamite hole; from time to time he estimated how much further we had to go down. When it seemed to suit him he dropped two of the sticks down the hole, one on top of the other. There was no tenderness in the way he handled that dynamite, inserted the fuse end into the copper tube detonator, crimped it with his teeth, and used a spike to work a hole into the third stick to receive the cap and fuse. He certainly knew how to handle dynamite. We watched him shove loose clay soil in around the sticks, tamp it firm with the bar. With his jackknife he split the free end of the fuse protruding from the ground. He took a match from his pocket.

"Hold on a minute," Melvin said. "Where do we – what do we – how long do we . . ."

"Once it's going there'll be three minutes," Peanuts said. "Plenty of time to take cover."

"What cover?" Fat said.

"Round the corner of the house," Peanuts said. "You may go there now if you wish. I'll come when the fuse is started. They're hard to start – it will take several matches."

We stayed. The fuse took life at the third match. Fat and Fin and Melvin and I ran the hundred yards to the house. We looked around the corner to Peanuts coming towards us. He did it by strolling. I had begun to count to myself so that I could have a rough notion of when the fuse was near the end of its three minutes. I had reached fifty-nine when I heard the Arbuckle screen door slap the stillness.

Fin said, "Judas Priest!"

Melvin said, "He's headed for the backhouse!"

Fat said, "He's got his knapsack and his hat and his cane on – maybe he's just going out to get lost."

Melvin started round the corner of the house but Fin grabbed him. "Let him keep goin', Mel! Let him keep goin' so's he'll get in the clear!"

"I'll get him," Peanuts said.

"He's my grandfather!" Melvin said.

Fin said, "There ain't even a minute left!" I had no way of telling, for I'd stopped counting.

The site of our proposed cave and, therefore, of the dynamite with its burning fuse, was halfway between the back of the Arbuckle house and the privy. Melvin's grandfather stopped by the woodpile. He shook his head and he spat. Peanuts launched himself around the corner of the house, belly to the ground towards the old man. Melvin's grandfather must have thought the running footsteps behind him were those of either Louis Riel or Gabriel Dumont, for without looking back he covered the open ground to the privy in ten seconds, jumped inside and slammed the door. Right in stride, Peanuts pounded past and out to the prairie beyond. There he was still running with his head back, chin out, arms pumping, knees high, when the dynamite let go.

The very first effect was not of sound at all. Initially the Arbuckle yard was taken by one giant and subterranean hiccup. An earth fountain spouted; four cords of wood took flight; the privy leaped straight up almost six feet; two clothesline posts javelined into the air, their wires still stretched between them in an incredible aerial cat's cradle. Not until then did the lambasting explosion seem to come. For several elastic seconds all the airborne things hung indecisively between the thrust of dynamite and the pull of gravity. Gravity won.

The privy was the first thing to return to earth, and when it fell its descent obeyed Newton's Law of Falling Backhouses, which says: "A falling privy shall always come to rest upon the door side." The corollary: "A loved one trapped within cannot be taken out on the vertical, only through the hole and upon the horizontal."

At the back of the house we looked at each other wildly; we swallowed to unbung our ears, heard the Japanese chiming of glass shards dropping from Arbuckle windows, the thud of wood chunks returning to earth. I saw Melvin lick with the tip of his tongue at twin blood yarns coming down from his nostrils. No one said anything; we simply moved as a confused body in the direction of the privy. We skirted the great shallow saucer the dynamite had blown, and I remember thinking they would never fill it in: the dirt was gone forever. At the very centre it was perhaps ten feet deep; it would have taken all the lumber from a grain elevator to roof it over for a cave.

"Grampa – Grampa –" Melvin was calling – "Please, Grampa. Please, Grampa."

"We'll have to tip it up," Fin said, "so's we can open the door."

"You're not supposed to move injured people," Fat said.

Melvin squatted down beside the fallen privy and put his face to the hole. His frightened voice sounded cistern-hollow. "Grampa!" Then he really yelled as the tip of the varnished willow cane caught him across the bridge of the nose. He straightened up and he said, "He's still alive. Give me a hand."

It took all of us to upright the privy and Melvin's grandfather. He swung at us with his cane a couple of times when we opened the door, then he let us help him to the house and into his own room off the kitchen. Seated there on a Winnipeg couch, he stared straight ahead of himself as Melvin removed the boy scout hat, slipped off the packsack. With an arm around the old man's shoulders, Melvin eased him down on the pillow, then motioned us out of the room. Before we got to the door the old man spoke.

"Melvin."

"Yes, Grampa?"

"Sure they're all cleared out now?"

"Yes, Grampa."

He released a long sigh. "Get word to General Middleton."

"For help, Grampa?"

"Not help." The old man shook his head. "Sharply engaged enemy. Routed the barstards!"

We were all whipped that evening, and the balance of our merciful catharsis was earned over a month's quarantine, each in his own yard. When his month's isolation was up, Melvin gained a freedom he'd never known before; he didn't have to knock on another door, for his grandfather never wandered again. He sat at the Arbuckle living-room window for the next three years, then died.

One of Khartoum's most famous native sons, Roddy Montgomery had called him at the Chamber of Commerce birthday party in the Elks' Bar: Dr. Melvin Arbuckle, Portland psychiatrist and mental health trail-blazer – in shock therapy, of course.

4

⁓ഓ⁓

The Day I Sold Lingerie in a Prairie Whore House

In 1952 W. O. *first used this childhood experience as the basis for one of his* CBC *radio "Jake and the Kid" episodes, "Earn Money at Home." He recalls an occasion in 1965, during a benefit performance at Calgary's Mac Theatre, when a woman laughed so hard during his performance of this piece that she "vomited in the aisle" and two ushers had to help her to the ladies' washroom. His sense that he, like his grandfather and father before him, is tone deaf has been borne out by his attempts to sing "Doodle dee doo," the song he remembers being carried to him "on the prairie wind" from Miss Rossdance's cottages.*

This first-person reminiscential version was first published in Maclean's (May 1964) and it was later worked into The Vanishing Point (1973).

❧

Wendell Coldtart got me into it, actually, even though he wasn't such a close friend of mine. He didn't live in our end of Khartoum or go to Haig School with me and Fat and Hodder and Fin and Peanuts and Mate and Ike. Quite often, though, he would be in our part of town to visit his aunt who taught us in Grade Four. He would always come down Sixth Street, most of the time by walking on his hands with his head up and back arched, his knees spread slightly and legs loose so that his toes kept tapping the top of his head. Behind him Gusty spraddled along with eyes rolled upwards so that four-fifths of the whites showed, slobbering and snuffling with chronic sinusitis. Wendell had won Gusty with 46,529 Bulldog Orange wrappers. Wendell always stopped at our place because he was determined to walk downstairs on his hands, and our front porch had five shallow steps for him to practise on. Eventually he was able to walk downstairs on his hands, an impractical accomplishment really, because the Coldtart house had no front steps at all; their house was not even a two-storey house. Ours was three.

Every time Wendell came by either on foot or on hand, always with Gusty behind, he was a living proof to other Khartoum boys that contests could be won. He had won a bulldog simply by collecting a higher number of Bulldog Orange wrappers than any other boy in Manitoba, Saskatchewan, Alberta, and British Columbia: 46,529. Wendell's father was the southern Saskatchewan manager for Watkin's Fruit Wholesale. It was therefore in a way Wendell Coldtart's fault that I got mixed up in the Ten Thousand Dollar Contest advertised in the back of our housekeeper Olga's *Ranch Romances* magazines.

The contest was illustrated with the picture of a lovely woman who had just been splashed with mud from a passing Stutz Bearcat; the balloon issuing from her mouth contained a lot of jumbled-up numbers. By substitution of "a" for 1, "b" for 2, and so on, you were to decipher what she said. The result was enigmatic to me: "Oh my, now you will have to buy me new hose. The best is none too good for me. It will have to be Tite-Wove Lingerie for real value, style, and freedom of action!" I told Olga that seemed a funny thing to have in a Ten Thousand Dollar Contest. Olga said that it was their ten thousand dollars, that probably they'd put it in to make the deciphering that much harder.

We mailed our solution and waited with impatience. We knew we weren't likely to win the three-thousand-dollar first prize, or perhaps even the second-place two thousand or third-place one thousand, but there were forty consolation prizes of one hundred dollars each and we were sure to get one of those. I suppose the reply to our entry came as soon as such replies generally do, though the time seemed to stretch elastically. When the answer came it was a large carton containing among other things a letter:

Dear Miss Mitchell:

You have perfectly unscrambled the numbers in our Grand Ten Thousand Dollar Contest, which has placed you in the semi-finals along with nineteen other successful contestants. The next step, in order to determine the winner of our first prize of three thousand dollars cash, explains to you our shipment of a consignment of Wear-Rite Beauty Garments and Tite-Wove Lingerie. All you have to do is sell these lovely, waffle-knit, misty sheer garments in plum, puce, magenta, coral, and petal pink to your friends. See how delighted they will be. Points will be awarded you per unit sale and so the deadlock will be broken. Good luck, contestant!

According to the price list enclosed there was fifty dollars' worth of lingerie; my friends were Ike and Fat, Hodder, Peanuts, Mate, Fin, and I could tell right away how delighted they would be. There were, however, my mother, my auntie Josie, my grandmother, Olga, the thirty members of my mother's Burning Bush Chapter, the twelve female singers of Knox Presbyterian Church choir, in which my

mother sang alto, her bridge club, and the Ladies' South Khartoum
Golf Club. There were as well those friendly individual women along
Sixth Street, at whose homes – for a price – you left May baskets
fashioned of wallpaper and filled with crocuses, where you were
sure of Hallowe'en generosity: Mrs. Campion and Mrs. MacKinnon,
Mrs. Zabel, Mrs. MacLean, Mrs. Oncough.

Included with the inventory list was descriptive literature intended
to be helpful. Stockings were said to be "whisper light" and "cobweb
delicate"; chemises had "self-flounce in bottom of full hem." This was
simply unintelligible, but the rest was unrelieved pornography.

I sold stockings to my mother, my auntie Josie, bloomers to Olga,
who actually would have preferred stockings, but I explained to her
that I anticipated no difficulty in getting rid of them. I was right, for
I had sold them all before I got down to the Ladies' South Khartoum
Golf Club. Now, pulling the carton behind me in my brother's wagon,
I had the distasteful task of selling the other stuff from door to door
and to ladies I didn't know. It was like trying to commit an inept crime
over and over again. I had to twist door bells and interrupt ladies at
their baking or ironing or napping; it was a sort of wrongful and mor-
tifying assault – to enter strange homes uninvited. I was quite unsuccessful, and after my tenth attempt without selling a single article, I
commented to Olga that it looked as though Khartoum ladies didn't
go in much for underwear.

I had worked our entire end of town and moved to Government
Road with no sense of adventure at all. I knew in my heart that there
wasn't a chance I could break the deadlock to win the Ten Thousand
Dollar Contest. And if I couldn't sell the lingerie I didn't know what
I *could* do with it. The contest people had assumed in good faith that
I would sell it, and it would be cheating of some sort to return it unsold;
quite possibly it would be breaking some sort of law.

Mrs. Halstead had closed the door gently in my face: she had been
kind without buying anything, and I stood disconsolate and ashamed
on the front porch with the iodine smell of old paint hot under the

sun bitter in my nostrils. Here it was the second Saturday afternoon in May and I should have been out on the prairie drowning gophers or watching William S. Hart in the Hi-Art Theatre. I pulled my wagon and its carton of obscenity to the corner and stood there uncertain. I'd run out of houses: in the next block south came the Co-Op Creamery, Stuarts' Livery Barn, then the Massey-Harris implement sheds. To the west lay the Fair Grounds, beyond that open prairie and then Sadie Rossdance's.

Miss Rossdance was a milliner and lived in three little cottages with bonnet roofs, an optimistic fragment of street some contractor had built in the early 1900s when Khartoum had been exuberantly subdivided for a mile in every direction. The prairie between Miss Rossdance's and the Fair Grounds was exciting, for here camels and elephants were staked and circus tents pitched whenever they came to town: this was the camping ground for gypsies, and since these were the immediate post-First Great War days, flying aces with white silk scarves landed their Jennies here, staked them down against the prairie wind, did wing-walking and trapeze-swinging, and took up passengers for ten cents a pound. These were short-lived and seasonal gaieties which somehow seemed to infect the Sadie Rossdance houses with carnival spirit. Each had a piano and someone to play it. From opened windows came "Roses of Picardy," "Barney Google," "Marquita," "Let Me Call You Sweetheart," and "Yes, We Have No Bananas."

I can't remember the day my younger brother and I visited Miss Rossdance's first and got a glass of milk and cookies, probably a Saturday morning on a return from a gopher hunt in the prairie beyond. After that it was a regular port of call. Miss Rossdance was a slender woman with very blonde hair and pale eyes. She had a tight energy that made her talk quickly; she laughed a great deal and had a way of cocking her head as though she were listening with comradely amusement. As only a child can tell, she liked children with an impromptu affection.

Standing on Government Road I was suddenly not so disconsolate or ashamed: I began to pull my brother's wagon filled with contest-breaking chemises and slips and nightgowns over the virgin prairie wool towards Sadie Rossdance and all her friends. The bright song of a meadow lark dropped again and again, then borne to me on the prairie wind, the piano:

"Doodle dee doo, doodle dee doo.
I like the rest, but what I like best is
Doodle dee doo, doodle dee doo!"

I came to the edge of Vandedreische's oat field with the moist May wind rolling waves through the shrill green. I saw a gopher sitting upright at her hole, paws held up before her fawn belly swollen with spring and young. Woman laughter drifted to me as I came up to the backs of the three beehive houses.

They were all on the porch of the second house, in kimonos or wrappers, seated on the rail, three of them on kitchen chairs there. They were drying their hair and leaning forward so that it curtained their faces, and they were laughing and laughing all the while the piano played inside the house. It wasn't as though they were happy sisters in the same family so much as though they all belonged on the same girls' basketball team.

Miss Rossdance gave me cookies and a glass of milk: I finished them and then sat on the edge of the porch, not knowing how to begin. I started finally by telling about the Grand Ten Thousand Dollar Contest. Miss Rossdance got me to bring the carton up onto the porch. I didn't have to do any selling. The dark woman with thick black hair and full cheeks, the one with the narrow face and wide forehead with the fair hair that seemed to spring from her temples rather like the hirsute wings that go with the balding and professorial clown, even Miss Rossdance herself, bought: "bud-burst brassières with elastic inserts for better control and floating-action circular bust cups," "petti-panties cut in one piece for extra comfort and longer wear, with opaque silk tricot and non-chafing double-crotch." The girl with the black eyes and cream skin, the very lovely one, took my last nightgown with "eyelet embroidery on bodice with overlays of lace – daisy white."

I sent all the money away and waited for the contest results. Three weeks later there was another carton with an enclosed note telling me that the deadlocked contestants had been thinned down to nine. The carton contained a gross of little bottles of perfume.

My mother made me return them. I could have sold them all inside of five minutes out at Sadie Rossdance's.

5

⟨⟩⟨⟩

Old Kacky and the Vanishing Point

This episode from The Vanishing Point
*(1973) is one of W. O.'s favourite perfor-
mance pieces from his novels. He finds this
piece particularly effective when reading for
audiences of teachers and students. It grew out
of memories of his Grade Eight teacher, an art
class, and, years later in 1943, his first day at
the office as principal of the school in Castor,
a small Alberta town. On opening his desk
drawer he found the calling card of a student
who had obviously been unhappy with the previous principal – or who may
have been welcoming the new principal.*

⟨⟩⟨⟩

Right from the time Carlyle had entered the boys' door of Sir Walter
Raleigh School, he had flinched from his inevitable destination in Old
Kacky's room. But five years later June had come, and then the day
that he and the others must leave the Three-Four-Five room, delicate
with paste perfume and thick with the smell of plasticine, with rabbit

35

and lamb and butterfly cutouts against its windows. Leave consistently gentle Miss Coldtart.

Then September happened. They must enter Old Kacky's room, with its long maps rolled above the blackboards and, between his desk and the window, an iron tripod stand with sickle-shaped external axis holding the world bubble ready to spin at a finger touch. And now he owned a flat, tin geometry box, with its metre ruler, short and metal, a protractor, a compass, and a hard, hard pencil that had to be needle-sharp so that length and breadth and loci would be exact. Hygiene wasn't about washing your hands and brushing your teeth any more; it had grown up: all the body's Latin bones, its circulatory and respiratory and alimentary and terminally incomplete urinary systems. The reproductive system was mentioned not at all; sex surfaced only in grammar, with the personal pronoun possessing the gerund and the chaste union of subject and predicate by non-thrusting copulative verb.

Old Kacky was just as frightening as imagined, especially when he stood behind a person and confused him at per cent on the board; Carlyle could tell without looking around that Old Kacky's scalp had turned scarlet through the fine white hair. When he was angry, his smell grew strong. Little number footnotes at the bottom of addition columns inflamed him. They hadn't bothered Miss Coldtart, if you rubbed them out when you were all done. Old Kacky said they were a remembering-to-carry crutch; once it was used, a person would need it all his life. It had taken him some time to recognize Old Kacky's anger smell: oatmeal porridge.

Possibly Old Kacky scared Billy Blake the most. Billy's nose bled easily and melodramatically; often it happened in running, shoving, mêlée games: flying red rain spattering all over a person's sleeve or down the front of his blouse. He bled on the kitchen linoleum of other people's houses; there was still a rust trail over the MacGowan living-room carpet from their couch to the hall door. One twenty-fourth of May he bled so badly out at Tourigny's swimming hole, it had showed in the silty water; if it had been the Rio de Paraguay or the Amazon instead of the Little Souris, it would have bannered down stream and alerted millions of deadly piranha. Actually he could make his nose bleed, particularly if it had recently bled, by simply blowing it hard till the clot came free. If that didn't work, he could put his arms on the slope top of his desk, cradle his head there, and bunt his nose sur-reptitiously till it happened and Miss Coldtart ran to Old Kacky's office for cotton batting and gauze from the first-aid kit. Then, after it was stuffed, she'd tell him he could forget the rest of his after-four deten-tion and go home. Old Kacky let it bleed.

Old Kacky frightened Maitland Dean the least. Mate was the new Anglican parson's son; there were just Mate and his father in the rectory next to the church. Mel said they had come to town so they could be near Mate's mother who was crazy in the mental hospital. Mel went to the Baptist church. Also, through some cruel sort of mus-cular self-discipline he could pass wind at will. On request he could let off a whole repertoire: whisper, explosion, two-tone, or in a long string skipping like a flat pebble over water, always without the slight-est change of facial expression. Never evidence of effort; the fart that concealed art. To Carlyle he had seemed immediately the most sophis-ticated boy in North America.

To begin with, history in Old Kacky's room seemed interesting enough – when the great maps were pulled down over the board to show the voyages of Columbus and Champlain and Cartier. The Iroquois were quite exciting, especially in their torture methods: having their victims run the gauntlet, making human porcupines of their captives by pricking them all over with pine-needle tufts. When the resin sputtered and flared, the victims took great pride in not showing their agony; the history book said that when they were ignited, Father Brébeuf and his brethren had conducted themselves well. But Canadian history soon became corrupted into an account of the way people governed and made laws and set up constitutions and Confederation.

Art was a half-hour once a week. They spent a long time on trees; for a hundred miles in every direction from their town there grew not a tree unplanted by man. Learning to draw a tree was complicated. First there must be a pencilled skeleton. Even though both were coniferous, pine and fir trees had different skeletons. Fir branches did not meet at the trunk, nor shorten to a point like pine branches; they laddered up and alternated. Poplars and birches kept forking. After the skeleton was drawn, it had to be covered with short hair-strokes – unless it was a deciduous tree, and then it was a matter of shading in puffy clouds of leaves with the side of the soft art pencil.

Next came sunsets, and a chance to use the paints like brilliant toffee squares in their little tin dishes. They had such a shallow, curving smell, and blue was Carlyle's favourite. The proper way to do sunsets, Old Kacky taught them, was to wet the whole sheet of art paper, then brush bands of red and yellow and blue across the top. The wet paper would dilute the colour bars so that they would fog each other and give you a glorious sunset. Carlyle's didn't; either they refused to fog each other, or they cried right to the bottom of the sheet, which as it dried shrank and pulled unevenly into a rippled mess.

Early in October they took up the vanishing point.

Mostly it was accomplished with the ruler, and it was a lot like geometry, only fun. Lower on the art paper than a person would think, the horizon had to run clear across. Then the vanishing point must be marked. It didn't have to be exactly at the centre, Old Kacky said, but a little to the left of centre if a person wanted. Perhaps because he hadn't been listening carefully, he got his off to the right, but because it was the very start he was able to correct his mistake. The next step Old Kacky gave them was to rule two lines wide apart at the bottom of the page, squeezing down to the vanishing point on the horizon. They travelled up the sheet, actually. These lines were the edges of the highway; another would determine the tops of the telephone poles, and on the opposite side of the road there was one to limit the height of the fence-post tips. Before the drawing was nearly done, there was a great skein of lines, very faintly traced, funnelling to the vanishing point.

When his drawing was finished, it was shocking; his eye travelled straight and unerring down the great prairie harp of telephone wires strung along tiny glass nipples of insulators on the cross-bars, down the barbed-wire fence lines on the other side of the highway. And as the posts and poles marched to the horizon, they shrank and crowded up to each other, closer and closer together till they all were finally sucked down into the vanishing point.

There wasn't the faintest shadow or smudge from the temporary guiding lines; he'd rubbed them out carefully with the corner of his art eraser. No accidents as the yellow cube rolled off springy crumbs that reminded him of skin from the wrinkled backs of his heels and his kneecaps when he towelled after a hot bath. He could not get over how doing something so crazy should end up looking just right. Things didn't look the way a person thought they did at all.

But very soon – before art period was over – his drawing didn't satisfy him. Empty. It needed something. Maybe a meadow lark on a fence post – a killdeer near the road – goshawk hung high. A tiger wouldn't do, of course, unless he put in a circus tent for it to have got loose from. Nothing dangerous went slinking along the highway or the CPR tracks over prairie. There were no man-eating plants or quicksand around Sadie Rossdance's three little cottages; nor did lions and leopards prowl down after dark to drink from Tourigny's swimming hole. Deadly five-minute snakes and hooded cobras, walnut-coloured natives with white turbans on their heads, and rocking giraffes with necks like swaying telephone poles lived far away in their native land – or in *Chums* – or on the screen of the Hi-Art Theatre, where Mel's father played the piano and drums for Ken Maynard and Charlie Chase and Harold Lloyd. This, in a way, gave Mel an extra right to them; he also claimed special knowledge of stinging scorpions because his Aunt Vera was in the mission fields of India for the Western Baptists.

The drawing had to have something more – some gophers, like tent pegs – clump of wild roses – buck brush. That was it! A tree! In the front and to the left, as high as the first telephone pole, he put in a poplar the way Old Kacky had showed them to make poplars. And then another – a pine on the other side of the road, almost halfway to the horizon. They looked great! Maybe some gophers and the curved Vs of flying . . .

Oatmeal! He looked back and up over his shoulder. Old Kacky in the aisle reached down, took up the drawing. As he looked at it, his scalp turned scarlet.

"My office!"

With the drawing in his hand, he followed Carlyle there. He closed the office door. He went round the desk. He dropped the drawing. He sat down.

"All right. Why did you do that?"

Badly as he wanted to, he could not find the reason that he had put the trees in his drawing. It had been a sort of an accident.

"You knew we were doing the vanishing point and perspective. You were told to do that. Simply."

He nodded.

"But you went ahead – you disobeyed. Put those trees in as well as the fence and the telephone line."

He nodded again.

"Deliberately."

He nodded.

"Haven't you anything to say – any explanation – excuse?"

He did know that Old Kacky was not interested in an excuse, whatever its excellence. "No, sir . . . it . . . just happened."

"It couldn't. The trees had to be outlined. They had to be shaded. Coniferous or deciduous – they can't draw themselves. Can they?"

"No, sir."

"So, you put them in deliberately."

"I guess I did, Mr. Macky."

"Do you mean you know you did?"

"Yes, I guess . . . yes, sir . . . I knew – know – after they happened – accidentally."

"What?"

"I mean after they – after I happened to think them – doing them – putting them in there – then I – drew them deliberate."

"Deliberately."

"Deliberately."

"What if a boy did this sort of thing in arithmetic? History? Geography? Do you see what I mean?"

"Yes, Mr. Macky."

"Deliberate disobedience."

"Yes, sir."

"You know I have to strap you."

"Yes, sir."

Five on each hand. Nothing before in his eleven years of life had hurt that much.

After Old Kacky had put the strap back into its drawer, he told Carlyle that he had conducted himself well and in a manly fashion. He said Carlyle could remain in the office for five minutes before returning to the classroom.

As soon as Old Kacky had closed the door behind himself, Carlyle thrust the incredible pain between his legs; with one knee lifted, he squeezed the hurt, then, with wrists loose, tried to shake off stinging drops. He rubbed his hands up and down on the front of his pant legs.

With some surprise he realized that he was not sorry for the trees at all. It wasn't trees he'd thought of putting – first. A tiger – with satisfied jowls and lovely stripes shaded in with his art pencil. But a tiger would have been ridiculous on prairie. So would Old Kacky. He'd be safe enough on prairie unless he broke his leg and lay out there in forty-below; or maybe in spring, when they ganged up for mating, coyotes might catch his smell and ring him and wait for him to die! In the deep rainforests or the rubber jungles of the Amazon, though, he'd be in trouble. His strong, scared, oatmeal scent would telegraph him to head-hunting Indians and black, man-eating jaguars. Boa constrictors went by smell too. Yes! Behind the flat head – just like a sack of coal struggling in the boa constrictor's neck!

The pain had completely evaporated; his palms were just warm now. Red as sunburn. He could see there was a slight puffing. His hands trembled. He couldn't stop them; it was a little like looking at them through the lifting drift and shimmer of heat waves. They blurred. Then they starred. He looked up and away from them to the picture over the filing cabinet. The soldiers had bloodied bandages round their heads, just like Billy Blake's handkerchieves, or the newspaper wrappings left over from the farm kids' sandwiches' hemorrhaging strawberry jam. Two artillery horses lay in their harness, all tangled up, legs thrust out into the air as though they didn't belong to them. The legs had been stuck onto their bloated bellies. And now he could read the brass plate underneath: SOMEWHERE WITH A VETERINARY UNIT IN FRANCE. Donated to Sir Walter Raleigh School by KITCHENER OF KHARTOUM CHAPTER IODE.

Suddenly he realized how very still it was in Old Kacky's office. And lonely. Here he stood by himself, and outside the office walls were all the others properly together and busy all around his own empty desk. He had vanished from them. Old Kacky had vanished him from them to vanishment. And then the really crazy thought happened. He was being vanished from himself . . . stepping outside and apart and walking away farther and farther from himself, getting smaller and smaller and smaller . . . dwindling right down to a point. That was crazy and enough to scare the shit out of a person!

Literally.

His stomach had cramped sharply. His five minutes were up! There wasn't nearly time to go to the boys' basement. He'd fill his pants! If he used the wastebasket, Old Kacky would see it right away. He could spread some paper on the floor and then gather it up and . . . This time it came lower and worse! He looked at Old Kacky's desk.

The bottom drawer on the left-hand side brimmed with cardboard folders lying flat. He lifted them out carefully and quickly. He set them down on the desk top.

Just in time!

He replaced all the folders – tenderly. Then he closed the drawer. It had taken Old Kacky a whole week to find it.

6

❧❦❧

Saint Sammy's Creation of the World

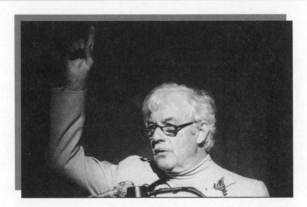

In this episode from Who Has Seen the Wind *(1947), eleven-year-old Brian and his friends Fat and Ike are on their way to visit Saint Sammy, a prairie hermit who lives in an Old Testament fantasy. As Brian's Uncle Sean puts it, Saint Sammy is "crazier'n a cut calf" – "years a gittin' rusted out an' cutwormed out an' hoppered out an' hailed out an' droughted out an' rusted out an' smutted out, he up an' got good an' goddam tired out." This latter-day Old Testament prophet, "Jehovah's Hired Hand," looks after the Lord's herd of wild Clydesdale horses named after various Biblical characters such as Lot, Habbakuk, Naomi, Ruth, Malachi, and the two colts, Corinthians*

One and Two. Bent Candy, the richest farmer in the area, lusts after Saint Sammy's Clydes. As the three boys approach the piano box in which Sammy lives, they are stopped by the foul stench of something that has died. Fat has refused to go any further and is walking back to town.

Anyone who has heard W. O. perform this piece will hear, when reading it, the high sing-songing cadences and the rhythms of Genesis which W. O. gives to Sammy's voice. It was first published as a short story in Atlantic Monthly *(August 1946).*

ᥱᥩᥰ

The smell grew stronger and stronger till it was a solid thing upon the air.

"There's where he lives," Ike pointed out to Brian. "That's his piano box – an' there's his c'rral."

"But – where's *he*? I don't see him anywhere around."

"Probably inside out of the flies," guessed Ike.

"That smell's coming right from his place."

"Yeah, seems to be comin' from there."

As he neared the place, Brian felt a welling of uncertainty. "You sure, Ike?"

"Sure – I'm sure." Ike's voice lacked the clear ring of conviction it had when he argued with Fat.

"That stink's bad," said Brian dubiously. "I bet it's as bad as when your dad –"

Ike had bent down to his pant leg and seemed intent on picking spear grass from it. His voice was muffled. "Think we oughta get any closer?"

Brian looked back over the prairie to Fat's black, pygmy figure in the distance.

"We gotta go now." Ike straightened up. "Or else we – what'll Fat say? He'll say we're scairt too."

"An' that – hey – there he is – he ain't dead!"

"Like I said!" cried Ike.

Brian saw the man ahead, walking over the prairie with a lilting lift as though he had a spring under one heel. One arm swung wide, and he carried his head to one side. The boys saw him stop, then slowly bring his arms above his head and just as slowly down.

"Come ontuh me where I dwell in thuh midst a my critters – come ontuh me with the jacks an' badgers an' weasel, an' skunk an' gophers too! Come ontuh me, boys!" he called out to them.

He was unbelievably whiskered, with a long and matted beard that grew in semicircles under his eyes, completely hiding his mouth except when it opened into a small dark well. Like his beard, the womanish hair that hung to his shoulders was grey. As he drew nearer to Ike, Brian saw that the old man's eyes were water-blue, with a staring fixity and an indefinable mixture of wildness and mildness. Perched on the very top of his head to give it a tipped-up appearance was a child's cap centred with a cloth button, from which ran down quartering creases.

"Come ontuh me, boys, with the creepin' critter that hath life an' the fowla thuh air an' thuh whole host a them about me – minus one – Lot's wife – she up an' died last month!"

The boys stared with mouths ajar.

"Moreover an' behold, she is behind you!"

As one they twitched around to see only the poplar poles of the corral.

"Lot knew her an' she was with calf an' she died an' the Lord He visited me with a plague a rheumatism, so I couldn't haul the bresh to burn her there."

With his stomach delightfully anxious, Brian stared at Saint Sammy. The old man walked a step away, then wheeled with his long arm up.

"The Glory a the Lord come outa the East, an' His voice was the wind in the smooth-on barley field! An' I called out to the Lord; He answered me from the belly a the burnin' prairie. 'Bent Candy won't git 'em,' He seth ontuh me. 'They shall be shod with silver horseshoes – dimonds an' em'ralds shall be in their britchin', an' their halter shanks shall be of purest gold! I say ontuh you, Saint Sammy, don't sell them there horses ontuh Bent Candy!'"

His arm came down and he advanced upon the boys, who drew back an involuntary step. "I got a lotta blue labels now," he said in a mild and confiding voice, "All offa underwear, an' I say ontuh you, 'tain't easy to git the red ones." He twitched around and dived into his piano-box home.

Craning their necks, Brian and Ike saw him plunge his hand deep into the binder twine bits and raw sheep's wool that made up his bed. He backed out, turned, and sat suddenly upon the prairie with a battered tin box in his hand. He lifted the lid carefully, looked up to the boys suspiciously, then down to the box again. "Matchboxes," he said. "An' I say ontuh you I ain't got no new matchboxes whosoever kin number the sands a the sea – got any red labels?"

They said that they had not.

"I saved them – labels an' matchboxes – saved the saved matchboxes – saved the saved labels – the drops a rain an' the days a eternity – saved an' it come to pass that all was saved! Sammy saved them all!"

A yellow butterfly flickered past; Sammy leaped to his feet, whipping his cap from his head, letting the tin box fall to the ground so that it spilled out its contents of labels and matchboxes, bits of twig and stone, broken china, stove bolts, safety pins, pencil stubs. In a broken run he followed the butterfly, then tossed his cap over it as it alighted. Carefully folding the edges of the cap in, he came dotting back. "Cigarette boxes? The Lord created He them. You ain't got no cigarette boxes?"

"We don't smoke," said Ike righteously. "You save butterflies too?"

Saint Sammy slowly opened his cap, and took the fluttering butterfly out between his thumb and forefinger. "All kinds a yella ones over the breadth a the earth an' white ones an' the voice a the Lord come ontuh me sayin', 'Sammy, Sammy, save me the brown ones' – on'y there ain't but yella an' white ones an' they are round about me." He let the butterfly drop; it lay with futile wings on the grass.

"I have went an' rubbed the dust from off of its wings," said Sammy forlornly.

"What's Heaven like?" asked Ike. On the way out he had told Brian and Fat that Saint Sammy really got going when he talked about Heaven and how God made the world.

"Wherefore it cannot fly no more."

"What's Heaven like?" persisted Ike.

"Sometimes nothin's not no good no more."

"Sammy, tell about when –"

Sammy's blue eyes stared at them. "He give them a few days an' accordin' to the Image an' His eyes on their hearts. Their eyes ain't seen the majesty of His glory ner yet the greatness a His work, but their ways is before Him an' cannot be hid." Sammy's arm with its hand clawed, lifted, and pointed out the town low on the horizon. "Fer they have played the harlot an' the fornicator in the sight a the Lord!" His old voice trembled, thinned, and clutched at a higher pitch. "An' there is sorra an' sighin' over the face a the prairie – Herb an' the seed thereoff thirsteth after the water which don't cometh! The cutworm cutteth – the rust rusteth an' the 'hopper hoppeth! Sadness hath come to pass an' they put no more little, red labels on the underwear – no more but the yella an' the white!" He shook his fist at the buildings dwarfed on the horizon. "He shall rain ontuh them fire an' brimstone – down on the bare-ass adulteresses –" His voice broke off and went ringing on in the boys' ears.

Looking into Saint Sammy's face unexpectedly calm now after the squeezed intensity of the harangue, Brian felt stirring within him the familiar feeling, coloured now with sickening guilt.

"What's Heaven like?" asked Ike. "What's it like, Sammy?"

In a monotone, with the sing-songing stress of a child's Christmas recitation, Saint Sammy began:

"To start with He give a flip to the flywheel a thought, an' there was Heaven an' earth an' Him plumb in the middle. She had no shape ner nothin' on her. 'Let there be light,' He seth, an' there was some. 'Suits me fine,' He seth, 'an' I'm a-gonna call her night, an' I'm a-gonna call her day.' He took an' He gathered all the water together so the dry land stuck up; 'that there is dry earth,' He seth. 'Grass,' He seth, 'let her come.' An' she come. She jumped up green. He hung up the moon; he stuck up the sun; he pricked out the stars. He rigged out spring an' fall an' winter an' He done it. He made Him some fishes to use the sea fer swimmin' in – some fowls fer to use the air fer flyin' in.

"Next he made the critters.

"An' He got to thinkin', there ain't nobody fer to till this here soil, to one-way her, to drill her, ner to stook the crops, an' pitch the bundles, an' thrash her, when she's ripe fer thrashin', so He took Him some topsoil – made her into the shape of a man – breathed down into the nose with the breath of life.

"That was Adam. He was a man.

"He set him down ontuh a section to the east in the districk a Eden – good CPR land – lotsa water.

"The Lord stood back, an' He looked at what He done inside a one week an' she suited Him fine.

"He laid off fer a few days whilst Adam named over the critters. Then He remembered.

"He took Him one a Adam's ribs – whittled him a wife.

"That was Eve. She was a woman."

Steadily sibilant the wind washed through the dry grasses all around, bending them, laying them low, their millions yearning all together.

"You better git, boys," said Sammy. "Tarry not, fer the Lord's a-waitin' on me." His arm went up and around pointing out his horses, great, black beasts with their tails blown along their flanks, their thick necks arched and pointing out of the wind. "He waits fer Sammy in the east corner a the pasture – the Lord's corner." Without another word he turned and took up his spry way in that direction.

High above the boys as they walked back to the town, the wind went winging on, singing its lost and lonely song, transcendent vibrance filling universe with utter fierceness of its sound, willing grasses down in unison, relentless – unstilling – wild.

Brian walked with his eyes on his shadow long in the evening sun, undulating as the grasses rippled from him. He could feel the wind compelling him, urging him forward. He was filled with forlornness. Looking out over the prairie he saw the steeple of the Catholic church, a narrow spire pointing out the dizzy sky. The steady hand of the wind on his back was the hand that moved the sky with grey and sifting cloud.

Down the ribbon of the road unrolling to the town, the wind sang a higher, shriller song; it whined and thinned along the pulsing wires strung down the marching poles, growing smaller and smaller with dis-tance – black, minute crosses where the town was. Ike had grabbed the corners of his jacket; he held them out at his sides and leaned back upon the bellying wings he'd made. He turned and walked backwards aslant against the solid wind.

7

relopen

Jake Invents the Jumping Pound

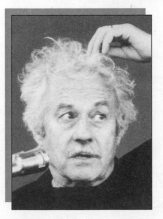

Listeners to the CBC's *"Jake and the Kid" radio series in the early 1950s particularly delighted in Jake Trumper's tall tales – and his "voice" as portrayed by John Drainie (who claimed that he was simply imitating W. O.). Jake tells the Kid that he invented hay wire, "made Chief Poundmaker give in at Cut Knife Crick," was a close friend of Wilf (Sir Wilfrid Laurier), "drunk Catawba wine with Sir John A," and threw Louis Riel in a wrestling match making him "say uncle three times – once in English, once in Cree, and the third time in French." The Kid's teacher, Miss Henchbaw, is a stickler for historical fact and the Kid often finds himself in hot water when he uses Jake's versions of history in his school projects. In the following tall tale from "Old MacLachlin Had a Farm" Jake tells the Kid how he invented the buffalo jumping pound. "Old MacLachlin Had a Farm" first appeared in Maclean's (September 1944), then aired a number of times on* CBC's *"Jake and the Kid" series in the early 1950s, and was published in Macmillan's collection of stories,* Jake and the Kid *(1961).*

❧

"Jake, I got H in school today."

"Whut!" Jake straightened up, and he had grease clear across his face. "Has Miss Henchbaw bin gittin' after you?"

"No, I mean I got a good mark again in History. Brought in a couple more buffalo skulls."

"Oh," Jake said, "that's nice. Whut the heck's skulls got to do with her?"

"We're takin' up about the Indians and the buffalo. Say, Jake, did you ever see a pound?"

"Dang right. Ain't I had tuh go git Queen and Baldy outa . . ."

"Not that kind. Like the Indians had, where they run buffaloes so's they could kill a lot and git meat fer pemmican."

"Oh. Why shore. A course I seen 'em."

"What're they like anyway?"

"Why they're – uh – she bin tellin' you fellas whut they wuz like?"

"All she said was they was a sorta place where they run buffalo, herded 'em, then killed 'em."

"Well, I tell yuh. I seen plenty of 'em, and there wuz one partic'lar kind I – uh – invented myself."

"Did yuh, Jake?"

"Yep." Jake was looking off toward the coulée. "Whut they call a buffalo jumping pound – run 'em over a cliff like – well – see that there coulée?"

"Yeah."

"Why do yuh figger yuh found so many arras an' skulls round there?"

"Why . . ."

"She's a buffalo jumping pound, the one I'm tellin' you about, the one I figgered out fer Chief Weasel Tail of the South Blackfoot in the early days."

"You mean Mac's coulée!"

"Yep, Mac's coulée. I can remember her like yesterday. Weasel Tail he come to me an' he says, Jake, he says, we gotta have buffalo. We need her fer meat, an' we need her fer tepees, an' we need her fer moccasins. We need her bad, real bad. There's bin a sorta flint drout around here an' we're all outa arras. The pemmican we was savin' up from last year, the kiyoots got at her. He hitched up his britch clout – he hitched her up, an' he says, my braves ain't touched off but a couple a buffalo fer two months. What we gonna do, Jake? I dunno, Weasel Tail, I says; an' he says, Jake, they's a lotta buffalo hangin' around only we can't git at 'em. You gotta give us a hand, Jake. She's got me beat, I says to him; an' he hitches up his britch clout agin the way it was all the time slippin' down on account of his belly bein' so shrunk up not havin' enny buffalo to eat. Jake, he says, you gotta figger her out fer us. Ef we don't git no meat fer our stummicks we might as well go throw ourselfs over the side a that there coulée. Well, sir, right there she come to me, she come to me how tuh git them pore Indians some grub inta their stummicks. Weasel Tail, I says to him, you go git you all your braves, build yuh a fence anglin' tuh meet that there coulée where she's steep, then go round up ever' buffalo fer a hundred miles around – herd 'em with a hundred drags behind and two hundred swings to the side, trail 'em right into that there coulée, an' there's yer grub."

"Gee, Jake!"

"Buffalo!" Jake said. "You never seen so menny in yore life. Thousands an' thousands of 'em, thicker'n grasshoppers, large an' small an' medium-sized. Cows with their calves a-bellerin' after 'em, beardy ol' bulls roarin' so's you couldn't har'ly hear yerself think. An' dust – they riz a dust that made her just like night fer fifty miles around. They come on the run, slaverin' at the jaws . . ."

"But if she was . . ."

"Stampedin' like they wuz, the shrink musta bin somethin' awful on all them buffalo – musta dropped a thousand ton to the mile – made a fella shudder tuh . . ."

"With all that there dust how could you see 'em?"

"See 'em! There wuz a million red lights a-shinin' through the dust, a million red lanterns where their eyes wuz, two million blood-shot eyes that lit her up. An' the smell – she wuz enough tuh give a badger the heartburn – like the inside of a blacksmith shop a mile square with a million blacksmiths shoein' a million horses – that wuz how she smelled. They wuz runnin' on smokin' hoofs – red hot, they wuz comin' so fast. An' then they hit that there cliff where the fence angled in. They wuz water there in them days. Soon as them buffalo commenced to go over, there come a hissin' an' a roarin' an' a blowin' – cloud a steam came up from them four million hoofs hittin' that there water – scalded fifteen braves and fifteen ponies to death. The rest got caught in the blizzard."

"Blizzard!"

"Yep. Never seen nothin' like it. Steam hit the dust, turned her to mud, an' she started in to mud. She mudded fifteen feet a mud in half an hour – the first mud blizzard I ever see – fifty Weasel Tail's braves got smothered to death a-sittin' on their ponies."

I looked at Jake a minute. "Jake," I said, "that's real hist'ry. That's – hist'ry!"

"A course," Jake said, "I wouldn't go tellin' that to – to folks that are fussy about hist'ry book hist'ry – the kind that like her sort a watered down. She might be a mite too rich fer Miss Henchbaw."

But there was where Jake was wrong.

Right about there I thought of something. "Jake," I said, "you claim there was a million of them there buffalo?"

"Yep."

"And they run 'em over the cliff?"

"Yep."

"Where's the bones?"

"Huh?"

"Where's all of them bones? Oughta be more'n a few skulls left outa million buffalo."

"Yeah. Ye're right there, Kid. Uh – why – the way she wuz – say, that there water jug looks kinda dry. Mebbe yuh better – oh – now I – they shore wuz a lotta them bones, a whole mile along that there coulée, hundred feet deep, wide as the coulée. Then we had them real dust storms a coupla years after – covered 'em plumb over. Jist take a look at that there coulée – only 'bout fifty foot deep, ain't she?"

"Yeah."

"Useta be she wuz two hundred in Weasel Tail's time. Them bones filled her a hundred feet; dust covered her over about fifty. Now she's only fifty – see? What you might call a reg'lar buffalo mine down there, Kid."

"Jake," I said, "like I said, that there's hist'ry."

I headed for the house to fill the jug for Jake.

8

Love's Wild Magic

In this episode from the "Jake and the Kid" stories, Jake Trumper tells of coming to the rescue of his long-time friend, old man Gatenby, who had fallen into the hands of Violet Bowdry. Violet is a complicated mix of Florence Nightingale, Keats's Belle Dame Sans Merci, and what we refer to today as an ambulance chaser.

"Love's Wild Magic" first appeared as a radio play in CBC's "Jake and the Kid" series in 1952 and then was adapted into a short story for McClelland & Stewart's collection of stories, According to Jake and the Kid (1989). W. O. naturally chose to read this story at Toronto's Harbourfront Reading Series, which is directed by Greg Gatenby.

❧❦❧

I never known anybody more stubborn than old man Gatenby is. Once he gets an idea into his head, stumping powder won't blow her out of there. Hard to say what gets Gate into more of his mix-ups: being stubborn or that temper of his.

Last winter we come close to losing Gate. Had Doc Fotheringham stymied. And after Violet Bowdry moved in to look after Gate, it turned real serious. Violet, she's a widow – four times. She all the time tells folks how them four fellows of hers went west:

". . . and Albert felt that bundle fork go. Caught one of the tines in the feeder and ripped it right out of his hands and he leapt up onto the feeder track to get the fork before it would go through the thrashing machine. Poor Herb didn't make it. I mean *Albert* didn't make it. And the fork went right through the – aaah . . . !"

She never did say how many bushels the wheat and Albert went to the acre that crop year.

". . . year after Albert passed away I married Herb and he got to feeling peaked – turned yellow as a buttercup, and Dr. Fotheringham said to me, 'Violet,' he said, 'I got to operate.' Herb never got down off that table. Gald stones. Nine of them. I still have them in that Mason jar on my bedroom dresser.

"I lost two to the knife, one to the thrashing machine. Harold – my last – kicked to death by a mule . . ."

Violet has to be about the most un-cheerful woman in all Crocus district. Or the province of Saskatchewan. Or Canada. She was the one damn near put the finishing touch on Gate.

First I knew something was the matter with him was the night last January he came over for an evening of rummy. Just me and Gate at the kitchen table. Kid and his ma visiting Tinchers'.

"What's eatin' you, Gate? You let the five of spades go by for a run of three an' it would've put you out."

"Was it."

"And that hand before – you end up with a whole slew of face cards and aces – they count high, you know. Can't get caught with face cards and not suffer."

"Ah-huh."

Gate sure loves to win. At anything. Something must've been eating him real bad. "What's botherin' you, Gate?"

"Nothin'. Nothin'."

"You ain't buildin' up for – haven't had your lumbago botherin' you?"

"No." He sighed a long one. "Uh-uh."

"Started up another them crazy diets? What is it this time – alfalfa and pigweed porridge?"

That should've got a rise out of him. It didn't. He just grunted.

"Reminds me of a fellow I knew out Hairy Hills way. Name of Clifton. Arley Clifton," I said.

"Mmmh."

"Arley Clifton – always tormented – always bothered with trouble. Women trouble."

"Ah-huh . . ."

"Worst I ever seen him he got tangled up with a woman nickname of 'Scatter-Piss Annie.' He spent whole month flat on his back with a beaver pelt on his – and a rock he kept on the window-sill, to keep it froze cold so he could put it on the end of – no, serious, Gate – what is the matter with you? Puttin' you off your rummy game."

"Jake, Jake – she's been an awful year for me."

"I never noticed that."

"Every way you look at her."

"Oh, I don't know, Gate."

"Late, cold spring, no summer to speak of at all. Humid – more like Ontario – kind of smothery. Then winter set right in. You know, Jake – this year there's been snow every month but July."

"That's what's gettin' you down – weather, Gate?"

"Not just the weather. She's been a bad year – for humans and for critters. Look at Old Candy Sangster."

"Well now, Gate."

"Went west."

"He was to go any time, Gate. The weather didn't have nothin' to do with . . ."

"Candy Sangster an' me homesteaded together – way back when the West was in knee-britches."

"Sure, sure," I said.

"Mort Dewdney. He got it, too."

"Yep."

"Then there was . . ."

"Now look, Gate. Ain't good to let your mind brood over depressin' stuff like . . ."

"I had a birthday – last week – Tuesday."

"Did you now! That's real nice. Happy – happy returns, Gate."

"Thank you, Jake. Ain't likely to be."

"Ain't likely to be what?" I said.

"Many happy returns. Jake – seventy-three. Seventy-three long years I been livin' an' breathin' an' eatin' an' workin' an' sleepin'."

"Don't have to lick all over her like a all-day sucker! Other folks done alla that with their eyes shut an' one hand tied behind their back."

"Ain't gonna be with you much longer," he said.

"Takin' a little trip?"

"Takin' a *long* one, Jake. One-way ticket, an' she ain't CNR. I got death settin' on my wishbone."

"The hell you have!"

"Oh, I may hold out till next spring, but not till much after. Seventy-three . . ."

"That ain't old!"

"Runs in our family – always run in the Gatenbys."

"Dyin' runs in just about everybody's family!"

"Put the rummy deck away at seventy-three. My father. Died at seventy-three. My grandfather, he went west at seventy-three. My mother – no Gatenby ever got past seventy-three. I am *now* seventy-three."

"I never thought you was superstitious, Gate."

"I ain't. In our blood an' in our bones. Feel it in my bones all year. What they call a fore-boddin'. She's comin' one way or the other. Don't matter how. She's comin' for Samuel Titchener Gatenby."

"Who's comin'?"

"Death."

"Aw shee . . ."

"Like an old lady in spring to get this old horse outa the pasture. 'Come on, Sam,' she'll holler, sweet an' coaxin'. 'Come on, Boy. We ain't gonna bother Doc Fotherin'ham – just you an' me an' away we go.'"

It ain't easy, but I'm fussy about Old Gate. About *Gate*. I didn't argue when he cut off the rummy early and headed home. When the Kid and his ma showed up, I told her how worried I was about Gate. She was too. And the Kid. He's all the time listening in.

Just before we turned in he said, to me, "How old are *you*, Jake?"

"Kid, I quit countin' before I come to work for you an' your ma."

"How long do you figure you've got . . ."

"'Bout as long as Old Man Sherry. Had lotsa sleep alla my life – good hard back-breakin' work from daylight to dark – out in the open from time I kicked the doo off the stubble till the springs creaked at night. Same as Gate."

"Well, if Gate's going west this spring . . ."

"He ain't. He ain't. Don't pay no attention to him. He's healthier'n I am. Gate's never had nothin' ailin' him in his whole life a couple tablespoons of Professor Noble Winesinger's Lightnin' Penetration Oil and Tune-up Tonic wouldn't fix up."

"But the way you said he was talking tonight . . ."

"Just talk. Just talk. Worst he ever had was a cold in the head."

"What about rheumatism – lumbago?" Kid said.

"Hell – them ain't bein' sick. Not *bad*. Just sort of a pest attackin' folks. Like horseflies or – Sam, he's too stubborn to die!"

Ma and me talked quite a bit about Gate the next week.

"I don't understand what's gotten into him," she said. "At first I rather liked the change in him. Gentler – quieter. But now I'm not so sure. He's lost weight, Jake."

"Nah. Always was a prune type, Gate. Tough – elastic – kind that bounces right back."

"Several people have noticed a change in him," she said.

"Just ain't arguin' with folks so much or screechin' his head off, that's all. Gate's all right."

"Well, he is getting on. It isn't just lately, but I've often wondered why he didn't have himself a housekeeper. To cook regular meals for him. *Proper* meals. Or if something did happen . . ."

"Nothin's gonna happen to that old . . ."

". . . an accident. He sleeps soundly, you know – he ought to have somebody there to take care of – just in case."

"Ain't ever had a hired girl – ain't likely to. An' nobody could do it to suit him anyways. Wouldn't last one minute. You can't find a soul in this here district would be willin' to put up with Gate long enough to boil him an egg an' butter a slice o' toast."

"You may be right. But all the same – all the same."

"I know I'm right!"

Whenever Gate goes off half-cocked on some whim of his, it's too bad that folks got to get pulled into her. All the time false smoke signals and a fellow runs to help him out an' it's like runnin' into a buzzsaw. Or Violet Bowdry's Albert through that thrashing machine. Wasn't just us an' the neighbours worried about Gate. Folks in town was concerned about him, too. I found that out in Repeat Golightly's barber shop.

"Autumn of his days. I say Old Man Gatenby has reached the long shadows of the fall of his life."

"Mm-mmmmh."

"The wick is turned low in the lamp chimney. All it needs – puff of wind – out – goes – the – lamp. Gatenby's lamp."

"He's got a lot of coal oil left in his lamp yet," I said.

"Those are the ones that fool you, Jake. Never tell. Never tell. Been a bad year. Lost a lot of our beloved ones this year. Take Candy Sangster . . ."

"Now look here, Repeat. I heard all this bull –!"

"This was Candy Sangster's year."

"Candy Sangster might just as well've got it any year since Ought-Four. He's been drivin' straight from the Maple Leaf over the CNR tracks with a hide-full of beer long as I knew him. Just a matter time till him an' the mules an' the wagon an' the Sooline 4:10 would hit her the same moment."

"Thing is, Jake, *this* year, they did. And Mort Dewdney – another old friend of Gate's – Mort Dewdney."

"Been sick for over five years."

"Helga Petersen."

"You sound more an' more like Violet Bowdry every . . ."

"Wonderful woman, isn't she," Repeat said. "Seasoned."

"With what!"

"There is one who had gone down into the valley the shadow . . ."

"She didn't. Just her husbands did – four of 'em."

"Sensitive – sensitive to the darker side of life. Serious. There is a woman."

". . . to give a gopher's ass the heartburn!"

". . . a woman has brought solace and understanding and comfort to countless folks – on their bed of pain – in their time deepest sorrow."

"All I ask, if I ever get laid out – one way or the other, sick or dead – keep her away from me!"

"Gentle ministrations – healing and soothing. Tell me she did twenty-four-hour duty with Mrs. Petersen. There to the very last."

"Mmmmh."

"Can't get specials down from Regina. Dr. Fotheringham been leaning heavy on Violet the past couple years. Doesn't know what he'd do without her. They say she read to Helga Petersen right up to the very last."

"That'd be better'n listenin' to her."

"No formal training, but she's what you might call an instinctive nurse. No formal training – sympathetic heart tells her what to do next. Nightingale – Florence Nightingale."

"I heard of her," I said, "but I didn't know she was a Crocus district girl."

"And when Sam Gatenby's time comes – as he feels it will, this year – it'll be Violet Bowdry that'll smooth his fevered brow. Be her sweet voice and tender care will soften Gate's last hours pain before he . . ."

"Repeat, for the love of – what the hell did Sam Gatenby ever do to you!"

"Jake, I count Samuel Titchener Gatenby one of my best friends. And when he goes it'll be a great shock to me – to the community he's served so well. Wet or dry?"

If there is a hell like the preacher says – and I got no reason to figure there ain't – there's something that'd be pretty close to her right here on this earth: a fellow laying flat on his back – with Violet breathing down his neck.

She's a great reader, Violet. All them glossy magazines in Pill Brown's drugstore – the ones with the woman's head on the front cover with real nice teeth – *True Story, I Confess, Revealin' Love Stories, Appallin' Love*. She don't read them just to herself. She reads them to them poor sick women. She's – indecent!

Wouldn't you know, after a bellyful out of Repeat, when I get home there she is, in the parlour with the Kid's ma. Having tea. Kid's ma invited me to join them. I said there was chores I had to do.

"Oh, chores can always wait, Jake," Violet said. "Set a minute. Cup of tea'll revive you. Nothing like the lift a cup of tea *or* coffee gives a person when he's feeling all draggy and done in."

"I'm feelin' fine. Just fine. Never felt better – I don't need no lift."

"Just like Carl," Violet said.

"Carl?" Ma said.

". . . Binestettner, my husband – was – third. Carl was always protestin' – nothin' wrong with him, he was all right, right as could be – an' all the time that growth in there in his . . ."

"I gotta go out to them chores."

"Always on the go, never let up. I said to him when he was just slipping off. 'Carl,' I said, 'it ain't the sarcoma, Carl, it's the top speed you always went at. You've depleted your reserve energy. Worked your fingers to the bone, never time to take the load off your feet.' I'm the same way. You take those varicose ulcers. That's just because a woman's on her feet twenty-four hours the day – on the go."

"Well, I got to go out an' finish them . . ."

"Breathless rush – overworked body can only take so much, I always say. Or rather Herb used to say. Now Herb . . ."

"Your cup's empty, Mrs. Bowdry," Ma said. "Another . . ."

"Thank you. If folks could only learn to ease off on their oars – relax."

"I relax all right," I said.

"Readin'. I always say readin' has been the savin' of me. Read all the time, whenever I can. Broadens a person, deepens their understanding of human nature. Why, I always – thank you, no cream, thanks, half the usual sugar, kidneys – I guess I'm no different from a hundred other women. Have their problems, make mistakes, tryin' to enrich one's life. Set – set, Jake."

I did. I needed to!

"Happy as a lark makin' a home for a loved one – all four times – and it was true-to-life stories of other women which helped me the most, all through the bitter and all through the sweet. Lots of lessons to be learned from these stories – on lovelier livin'. I've enriched my life, an' my husbands' . . ."

"All four," I said.

"Physically – spiritually – morally – emotionally whilst we made a life together. I think *I Confess* . . ."

"To what?" I said.

Kid's ma glared at me.

"*I Confess* has given me more comfort and help. I have the January copy with me now. I – here . . ."

"I guess I could use a cuppa tea now," I said.

"Titled 'The Unmarried Bride' . . ."

"Usual – four spoons."

"Yes, Jake. I know," Ma said.

"Ah, here. Just listen to this: '*After the bright rapture of the honeymoon comes the dawn of understanding. The grey dawn of the betrayed. Kirk had forged the wedding certificate and Veronica knew finally . . .*'"

"Slurp," I said.

"'*. . . that she was the* unmarried bride.'"

"Rather unusual situation," Ma said.

"Oh, it's the way it's written – it's so true to life . . ." She went back to the goddam magazine.

I had another cup of tea.

"'*With a snide little laugh Sabra turned to Veronica. "So you two have been playing at marriage, have you?" she said.*'"

I had two more cups of tea while she finished "The Unmarried Bride." She started in on another one.

"'*My trousseau was modest, but in one fling of extravagance I had bought a dramatic negligée of pale rose-dawn coloured lace and chiffon – delicate but daring. I fastened it about me.*'"

In this one a fellow name of Raymond turned out to have two other wives he hadn't told Kimberly about.

"'*I sat shivering until the pale fingers of morning lightened the room. My anguish deepened with each passing hour. After a long time I stripped off the negligée and groped my way, blinded by tears – to my clothes – young, vulnerable, bewildered. I stood frozen for an eternity.*'"

I knew exactly how Kimberly felt!

"'. . . then I collapsed on the sobbing bed – I collapsed sobbing on the bed. I saw now that Raymond's love for me was not on a higher, more spiritual plane. He had done his best to drag it down to the level of . . .'"

She closed up I Confess.

"You see what I mean," she said. "I'm not the weepy type but I think all of us – women – are happiest when we're having a good cry or worryin' over somebody else's problems. I've been told so many times I have a sympathetic ear, and I must admit I enjoy sort of ponderin' over other people's problems. Now, you take Old Mr. Gatenby down the road from you."

"No!" That really shook me!

"Oh, I don't think Sam Gatenby has any real health problem," Kid's ma said.

"I hear he's been failing," Violet said, "just in the last year – the last few weeks as a matter . . ."

"Sam's all right!" I said.

"I know he's been in to see Dr. Fotheringham several times now," Violet said. "They say he's spent several afternoons with Title Brown."

"What the – what's Title Brown got to do with . . ."

"Affairs – affairs," Violet said. "Getting them in order. So many of us leave our wills to the last minute. Till it's too late."

I skinned out of there to do them chores I didn't really have to do. I headed for Gate's. Found him in his rocker. Afghan throwed over his shoulders. All hunched up and staring at the mica belly-button of his Quebec heater.

"Pull out a chair for yourself, Jake." Didn't even sound like Gate. All breathy.

"Sure. Sure, Gate – dropped over – few han's of rummy."

"No-no . . ."

"Euchre?"

"No – I no . . ."

"Five hundred? Say, look Gate . . ."

"Sorry, Jake. Ain't got the strength to pick up the cards an' lay 'em down."

"Now look here, you gotta get a grip on yourself! You been lettin' this foolishness go too far . . . !"

"Foolishness? Foolishness? Jake – Jake – for your own peace of mind – so you won't be kickin' yourself after she's happened, watch yourself . . ."

"What are you tryin' to tell . . ."

"Nothin' hurts more than the unthinkin' harsh word spoke in thoughtlessness – remembered, when it's too late."

"You ain't ready for no shiny box with handles yet!"

"I'm more'n ready. All square with the world. Will's made out."

"Look, you're gonna carry this thing too far . . ."

"Borrowed time. Livin' on borrowed time . . ."

"The hell you are – any more'n I am!"

"An' I want to – now you're here – I want to ask you a favour."

"Why sure – ask away, Gate."

"I'd like it real well if you was one of my polar bearers. Active. Or if you ain't up to it – honorary."

"We'll bury you – we'll bury you in a banana crate out by the slaughterhouse the way we did with Chuck Swengle in Ought-Eight when he passed out at the old Arlington – only turned out he wasn't dead. Just passed out."

"No laughin' matter, Jake. Another thing – my favourite hymn is 'There's a Beautiful Land on High.'"

"Gate, I always knew you was the stubbornest fellow I ever run across, but this one time it ain't gonna do you no harm nor no good. You ain't gonna die this year nor the next – nor the next – and it don't matter a whoop how hard you try to do it, you – ain't – gonna – die!"

Even back then, I wasn't all that sure about that. Got worse. Each time I dropped in on him he seemed to've sunk lower. I come to a conclusion. Me visiting him wasn't doing him one goddam bit of good. Matter of fact, just the opposite. Only helped him to feel sorrier and sorrier for himself. Maybe if I stayed away and he got to wondering why I wasn't visiting him, might upset him enough to make him perk up.

Even though I wasn't checking him out regular all that week, didn't mean I didn't know how he was doing. Kid's ma, she answers a lot of rings on our party lines that ain't our ring. She picked up more about Gate's condition than I wanted to hear about.

"Martha Tincher's seen Dr. Fotheringham's car go past their windbreak three times since Tuesday."

"Maybe he wasn't headed for Gate's."

"Oh, he was. Shirley Totecole saw him turn in there."

Totecoles are right next to Gate's place.

"She dropped in after Dr. Fotheringham left the last time. She says he's staying in bed. Isn't eating. Cheeks all caved in . . ."

"Probably had his dentures out," I said.

"Jake, maybe you ought to go over and – why don't you . . . ?"

"Because I am tryin' to get him stubborn in the opp'site direction!"

"Evidently it's not working."

I was afraid she was right, but what the hell could a fellow do? I decided to drop in on him next morning. I changed my mind when the Kid got home from Rabbit Hill school.

"He's got a housekeeper now, Jake."

Well at least that was something good for a change.

"Stevie Kiziw's dad drove her out there this morning. She's going to cook and clean for Mr. Gatenby."

"Thank goodness!" Kid's ma said. "Just what I've been saying all al . . ."

"Mrs. Bowdry," the Kid said.

"Shee-yit!" I said.

For the first time since I ever said that word in front of the Kid, his ma didn't take me by the face. I didn't wait till *morning* to go over to Gate's.

She was there all right.

She stopped me before I could get into his bedroom.

"I just don't know what we're going to do. He won't eat. Even soup or tapioca." I happen to know that Gate hates both of them equal.

"Not enough to keep a sparrow alive."

I noticed sparrows eat a lot of what Baldy and Queenie drop out there. For their size. The sparrows.

"That's probably all what's wrong with him," I suggested. "A couple of rare steaks an' . . ."

"Oh no, it's much worse than that, I'm afraid – goes deeper. I have a feeling – though I'm no doctor, goodness knows, but I've seen enough of them – I have a feeling there's a growth – malignant . . ."

"That's for Doc Fotherin'ham to . . ."

"Yes, but sometimes even the doctors are helpless. I'm afraid it's so with Mr. Gatenby. I'm doing my best. And tomorrow Martha Tincher's dropping in to relieve me so I can get into town."

"Mmmh," I said.

"I can tell when the end is near. He's lost all interest in this life, Mr. Trumper –" she sighed. "Too bad he isn't a woman."

Now what the hell did she mean by that? "What the hell do you mean by that!"

"Ssssh! Lower your voice! He can still hear! My reading to them – women – works wonders for them, but the appeal is only to women. I did try it with Harold, hoping he would rally, but he didn't. Too far gone – seemed to sink even faster. If only Sam were a woman patient of mine, I'd be right in that bedroom beside him, reading aloud to him these wonderful and inspirin' stories . . ."

"Yeah! Yeah!"

"I read to Helga Petersen – near the last – for twelve straight hours."

"You thought of tryin' it out on Gate?"

"Oh no – he's a *man*."

"Yeah. Noticed that. All the same, even though it didn't work when you tried it on Herb . . ."

"Harold."

". . . just the once with a fellow."

"You think so?"

"Can't tell if you don't try it, can you?"

"I suppose not," she said.

"Gate, he'd never ask you to read to him. Never did read much himself – *Crocus Breeze, Nor'west Prairie Farm Review*, like of that. Might not be so bad a idea for you to read to him some of them wonderful stories out of *Appallin' Love* . . ."

"*Appealing Love.*"

"If you really want to do your best for Gate . . ."

"I do! Oh, I do!"

"All right, then. You said Martha Tincher's drivin' you into Crocus . . ."

"First thing tomorrow morning."

"So – you go into Pill Brown's an' get a pile of them shiny magazines an' you take an' read 'em to Gate. No matter what he says – or does. I got a notion that's just what he needs. Might just turn the corner . . ."

"You really think . . . ?"

"Sure do. You read to him. Like you did with Helga an' all them other women. Here. This oughta cover it." I handed her the ten-dollar bill. "You read to him till your voice gives out."

We didn't wait for Martha Tincher to pick her up. I got on the phone to her and said *I'd* take Violet in. Then I phoned Pill Brown an' he agreed to come to the store and open her up for us. Ten dollars bought one hell of a lot of them magazines – enough to fill a bundle rack. After we got back to Gate's I took as much as I could of it the rest of the evening:

"'. . . *didn't know marriage could be like this. She had thought it would be all love and kisses and tenderness. When Darryl kissed her brutally, then revelation dawned in her hitherto blinded heart . . .*'"

Gate, he just laid there with his eyes closed the way he'd been doing the past week, not saying a word.

"'. . . *life had been one long and carefree flirt. Little did Sandra care for the lives she had wrecked. Until debonair Lindsay came along. Here was a conquest that really mattered . . . !*'"

By the next story, Gate had started to make kind of grunting sounds.

"'. . . had Darby been deceiving her all along through those tempestuous three years they'd been together? Only Willa Lynne herself could answer that searing question! How could she ever be sure of his love for her? How could she find the answer her parched heart thirsted for?'"

I'd known Gate a long time and I seen that squeezed-up look around his mouth whenever he had them gas pains an' trots you get out of catching Looie Riel's Revenge from a bad water supply in summer. Salmon Nellie, Doc Fotheringham calls it.

I guess it was the morning of the second day Gate quit grunting and groaning. He'd opened his eyes to curse, but she kept her promise to me, went on reading to him. Only quit if he dropped off to sleep.

When I come by in the afternoon, she said, "He still won't eat a thing, but you were right. It does seem to be working. He threw the urinal at me this morning."

"Good sign," I said. If it was full.

I went in with her while she read to Gate some more.

"'. . . his lips on Carla's were sheer magic . . .'"

"Jake – Jake, for God's sakes . . . !"

"'. . . he was hers. Yet why did he draw back? Why was he keeping the check-rein on the untamed passion that coursed so wildly through his veins? Only time would . . .'"

"Stop it! Stop it!"

"'. . . what strange force stronger even than his love for her was holding him back . . .'"

Me, I was wondering what strange force was still holding Gate back.

"'. . . she knew then the idea of marriage had never even entered his head. Or his heart. What a mockery it would have been if . . .'"

"Turn it off, woman!" Gate had made it up to sitting.

"Now just you lay back, Sam."

"Chuck them magazines!" At least that's what it sounded like he said. He didn't have his teeth in.

I nodded for her to go on.

"'. . . *what a mockery it would have been had I brought him round to it. Anything outside of marriage was unthinkable, of course, and yet I knew we both came from two different . . .*'"

"My pants! My goddam pants!"

"'. . . *worlds. There was no overlapping of those two different worlds really, except for this exquisitely torturing* physical *attraction . . .*' Mr. Gatenby!"

Gate had flang back the covers and most of his nightshirt with them. "Pants or no pants!" he yelled, "I'm runnin' you outa here! An' after her I'm takin' care of you, Trumper!"

He did, barefoot, his nightshirt flying, out the bedroom through the kitchen, the back stoop and into the backyard and past the chicken coops beyond, but it wasn't no physical attraction or untamed passion driving him on after her.

I skinned out of there before he got back inside to keep the rest of his promise.

Doc Fotheringham had to come out to him again, and the Kid's ma moved in to take care of Gate with the kettle steaming and a blanket over his head. Pneumonia from chasing Violet over the snow in twenty-below weather. He's just about over that now.

Same old Gate again.

9

❧

Brian's Skates

When W. O. selects pieces for a reading, he generally works on the principle of "make 'em laugh, make 'em weep." The following scenes from Who Has Seen the Wind *fall into the latter category. W. O. is particularly sensitive to the joys and disappointments of the child's world, especially those significant moments of initiation which are looked forward to by children but often feared by parents. This piece's poignant portrayal of Brian's desperate longing for his first pair of skates for Christmas and his subsequent disappointment moves both children and parents in the audience.*

❧

In the O'Connal family, Christmas began as a rule early in December, when the boys started to decide what presents they would like. Brian's second year of school, Christmas was called earlier to the parents' attention because with the beginning of winter Brian asked for skates.

Maggie's first response was unbelief; it was difficult for her to think that one of her boys was old enough to want skates. She told him that he was just past seven and that Forbsie Hoffman did not have skates yet. Brian answered that Artie Sherry had them. Artie, who was a year and a half older than Brian, had inherited a pair from an older sister; the high tops had been cut down; they had to be worn with three pairs of woollen socks so that Artie's feet would not slide around in the shoes – but to Brian, skateless, they were things whose beauty would endure forever.

Skates became a frequent topic of conversation at meals. At length the grandmother said she was tired and sick of hearing about them; would it not be possible to give the child a pair so that he could break his neck and afford them a few peaceful meals? Maggie forbade Brian to mention skates at the table again.

The day that he saw the new tube skates in the hardware store window, Brian called on his father at work.

"Why can't I have them, Dad?"

"Because your mother says you're too young for them."

"But I'm not – I'm –"

"Seven's pretty young for skates."

"I was seven a long time ago – in the fall – I'm past seven!"

"You're still too young – when you're older – next year, perhaps."

"I'll be older at Christmas. That's a long ways away. May I have them for Christmas?"

"I don't think so, Spalpeen."

After Brian had left, Gerald felt a pang of remorse; it was difficult to see why the boy could not have skates. That night he had a talk with Maggie.

"– perhaps by Christmas time?" he asked her. "He'll be almost seven and a half by then, Maggie."

His wife looked at him a long time before answering him. "You know – I love him too, Gerald. I hate to deny them things as much as you. It's just that he seems so – do you think he's old enough? Do you – honestly?"

"I think so, Maggie."

"It isn't because he wants them so badly?"

"Well – he's old enough – let him skate."

After a decent interval Brian was told that he might possibly get skates for Christmas. Bobbie then insisted that he should get them too, but he finally settled for a hockey stick and a puck.

Brian looked forward with eagerness to the promised skates. He thought of them often – during school hours – whenever the boys gathered after school with worn, sliver-thin sticks to play a sort of hockey between tin-can goal posts and with a blob of frozen horse manure for a puck. The more he thought of them, the less envious he was of Artie with his "wimmen skates." There would be nothing feminine about *his*; they would be sturdy tubes with thick, felt tongues.

The night before Christmas he was almost sick with excitement and anticipation as he lay in his bed with Bobbie beside him. He could see the skates clearly with their frosted tubing and the clear runners that would cling to his thumb when he ran it along them to test their sharpness. He could see himself gliding over the river, alone on shining ice. With a twist and a lean – a shower of ice snow – he came to a breathtaking stop.

Bobbie stirred in his sleep.

"You awake, Bobbie?"

Bobbie did not answer him.

Perhaps there would be straps over the ankles; not that he would need them, for his ankles were strong. His feet wouldn't slop. He flexed them beneath the covers – stronger than anything. Maybe they were too strong, and when he pushed, he would push the ice clean full of cracks.

He got up and went to the window of the room. The streetlight outside was starred in the clear winter night; it made him think of the Star of the East and men on camels. Over the house across the street he could see the Northern Lights in a curtain shifting delicately, tinting green fluted and rippling, with here and there a pale blush of pink. He watched them melt and reappear against the dark sky.

As he climbed into the bed again his excitement was smothering him. He closed his eyes tightly. If only he could get to sleep the time would pass more quickly. When one slept it was nothing – swift as a person on skates – swift as the wind –

"He came, Brian! He came!"

Bobbie was jumping on the bed, his hair bright in the winter sunshine that filled the room.

Brian jumped from bed. "C'mon!"

Their stockings lumpy with oranges, each with a bright, cardboard clown protruding from its top, hung from the mantel of the fireplace. Bobbie's sleigh, that could be steered, was before the tree. Bobbie threw himself on the parcels.

"Wait a minute!" cried Brian. "They're not all yours – just with your name!"

He began to sort out the presents upon which Maggie the night before had printed in the large block letters which Brian could easily read.

Anxiously Brian watched the growing pile of parcels beside him. He opened a deep box to find it full of coloured box cars and an engine, in little compartments. He opened another – a mechanical affair which when wound caused two long Negroes to dance galvanically, all the while turning around. Slippers were in one promising-looking parcel. As he opened the last of his parcels he was filled with the horrible conviction that something was wrong.

Then he saw a parcel behind the Christmas tree. His name was on it. He opened it. They were not tube skates: they were not single-runnered skates; they were bob-skates, double-runnered affairs with curving toe-cleats and a half-bucket arrangement to catch the heel of the shoe.

For a swift moment Brian's heart was filled with mixed feeling; disappointment bitter and blinding was there, but with it a half-dazed feeling of inner release and relief that he had got skates. They were skates, he told himself as he turned them over in his hands.

"What's the matter, Brian?" Bobbie had looked up from his fire engine.

Brian got up and went into the living room; he sat on the window-seat next to the shamrock plant, the bob-skates upon his knees. When Bobbie came through a while later clutching a hockey stick a foot longer than himself, Brian paid no attention to him.

Throughout dinner he spoke only when spoken to. When his father and uncle were seated in the living room with lighted cigars and his mother and grandmother were in the kitchen, washing the dinner dishes, he went unnoticed to the hallway, put on his coat and tuque, and with the bob-skates went out.

As he walked, he passed other children pulling Christmas sleighs and Christmas toboggans, some with gleaming Christmas skates slung over their shoulders. Through the fiercely tinselled snow sparkling unbearably in the sunlight he walked, not toward the downtown bridge where children and adults swooped over cleared ice, but toward the powerhouse and the small footbridge. There he sat near a clump of willow, fitted the skates to his feet, buckled the straps over his insteps, and went knee-deep through the snow on the river-bank, to the ice.

Once on the ice he stood for a moment on trembling legs. He pushed with one foot; it skidded sideways; the other went suddenly from under him, and he came down with a bump that snatched his breath. He got carefully up and stood uncertainly. He pushed a tentative skate ahead, then another. He stood still with knees half-bent. He gave a push with one skate preparatory to swooping over the ice. He fell flat on his face. He got up.

He began a slow forward sliding across the ice, painfully, non-committal steps of a stroke victim just rising from bed. He was not skating, he was walking with an overwhelming feeling of frustration that reminded him of dreams in which he ran with all his might, but stayed only in one spot. He fell again, and felt his elbow go numb. He sat on the ice, looking at his own feet ahead of him.

He began to cry.

Brian's parents, his grandmother, and his uncle were seated in the living room when he got back to the house. He was carrying the bob-skates as he came out of the hallway.

"Been skatin'?" asked Sean.

Brian did not answer him. "Uncle Sean asked you a question, Son," said Maggie.

Sean's big, freckled hand reached out to take one of the bob-skates. "Damn fool question," said Sean. "Fella doesn't skate with bob-skates. Had somebody pullin' you, did you?"

Brian shook his head.

"What's wrong, Spalpeen?" Brian's father was looking at his tear-stained face.

Brian rushed from the room.

"What do you mean?" Maggie turned to Sean. "What's wrong with his skates? What did you mean –"

"They call 'em skates," said Sean. "Can't skate with 'em. Just teaches kids a healthy respect for ice, that's all. Got no grip at all – skid like hell. Never forget the first time I took Gerald on ice with a pair – 'bout the same age as Brian. He had one hell of a time – ended up hangin' on to me coat tails, whilst I pulled him around."

"But – then that means that Brian – he's –" Maggie got up and went swiftly from the room.

She found Brian at the kitchen window.

"Don't they work, Son?"

Still looking out the window, Brian shook his head.

"Aren't they what you wanted?"

"Tubes," he got out with difficulty. "Like in Harris's."

"I'm sorry, Brian." Maggie watched his shoulders moving. She turned his face around to her. "Don't – please don't! I'll fix it!"

She went to the phone.

"Mr. Harris? Have you a pair of – of tube skates left? Small size? I wonder if we – if you could come down to the store with me – my son – will you – will –"

"Mother!"

That night Maggie O'Connal stood at her children's bedside. With her white nightgown almost to her heels, her hair in two black braids, she looked like a little girl in the dimness of the room.

A glinting light caught her eye, and she saw a length of leather lace hanging down the side of the bed. Brian slept with his hand clenched around the runner of one tube skate, his nose almost inside the boot. Maggie reached out one hand and laid it lightly upon Brian's cheek; she kept it there for a long time. Then she gently took the skate from his hand.

She turned and with the flat, soft steps of the bare-footed, went from the room.

10

⁓

Take One Giant Step

W. O.'s grandmother Maggie McMurray figured prominently in his life as a child and adolescent, and he frequently drew on his memories of her for his stories. While the stories in this collection emphasize her Scots Presbyterian nature, W. O. also delights in his memories of her "earthy" side. In this piece he recalls how one Christmas she helped him take a giant step towards manhood.

The following is a combination of W. O.'s original reading manuscript and the version first published in the Imperial Oil Review *(December 1960). It was later worked into* How I Spent My Summer Holidays *(1981).*

⁓

For years as a writer and before that as an ordinary and sensible person, I have always been drawn to the very young and the very old; either end of the age stick has seemed so much more interesting than the middle. There is not anything dilute or luke about the emotions and

80

responses of children and of old people, almost as though we start out concentrated and we end up concentrated. This goes for the abrasive as well as the charming qualities, and I am a little worried about the sort of old man I may make thirty years from now, an undisciplined, cranky, vain, and dirty old man, I suspect. If only I could become something like my grandmother, I would be an octogenarian successful beyond my wildest expectations.

In spite of the wonderful homes for senior citizens all over our country, necessitated by the loss of the second storey from our houses, a very important and rightful influence has been stolen from the lives of our children. They are denied the privilege and the discipline of growing up with a grandmother or a grandfather or a grand aunt in the home. There is nothing quite like association with a grandparent to teach a boy restraint, the art of argument, consideration, patience, and an appreciation of both the Puritanical and the Rabelaisian elements in life. As well, he is prepared for that moment of truth sooner or later in his life when he must discover his own mortality.

My own grandmother taught me not to: whine, squeal, cheat at casino, tell tales, conform, settle for less, or grow up into anything but a Liberal. Her name was Maggie McMurray; she was of lowland Scottish descent, a Grit, and the most erect human I have ever known. Her person carried a ripe apple fragrance like that of shellac; I know that the same scent breathed from the crystal set my brother Jack built and very nearly got Regina with. She looked a great deal like a more finely drawn John Knox, if he had worn a black velvet ribbon high around his neck. Under the attached throat-piece of lace my grandmother kept a goitre. It was an *outside* goitre as opposed to an *inside* goitre. Had it been an inside goitre she would still have worn a black velvet band with a lace throat-piece.

At Christmas time and New Year's, on her birthday and election days, she delighted in a ruby glass of beet wine. She would tell and retell mirthful yet enigmatic stories about: Uncle Will and the bobcat – the hired man and his overalls – the Tory who bought votes in Huron County – an earthy fable about a smart-aleck coyote and the snow and "where there's smoke, there must be fire." The one which promised the most excitement, the time the Clinton town bell rang the alarm for the Fenian Raids, was not thrilling at all, for there had been no Fenian Raid.

The Christmas that I was eleven years old I took a giant step. My grandmother helped me take it, and I think it must have been a salient Christmas for her too.

It started out the same as any other Christmas in my life – wonderful and exciting. In the basement of Knox Presbyterian Church, Margaret Finlay had played Mother Mary again in our Sunday School concert. Sheeted, Fat and Ike and I had sat before a red tissue-paper fire glowing from the bulb in a plumber's extension light supplied by Mr. Kalman, our broomstick camels grazing nearby. Then Ike said, "Lo."

Fat said, "It is a star."

I said, "It is the star of the East."

We mounted and we galloped across the stage to the stable furnished with hay from Stinchcombe's Livery Barn and my gift for the baby in the manger was "frank-in-cents-and-meer," whatever that was. Jack Andrews played "The Robin's Return"; Bill Stinchcombe recited "'Twas the Night Before . . ." as also did Jack Graham and Willis Ballantyne and Russel Sales and Clara Gatenby. The week before Christmas our town generally had a surfeit of "'Twas the Night Before"s, since it was not a predominantly Presbyterian piece and was being done in the Anglican, Baptist, Methodist, and Catholic basements as well, or rather also.

In our home we had by then decorated the living room with special attention to the cuckoo clock, leaving it to the last and draping it just before the hour would strike; we could almost imagine that there was a surprised expression on the bird's face when it popped out. A week before we had unwrapped and pried apart the tree, which was the same age as my oldest brother, eighteen. It was made of shrill green feathers and wire, had been brought home by my father in 1907 when pine and spruce trees were not available on the Saskatchewan prairies. It looked now as though it had just made it through the terrible western winter of '06 and '07, for each year it had moulted more, but tinsel and the delicately spiral-ribbed Christmas candles clutched upright in the little tin claws at the ends of the wire branches revived it beautifully.

It did not smell of mint freshness of evergreen, but it did have a bouquet of its own. My grandmother liked her smaller gifts to be hung from the tree and each year one of these came very early in the season from a favourite niece of hers in Kitchener. I have suspected, in later years, that this niece had married well – and into cheese, for the gift she sent west was always a quarter pound of hysterical Limburger. Not a creature was stirring in our house the night before Christmas but Grandma's cheese could be smelled clear up to the billiard room on the third floor. I know that Christmas is traditionally associated with holly and pine, but my three brothers and I are the only living Canadians who will always associate it with feathers and Limburger cheese.

At any other time but Christmas and my birthdays, I took my grandmother seriously – indeed I loved her. Had she not been such a consummate craftswoman with needle and thread I could easily have loved her all the year round. My grandmother's Christmas presents held no surprise, for several weeks before Christmas or birthdays I could annually hear her arguing out in the breakfast room with my mother about which way the pattern should lie on the goods so as to save most of the goods and to hell with the bias. There was not really any need for this caution, for it was always material from a suit, a coat, a top coat of my grandfather's, my father's, my uncle's, my eldest brother's, or was salvaged from a dress, a duster, a skirt of my mother's, my grandmother's, my aunts', any one of many female cousins. From this reclaimed material let out at the seams and turned so that the worn and shiny side would be in, she might make a reefer coat with brown velour collar that had once been part of the dining-room curtains before they suffered smoke damage in the fire; striped pyjamas from a flimsy and exuberant dress my mother had relegated to the closet when she had gone into mourning for my father; a pongee blouse reclaimed from a kimono once the possession of Aunt Josie, Aunt Myrtle, my cousin Margaret or Mildred, or Lottie or Helen, or perhaps even some quite unrelated female human unknown to me. For my grandmother collected material, ostensibly for hooking rugs or making log cabin quilts, only half of which found its way into mats or quilts. The other half went into middy suits.

I hated these suits, which came in three parts: the broad-collared middy itself, the stovepipe pants, and a waist. The waist was a foundation garment quilted rather like a lifejacket that had been on a severe diet; it buttoned up the back with thirteen small buttons so that you pretty nearly had to share a bedroom with a brother in order to undress at night and dress in the morning. The pants buttoned to this waist; long snap garters dangled from the front of it to hold up stockings. After swimming had opened officially in the little Souris on the twenty-fourth of May, my brother Bob and I would walk over the prairie west of town, undress a quarter of a mile before we had reached the swimming hole, hide our clothes under a clump of brush and continue the rest of the way naked through prairie wool and spear grass, hoping thereby to avoid mortification. We were quite unsuccessful; it was known throughout the district as far as Brokenshell, Trossachs, Estevan, and perhaps even around Oxbow, that the Mitchell boys wore corsets.

I could not recall a Christmas or a birthday when my grandmother's gift had not been a detestable middy suit. This Christmas morning I spotted it almost immediately by its fat and shapeless bulk and by the spidery, angular handwriting which said: "For Will." I left it to the very last.

My two younger brothers and I were the only ones before the feather tree in the living room, bright with tinsel and redolent with the Yuletide scent of Limburger cheese as we opened our presents at least two hours before winter dawn. Some time after the first intoxication of Christmas morning had left me, after Bob and Dick had each stoically and dutifully unwrapped a middy suit (Bob's, blue serge via Uncle Frank; Dick's, pepper-and-salt tweed courtesy of Grandfather McMurray) I turned to mine.

It was wearing apparel, of grey flannel, but without the usual bitterness of mothballs – quite unfamiliar material. As I lifted it up and shook it out I was surprised that no white waist either dropped to or remained on the opened paper. Then I realized what my grandmother had made for me. Time can never dissolve those stunning moments that I held up my first pair of long pants.

I pulled them on over my pyjama bottoms and looked down at my no-legs. A balloon was inflating inside me and I had grown one foot. I was taller. I was male-er as I stared down the long and unbroken creases "with a wild surmise . . . silent on a peak in Darien."

Ah – there was a Christmas! There was a grandmother! There was the ritualistic birth of a man!

11

Of Tar Paper, Shiplap, and Shingles Made

This evocative memory of W. O.'s childhood home in Weyburn, Saskatchewan was written shortly after his mother died in the fall of 1960. It was her death which prompted the first of half a dozen first-person childhood reminiscential pieces beginning with "Of Tar Paper, Shiplap, and Shingles Made," "Take One Giant Step," and "The Day I Spoke for Mister Lincoln."

I think children have a right to expect a home to hold solid under them, an enduring platform on which to practise the anarchy of childhood. The restless drift of suburban society today must blur the home reference point a person needs in later life, to look back upon with fond if distorted nostalgia. So many children today live in new homes in new residential districts; they have not had the chance to meet a cricket, an earthworm, a caterpillar, bird, or squirrel, for neither these creatures nor children flourish in new real-estate developments where excavation dirt lacks oxygen and organic matter, where buggy whips of trees are unsatisfactory sites for nests.

A house, like a new pair of shoes, is not truly appreciated until it has been worn for some time. Many of today's children have not heard a home talk, for a house is mute the first three years of its life; only with maturity will it stir and creak at night and mutter faintly with concern for its sleeping family. Before that it simply doesn't give a damn.

Not that today's tighter, better-built homes are nearly so articulate as those born fifty or sixty years ago. The one of my own childhood had radiators which clanked peremptorily; when the north wind blew off the prairies carrying its message of mortality for all, the building hummed and thrummed through felt and brass weather-stripping like a dirging mouth organ. In spring it gurgled and lapped like the Lake Isle of Innisfree as the cistern under the dumb waiter filled with soft water, and in the basement kitchen a coal and wood stove was always cracking its knuckles.

Ours was a three-storeyed house on Sixth Street in the southern Saskatchewan town of Weyburn. The façade it presented to the street was very, very high and uncompromising, like my octogenarian grandmother, who lived with us. If she had been a house, this was the sort of house she would have been. The living room and the music room and the breakfast room and the dining room on the ground floor, were wainscotted with oak panels – the ceilings with oak beams. On the living-room wall by the door to the music room hung Mary, Queen of Scots and John Knox, both soapstone plaques with pinprick pupils. Both looked like each other, except that John Knox had a long and perfectly marcelled beard and held a Bible in one negligent hand, while Mary held a scroll of some sort. Also – both looked like my grandmother except that she (Mary) wore a ruff convoluted like the Christmas candies that came in wooden pails, while my grandmother wore a narrow black velvet ribbon with an attached lace throat-piece under which she secreted an outside goitre. As a child I toyed with the suspicion that Mary, Queen of Scots and John Knox might have goitres too, Mary's under her ruff and John's under his beard.

The dining room was magnificent for one thing – a chandelier made up of rows and rows of encircling prisms. In the sideboard drawer were spare prisms, which you could look through and they obligingly broke the light up into violet and raspberry and gold. The built-in sideboard had bevel-edged mirrors along the back and sides so that you could stick your head in and look down a long corridor reflecting thousands upon thousands of heads which had this to recommend them: they were all yours. Just the backs of the heads, that is – whichever side you looked down – just the backs of your heads.

The bedroom I shared on the second floor with my youngest brother was notable for its wallpaper: boys fishing. Not several but thousands of identical boys with similar rods at precisely the same angle, seated on a fragment of pier and fishing about six inches from each other – over each other – under each other – kitty-corner from each other. I can recall a faint contempt for the person who had painted the wallpaper, for he had done all the boys carelessly; you could see that his hands had skidded slightly so that they were all out of focus.

Perhaps the two most important rooms in the house were the billiard room on the third floor and the one across the hall, which was an unused room, or – I suppose – a play room.

This room, furnished only with strewn toys and sporting equipment out of season, had a clothes closet within which the plaster and lathe had been gashed, some mysterious while ago, I suspect now by an electrician called in for wiring changes or repairs. You could climb through the hole as you would into any secret passageway in any castle, and then, crouching, make your way along under the side slope of the house roof. Before you did this you made preparations. First you arranged for your brother to invite a victim, wooing him with the promise of a magic-lantern show. Before they had arrived you took in with you the great morning-glory horn from a deceased gramophone. When your brother had turned off the lights for the magic-lantern show you placed the horn against the wall and moaned through it. This was particularly effective the first time with Keith from the corner, who was a Baptist and had played rummy with you in the hut the afternoon before so that his conscience was bothering him.

Here was the magic lantern of blued tin with a stubby, fretted chimney. The door at the back swung out and it had clips for holding postcards and photographs. There were lots of magic lanterns in Weyburn in the second decade of this century but they showed simply transparent pictures on glass slides. Our magic lantern would project anything. If you put your hand in the back and focused the lens properly you could throw on the opposite wall a picture of a fat-fingered hand with the skin pores perfectly reported and folds standing out magnificently. Almost anything or any presented part of the body would be magnified, many times. I say any part, for one dull late-February afternoon Melvin and I . . . Melvin is a psychiatrist practising now in Seattle or Portland – somewhere on the West Coast, I believe.

Looking back to this house I am concerned for the well-being of most modern houses – specifically their vascular systems. The house of my childhood had one vertical master aorta, a clothes-chute tube which began in the hallway of the third floor, had an opening just outside the bathroom on the second floor, and its final opening in the basement kitchen. If a person happened to have left the door slightly ajar in the kitchen, he could sneak out of bed and, by holding his ear to the bathroom opening, could hear quite clearly every word that was said in the kitchen: how close, for instance, the widowed section hand came to getting Olga for the mother of his six children.

At one time, before my own birth, my oldest brother climbed into the square well on the third floor. His screams brought my mother, who extricated him just before his fingertips gave up. Doctor Eaglesham said that the boy could have been seriously injured if he had let go and plummeted down the sixteen-inch tube some forty feet long. Doctor Eaglesham generally made his points by understatement. At the kitchen end my brother would have ended up as strawberry jam, and I have often wondered in later years just how high – in that state – he would have filled the bottom end of our clothes chute.

One other thing about the clothes chute. When I was twelve I sent away for Ventrillo, a magic instrument costing ten cents, which would enable any boy to throw his voice easily. It didn't throw mine. As well, the instructions were disappointing, simply a stamp-sized thing of flimsy paper which told you to say the alphabet over and over without moving your lips. This I did religiously. The clothes chute seemed a very fine and likely place for throwing your voice that was supposed to sound far-away and muffled. I spent hours with my jaw and lips stiff, screaming in a choked and what I hoped to be a far-away voice: "Let gee out – let gee out – I'g dowg the clothes chute!"

Another, but shorter, house artery was the dumb waiter between the breakfast room and the kitchen in the basement. It brought up dishes and food from the kitchen, so that most meals in our house were interrupted by trips from the table to the dumb waiter and a shouted request for more mashed potatoes or salt or sugar or the gravy. This box of shelves in its well had ropes and the left-hand one pulled the thing up and the right-hand one let the thing down. It went down much easier than it came up especially with Melvin crouched inside it in the foetal position. It made my brothers and me very popular in our end of town, particularly with Melvin, who, as many as six times in a week, got me to pull him up and down until my arms were ready to drop off at the shoulder. He is now a psychiatrist on the West Coast somewhere.

And then there was the stair; from the third floor it made four curves right back upon itself, one for each floor and each landing between. You could start at the top and make a glissading descent, taking the last curve at about the same speed as a Winter Olympic bob-sled, your loose heels strumming the struts like a xylophone player ripping his hammers along the instrument.

But a house is not simply of tar paper, shiplap, and shingles made. Particularly to a child it is another and outer self. It lives on by a sort of Bishop Berkeley grace, for just as long as living people experience it and hold memory of it.

On a September morning two years ago when the fall wind went ticking through the leaves of the poplar for which I had once carried pail after pail of water – the lone survivor of eight – I walked up the porch steps with my youngest brother. We paused at the front door and before I turned the brass knob I looked around to see the dead Virginia creeper, whose dried leaves had made such good smoking some forty years ago. As soon as we stepped inside I saw that someone had condensed the living room, moved in the walls, lowered the ceiling with its oak beams and chandelier, and made the fireplace smaller. An erect woman with grey hair did not rise from the wing chair under Mary, Queen of Scots, and John Knox. The cuckoo clock did not tick one tick.

I glanced at my brother and from the stilled look upon his face I knew that the same realization had happened to both of us at the same instant. Her death had become a fact for us, and we knew truly that this afternoon she would take her place in the prairie cemetery beside her own mother and our father.

As each child grows up and leaves it, a house dies by bits. The house of a child must have vivid permanency. When a mother dies it's time enough for it to take its final and mortal blow.

12

~~~

The Shocking Truth About the Undefended Border

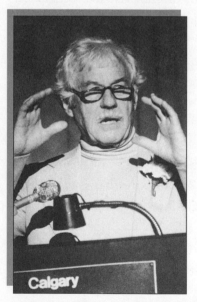

Throughout his life W. O. has run afoul of borders, which persist in declaring their existence in spite of his belief that they do not, or should not, exist. On one occasion, while on a winter vacation to Grand Cayman, he was suspected of drug trafficking. While waiting in line to go through customs, he took out his silver snuff box to have a few fixes of his favourite Wilson's Finest Menthol. A customs officer became suspicious of this old white-haired gentleman who periodically snorted brown powder off the side of his thumb. The officer took W. O. and Merna out of the line-up and demanded his snuff box. W. O. protested that it was only snuff, as should be obvious to the customs officer since it was brown, not white. The officer held out his hand saying, "Now you give it to me, mun!" W. O. complied and watched as the officer opened the box, took a pinch of the snuff, smelled it and then tasted it. Grinning from ear to ear, the *officer handed the box back and said, "Haven't you ever heard of Mexican brown, mun?"*

In the following piece W. O. recounts some of his experiences as an importer/exporter of such items as his grandmother, Mexican jumping beans, a duck-and-goose boat, banana plants, and himself. It was published in Maclean's (June 1961).

I wish that statesmen and public speakers (American and Canadian) would not keep on referring to the thousands of miles of unprotected border stretching from the Atlantic to the Pacific. I was born and now live just north of it. This smooth statement is quite false. One way and another I have tried unsuccessfully to breach that border for almost forty years: uniformed guardians in blue or khaki have repulsed me every time.

As a child in southern Saskatchewan I had a vague notion that there was a fence-line running from sea to sea, dead straight along the bottom of British Columbia, Alberta, Saskatchewan, and Manitoba, taking a southern jiggle down and around the Niagara Peninsula, then looping up rather unfairly under the throat of Quebec. I knew that it wasn't a picket fence or a barbed-wire fence, but probably an iron-pipe rail fence with quite sturdy cement posts every mile or so. When I was eight I discarded the fence concept as untenable; there was probably just a four-thousand-mile line like the blue line on the ice at the Weyburn Arena rink. Someone – Fat or Ike or Mate or Hodder – crossed it on a trip with his family, and reported back to the rest of us that there was nothing at all to define it; the spear grass and crocuses were the same on either side; a gopher's squeak had identical impudence whichever side he was on; a meadow lark could drop his bright notes from a Canadian haystack and a moment later from an American fencepost; the coyote left a steer carcass on the North Dakota side to trot across to his Saskatchewan den with nothing to declare. North Portal and Portal were just one straddling town; one batch of children attended a school under the Union Jack and sang *God save our gracious King* while a few steps away another batch under the Star-Spangled Banner had swiped the very same tune and were singing My *country, 'tis of thee* to it. Under these conditions it was difficult to take the border seriously, or to quench a faint distrust of anyone who would steal the tune of another country's national anthem. This might have explained the number of southern Saskatchewan youths, with patent-leather Valentino hair and bell-bottomed trousers, who drove yellow-wheeled McLaughlin-Buicks over the border with cargoes of Scotch and rye and rum that must eventually have found their way to the warehouses of Al Capone. I was too young for this, and before the twenties were done there were no opportunities left in rum-running for amateurs.

I think I was ten when I came to respect the border first; at that time I sent away to the States for a device called Ventrillo, which would fit under a boy's tongue and enable him to throw his voice. For weeks I badgered our postmaster and the express agent, who assured me again and again that Ventrillo had not arrived. They were telling me the truth, for in time I received a notification that a shipment was being held in bond for me at the border. It would be sent on when I had filled out the proper forms and paid the duty on it. When, with the help of my mother, my grandmother, and my oldest brother, I had done this, Ventrillo arrived. It proved to be a thin and disappointing wafer of tin folded over with a hole punched in the middle. It fitted easily under the tongue all right, but it did not assist you in throwing your voice at all. It simply made it possible for you to whistle without pursing your lips (which I could already manage) and to do bird calls if you practised to beat hell. In all fairness I did not (nor do I now) blame the Canadian Customs and Excise for my getting a whistling device instead of a ventriloquial aid, but I do wonder if it is not some childhood experience such as this that gave John Stuart Mill and Adam Smith and David Ricardo their initial shove down the road to Free Trade.

Two years after Ventrillo I learned that it was just as difficult to beat the border one way as it was the other; the fall that I was twelve we tried to export my grandmother to Oceana, California. Actually we travelled with her, my mother, my two younger brothers, and I, for Grandma was seventy-eight and her rheumatic right leg was encased in a metal brace from heel to hip. Without crutches or a cane and a pinching grip on the underarm flesh of a grandson, she was quite immobile. To break the trip we had taken the boat from Vancouver to Seattle, and during the two-hour stopover in Victoria my mother took my brothers and me to see the sights, leaving Grandma comfortably settled in a canvas chair on the upper deck of the boat.

We were no sooner on our carefree way when two plainclothes immigration men descended upon my grandmother. They asked her where she was from and she said she was travelling to her favourite niece's place in Oceana, which was just south of Pismo Beach where they had the clams and the abalones. Delighted that these two nice young men had come to visit an old lady sitting in the sun, she went on to explain to them that the niece was married to Will Clarke, who had been a piano tuner in the organ factory at Goderich but now ran a dance pavilion and she had herself come west from Huron County, with her son Will and her husband, John McMurray, in '98, travelling from Moosomin by buggy to their homestead stakes where they had built a sod hut and been hailed out and droughted out and rusted out and wasn't that an awful winter of '06 and '07! My grandmother was quite cavalier about time at this stage of her life so that she skipped with ease from the nineteenth to the twentieth century, and the immigration men got the impression that she was a penniless prairie Kulak living in a sod hut on harsh land that had not yielded a crop in the past fifteen years. They therefore took the crippled old lady who wanted to get to California and see real oranges and lemons and a grapefruit growing on a live tree before her time had come – and put her in bond.

We returned from the swimming pool beside the Empress Hotel to find ourselves charged with attempting to breach the

Anti-Grandmother-Dumping Law; the undercover immigration men had foiled us before we could cross the line and leave the destitute old lady to starve to death on Pismo Beach (with that leg, she couldn't dig clams) or become a ward of the American government. It took us three days to clear Grandma, but a notarized financial statement from her bank, running to five figures, accomplished her freedom. The three-day delay meant that we boarded the train in Seattle without berths. Mother obtained an upper for my two brothers and me so that we slept to Los Angeles with head and feet alternating sardine fashion. Mother and Grandma, however, spent their two nights in the smoker, which made Mother ill, for she could not stand the bitterness of shoe polish. It did not seem to bother Grandma too much, for when the porter was finished doing his dozen or so pairs of shoes, she played casino most of the night and took him for two dollars and sixty-five cents.

On our return a year later I brought back with me a matchbox of fourteen Mexican jumping beans from Tijuana, Mexico. They were intended as presents for Fat and Ike and Hodder and Mate, but were confiscated at the border. It was a sad blow even though my brother Dick pointed out that they had lost all their jump since before San Francisco. (Almost a year later he admitted to me that he had placed them over the Pullman heater to warm them to greater activity and had succeeded only in cooking them.) This information did not dilute my feeling toward border officials at all.

By this time I knew that the border was bigger than I was, but formative early years on the prairies, and a Presbyterian grandmother who had spoken only Gaelic till she was eighteen, can leave a man wishing for the rest of his life that he were made of the same stern stuff as Greek heroes and Covenanters; even if he wishes to, he cannot discontinue the hopeless fight against the powers of Fate and Customs and Immigration, implacable and much more powerful than any one mortal.

I was lucky or unlucky during university years to be exposed to the clean and burred logic of another Scot, a classical economics professor, Dr. A. B. Clarke, who opened each class by raising his clenched fist high over his head and declaring, "I am no pole-uh-titian. Our interest here is in the science of economics and its laws as they *are*, not as we *wish* them to be!" He would go on to tell us that Protection by Tariff was an abomination and Free Trade the salvation of man, invoking the utilitarian saints, Adam Smith, Mill, Ricardo. Dr. Clarke's influence is still upon me, for in the intervening years whenever I have crossed the border I have stuffed my pockets with packages of Chesterfields, credited my eight-year-old son on one occasion with two pounds of Sir Walter Raleigh pipe tobacco and two cartons of cigars, and my five-year-old daughter with a gallon of Old Grand-Dad Bourbon.

This sort of thing, I suspect, is a categorical imperative for all Canadians; but I wonder if they are visited as I am by the border-crossing feeling. It grows upon you gradually, starting about a hundred miles south of the line and strengthening as you near the gates. It is a compound feeling and here is my recipe: one part visceral tension, one part vague shame, one part excitement, one of trepidation, and two of who-the-hell-cares. I also get this feeling or one much like it whenever I go to the bank to plead for a note renewal; it once visited me before a ten-cent slot machine in Las Vegas and many years before that just as I was about to kiss a Williston, North Dakota, girl scout (Troop Nine) in our green Peterborough canoe in the middle of Carlyle Lake when I was fourteen.

From the time they put my grandmother in bond at Victoria till almost ten years ago I had taken part in few border incidents of any magnitude. There was, of course, the sectional fibreglass duck-and-goose boat I tried to import from Waseca, Minnesota. The stern half made it through Kingsgate to Lethbridge, south of our town; the bow slipped through Sweetgrass, Montana, and ended up at Okotoks, north of our town. This schizophrenic boat presented such a problem in international trade that I was successful in importing only one half of it legally and gaining for the other half a sort of special parole. Almost a year later I received a frightening registered letter from

Ottawa, warning me that since only official charity had cleared the fibreglass duck-and-goose boat stern, I was liable to a fine almost as great as five years' taxes on my house, or imprisonment for six months, or just both. Simply by taking three trips to Calgary, hiring a bondsman, and filling out forms in quintuplicate, I managed in the end to release my stern properly.

By this time I had become an addicted amateur importer. And now I must explain how I came to be compelled recently to import some banana plants into Alberta, aside from the pure challenge and daring of it, that is.

A year after they'd snatched my Mexican jumping beans from me, I moved to St. Petersburg, Florida, with my mother and younger brothers. This was because I had developed a tuberculous wrist that necessitated a mild winter climate. Here for four years at school chapel I sang *God save our gracious King* each day while the rest of the students belted out *My country, 'tis of thee* (same stolen tune). Back of our apartment with the palmettos and poinsettias, and the pecan, mango, and sour orange trees, there were several banana plants, such as a large one with brilliant but inedible red fruit called a Horse Banana, and a small one with delicious fruit called a Lady Finger Banana. The canoe-paddle leaves on these hung tattered and limp, whispering over and over in the tropical breeze "Lord and Lady Greystoke," and sometimes "Me Tarzan; you Jane." Two things happened during the three years in Florida: the tubercles in the wrist became dormant and my original forty-below-proof Saskatchewan blood was replaced by a dilute tropical variety with very tender corpuscles.

In the thirty-some years since, I have not once been completely warm, but I have built onto my house a thirty-five-by-fifteen-foot area of glassed-in tropics. With thermostatically controlled heat and automatic humidity it looks tropical; eighty-five orchid plants blow-torch pink and lavender and yellow; the utterly pure blossoms of gardenias breathe a heady and immoral fragrance, flamingo flowers lift scarlet as arterial blood. It has lacked only banana plants. Often I have imagined their leaves drooping with tropic languor, the blossoms of

Bird of Paradise with royal-blue bills and canary wings uplifted. I could hear myself saying to visitors, "Yes – that's *Musa ensete* – its common name is Abyssinian Banana."

Forgetting Ventrillo, Grandma, the Mexican jumping beans, and the sectional fibreglass duck-and-goose boat, I sent to Ottawa for a form to use in requesting a form for applying for an import certificate to import banana plants from Hawaii. Such a first form was sent to me. I filled out this form, which would get me a form for getting the import form I must fill out in order to import my banana plants from Hawaii. In turn I got from Ottawa the form I needed, filled it in with the generic names of the plants, the name of Mr. F. L. Kong of Hilo, Hawaii, the date the plants might arrive in Canada, the number of packages they might be in when Mr. Kong sent my banana plants from Hawaii. I sent the order with the import certificate number to Mr. Kong of Hilo, Hawaii, along with two sheets of instructions he must follow if we were to be successful in getting banana plants from Hawaii. I also sent the import certificate to the Chief Officer of the Plant Protection Division of the Department of Agriculture. I waited for Mr. Kong to send me my banana plants from Hawaii.

Mr. Kong was not idle. He alerted the federal inspector of plants for Hawaii to come with microscope and fumigator, to make out a phytosanitary certificate. He wrapped the plants in moist sphagnum moss, their roots in tree-fern fibre. He rushed them to the airport. Deep in their moist darkness they flew high over the Pacific, hardly aware that they had left their tropic birthplace.

They made it to Lethbridge within eighteen hours; the plant inspector jumped to his duties, gave them a free bill of health, and sent me a note that they had arrived safely.

I wired Mr. Kong in Hilo: "Banana plants cleared Pacific and border safely. Please send phytosanitary certificate soonest. Hurrah!" I believe I paid for the "!".

My plants did not reach me for eight more days; my home in High River is a hundred miles from Lethbridge; I have not yet established why after covering thousands of miles in eighteen hours it took them eight days to come a hundred. I checked back with the plant inspector. I got in touch with the postal authorities. Finally I discovered that the shipment was in bond; my long-distance phone call released them. When they arrived they were dead.

I sat down to write a letter sad and stiff with the formality usually reserved for elegiac notes of thanks composed after the funeral of a loved one.

"Dear Sirs," I wrote, "Today I opened my shipment of exotic plants from Mr. Kong of 1477 Kalaniole Avenue, Hilo, Hawaii. They were anything but exotic." I did not remind them of Ventrillo or mention my grandmother, nor did I bring up the matter of the fourteen confiscated Mexican jumping beans and the fibreglass duck-and-goose boat. I said simply, "The growing point on my Abyssinian Banana is black and desiccated; the Bird of Paradise leaves hang limp and jaundiced in death; the Heliconia is moribund."

"We are sorry to hear," Customs and Excise said, "that the banana plants reached you in poor condition and that a high percentage of them were spoiled beyond recovery. It is our consistent policy to expedite the release and clearance of perishable goods. As a matter of fact in expediting a clearance of your banana plants we circumvented Customs Regulations inasmuch as the banana plants were released prior to the duty and taxes applicable having been paid. Please send us the invoice for this shipment and your Import Certificate. On receipt of these we will forward our Postal Card showing the amount of Customs Duty required on this shipment."

I hadn't dreamed that there would be a duty on the banana plants and I wrote to the Chief Officer in Charge of Tariffs for Banana Plants for Western Canada: "What banana plantations does this duty protect in Canada?"

He answered, "It is noted, in your letter of March 10, that you feel that your banana plants should not be subject to Customs Duty. In this respect I would advise you that they are subject to an *ad valorem* duty of 12½% but are exempt from sales tax."

Actually I was not protesting the duty, simply trying to understand it. A tariff must serve one of two purposes, protection or revenue. Since obviously there were no banana plantations in Canada, the tariff must be levied to swell the treasury. I considered asking Customs and Excise to send me the figures for the past five years covering the amount of duties collected on banana plants imported into Canada.

I have since had notice that I will not be expected to pay any duty on the *dead* banana plants. This makes sense. The cultivation of *dead* banana plants in Canada is quite likely not in need of protection from the West Indies, Hawaii, South America. In Canada we have a definite advantage there, for in the tropics temperature and humidity conspire to make it difficult to raise anything *but* live banana plants.

Enough of ornamental banana plants. Years ago I took a blithe assignment from *Maclean's* to do a profile article on a Mr. George Ross, the flying rancher, whose ranch east of Milk River along the border was only slightly smaller than some English counties. He tended this principality and his Herefords with the aid of a couple of planes. Very soon after I had started my interviews with him, I came to admire him tremendously: he was beating the border magnificently and quite legally. At the time there was an embargo on Canadian beef, with a very thin annual quota for each rancher. Mr. Ross bought land in western Montana: he had it declared an American bonding post and there he sent his quota of beef each year, but in terms of early fall calves weighing perhaps twelve hundred pounds each – all of it on the right or market side of the border.

After my interviews with Mr. Ross I had no way to cover the seventy miles to Lethbridge other than to fly over the border with him, for he was leaving for his Montana leases. He obligingly landed the plane on Highway 91 just south of the border, picking a time when there was no traffic. Soon after his plane had roared off, I hitchhiked a ride with an oil truck, which let me out in the Montana border town of Sweetgrass. At 6:40 a.m. I walked up to the barrier carrying my briefcase and portable typewriter. Immigration Officers Scylla and

Charybdis were there, waiting for the morning's first smugglers and enemy aliens to sneak through. I told them that I wished to pass through to the country of my birth.

The one with his elbows on the counter asked me how long I had been in the States. I said about thirteen minutes and as I did the border-crossing feeling came over me for the first time.

The other officer, the one with his feet on the desk, said: "What was your port of entry?"

I pointed in a direction I thought was east and said, "About forty miles that way."

"There isn't any port that way for over a hundred and fifty miles." (He was exaggerating, of course. The next port wasn't even a hundred miles away.)

"I flew over," I explained. "About fifteen minutes ago."

"By hand?"

"No – this rancher had his plane – he was flying over the border anyway to go down to his cattle he has in bond on his ranch. His ranch in Montana is a bonding post. It's the embargo – that's the way he – ah – gets around – handles the beef embargo. It was his plane."

"Did you parachute?"

"Oh no." That was an easy one to answer. "He just landed it on Highway 91 and I got out and caught a ride with an oil truck and – here I am."

They were much more than officially unreceptive. The nearest man was no longer leaning on his elbows; the other had swung his feet down from the desk top and come over to the counter. "He's a very well-known rancher," I explained, and added, "in Canada."

Compelled as I always am to talk too much, I hurried on to explain that I was a writer, that I had been visiting the ranch to do an article for *Maclean's*. Neither of them had ever heard of a flying rancher, nor did they believe I was a writer, that I was doing an article on a flying rancher. *Maclean's* wasn't even a toothpaste yet.

I spent the morning in Sweetgrass, unable to get through to the Ross ranch by phone. Finally my assurance that I would phone to

Mr. Arthur Irwin, then editor, convinced them that I was telling the truth.

But, they explained, that did not change the fact that I had made an illegal entry into the United States at a place other than a proper border crossing. This was bad. They left me to sit for the morning contemplating just how bad it was. Then at noon one of them came to me and said that he was going home to lunch, that the other would probably have to go to the washroom at the back, that the new man coming on would not get there for a couple of minutes, and why didn't I just stroll across to the other side in the convenient time gap?

I said, "What about the Canadian Immigration authorities?" He said, "That's their problem and your problem," and left.

As it turned out I did just stroll across. There was no problem at all. "You're a Canadian," the Canadian officer said, "and this is Canada."

For a brief moment I felt a warm glow, but it was soon damped. I am right about that border along with Adam Smith and John Stuart Mill and John Dafoe of the *Winnipeg Free Press*. I shall not ever forget Ventrillo, the Mexican jumping beans, the sectional fibreglass duck-and-goose boat. The Abyssinian Banana plant did not die in vain!

13

ल৴৹ও৴

Take Me to Your Cannibal Chief

Like many of W. O.'s characters, Daddy Sherry ignores borders or restrictions of any kind. In the following episode from The Kite *(1962) he succeeds in exporting a much larger item into the U.S.A. than anything W. O. ever attempted. David Lang is a Toronto columnist and television personality on assignment to do a magazine article on Daddy Sherry, who, at one hundred and eleven, is the oldest man in Canada. Daddy lives in the* foothills town of Shelby with his housekeeper, Miss Tinsley. While researching his article, David boards with Helen Maclean, a widow who lives with her young son and her mother, Mrs. Clifford. Daddy Sherry is Helen's great-grandfather.*

Daddy Sherry was inspired by a distant relative of W. O.'s (the oldest voter in the 1949 federal election), by two old war veterans, and by Tommy Tweed's imitation, at a CBC *cast party, of an old, old man. Tweed played the part of Daddy Sherry's forerunner, Daddy Johnson, in* CBC's *radio series,* Jake and the Kid.

⁌⁊

Most of Shelby's young had learned to swim in the Spray. The twenty-fourth of May signalled the official opening of shrill and merry hell along its slippery banks with: "Last one in's a monkey's uncle," "Petey-Petey – see the moon rise," "I can bottom it – I can bottom it!" On the river road virginity had been lost many times, first with cow ponies grazing near, then with buckboard or phaeton or buggy standing by, finally with moonlight glinting from chrome and enamel. In late March of 1927 something more precious had been lost when ten-year-old Jimmy Sangster had gone through rubber ice, to be found far downstream in a backwater, bloodsuckers over his body, his arms outflung and his head in Metherall's bearded barley field.

After Shelby the river flowed through the towns of Conception and Foxhole and Tiger Lily, much wider, much slower, its tepid waters shunned by trout and populated by mud-inhaling suckers, carp and gold-eye, scummed and tea-coloured, stinking of marsh gas, its edges reedy; an old and sluggish river, it slipped over the American border at One Star, Montana.

Each year with the glacial run-off late in May the Spray threatened Shelby with flood, and in 1925, in 1931, in 1945, and in 1954, property damage had been high. Now an earth and gravel breakwater protected the community, and most people felt that never again would their homes and stores be awash. "It was wonderfully exciting before the breakwater," Helen recalled. "1954 was the worst year of all – they used canoes and rowboats on Main Street. All of Mrs. Sorenson's chickens were drowned in spite of the Shelby Emergency and Disaster Relief Committee. It did frighten Mayor Fraser and his council into action and they had the breakwater built – it diverts the Spray from its natural course through the business district – and from Daddy's cottage."

The last flood had taken place two years after Helen had returned to live with her mother and to teach in Shelby High School. Daddy

Sherry had been one hundred and five that spring, had put in a winter uneventful in regard to health or to personally created incident. The last week in April, Helen had gone into Mayor Fraser's store, the Bon Ton, to settle her month's bill for groceries. She always paid by cheque so that she had a record, but Mr. Fraser had insisted, as he usually did, on making out a receipt for her.

As he bent over the counter he said, "And how are things in the Clifford household?"

"Fine, Mr. Fraser."

"What's this we hear about Daddy Sherry?"

"I don't know," said Helen, who had heard nothing.

"Hasn't eloped – held up the Royal Bank – dynamited the town hall – shot up the Cascade Beer Parlour." Mr. Fraser enjoyed a benign split personality; in private life he took nothing seriously, in public – everything. "There you are." He handed Helen her receipt.

"Thank you. Just what is it you hear about him, Mr. Fraser?"

"Understand he's taken the notion to travel."

"Oh? Where?"

"The South Seas."

"To the South Seas!"

"That's right. Honolulu – Fiji Islands – Tahiti. Wants to lie back in a hammock, he says – rocked to sleep by the tropic breeze – listen to the idle strum of native instruments – waiting for the bananas and paw-paw fruit to drop into his lap."

"I suppose we all think about how nice that would be," Helen said, "sooner or later."

"All he's been talking about for the past month. Miss Tinsley has been trying to get his mind off it . . ."

"She isn't taking it seriously, is she?"

"She takes everything seriously," Mayor Fraser said. "I told her not to argue with him about it."

"That's right."

". . . just sets him firmer. Of course – it's so ridiculous – I don't suppose there's any real need to worry . . ."

"With Daddy," Helen said, "you should worry in direct ratio to the ridiculous element in the situation."

Mayor Fraser considered that for a moment. "Yes," he said, "I suppose you're right."

On her way home she called in at the Sherry house.

"He keeps muttering about long pig," Miss Tinsley said. "And he seems quite set on it. Imagine – a hundred and five – why is it? – always in the spring he gets these silly – well – brain storms."

"You shouldn't pay too much attention to them," Helen advised her. "Just ignore him when he . . ."

"Ignore him! Have you ever tried it? He's out in the backyard – you go on out there and see how easy it is to ignore him – in anything!"

Daddy was well wrapped against the early spring air. "How are you, Daddy – what's this I hear you're plotting against the whites?"

"Aaaaah – day – day, girl – itch – itch – itch."

"Wait a minute – my time's valuable – can't waste it if you're not going to make some sense."

"Set – set." He indicated the empty chair on his left. "Mrs. Doc Richardson."

"You have the wrong girl, Daddy. I'm Helen Maclean – remember?"

"Didn't say you wasn't. Didn't say that."

"What did you say then?"

"Mrs. Doc Richardson – aaah – Mrs. Allerdyce – Sadie's headed for La Jolly California – Florence Allerdyce's slouchin' aroun' St. Petersburg . . ."

"Yes?"

"Me – I froze for ninety years on the prairies an' in these foothills – cold – cold – I ain't been warm since I cracked ninety!"

"That's too bad, Daddy."

"I aim to get warm."

"How?"

"Thin – I got real thin blood an' she's slow risin' this year, when she does come up she's gonna split the bark."

"You'll be all right."

"Nope. Nope. This is the year John Felix Sherry migrates."

"Where?" she asked him, just as though she didn't know.

"Bermuda – Mexico – aaaah Tobango – Durango – Sumatra – I'm goin' wherever the tropical breezes blows me – Tahiti where the warm trade winds can kiss my thin old hide an' warm her good . . ."

"Well," she said, "you can afford it – no reason you and Miss Tinsley . . ."

"Just what I told her . . ."

". . . shouldn't go down south – like Mrs. Richardson and Mrs. Allerdyce – Belva Louise can look after you just as well in Phoenix or Laguna or . . ."

". . . or Papeete – Easter Islands – Sandwidge Islands . . ."

"But those places are off the . . ."

". . . eat that there bread fruit – kick yams outa the dirt an' watch them grass skirts swayin' – listen to them guitars – lay on the silver sands an' see the hot sun settin' on blue doubloons . . ."

"Lagoons."

"Eh?"

"Lagoons – a sort of tropical slough."

"Coral Islands. Eat long pig for breakfast an' dinner an' supper . . ."

"Might not agree with you, Daddy," she said.

"How the hell will I know till I tried it?"

"And it's a little far at your age – you'd better settle for California or Florida . . ."

"Itch – itch."

"You have the travel itch?"

"Underwear – underwear. I ain't been outa scratchy underwear for a hunderd years. I'm goin' where I can take it off . . ."

"You can take it off in California or . . ."

". . . peel to the hide – right to the hide." He leaned forward, grunting with the effort. "Gimme your arm."

"Certainly, Daddy – you want to go back into the house?"

"You're gonna come downtown with me," he told her. "Today's the day I buy the tickets."

"Now – just a moment . . ."

"Sposed to had 'em ready ten days ago, then she stuck her nose into it. Cancelled 'em. I'll cancel *her*! An' him! First-class ticket – train – air an' windjammer – high-ballin' outa this deep freeze like a scalded kiyoot. Ticket – ticket – ticket. Mr. Rossdance's got 'em ready by now – like an accordeen – when she's opened out she'll stretch from here to the correction line! No – don't you hold me – let me grab holt of *your* arm!"

Helen suspected from the twitch of the front window curtains that Miss Tinsley saw them leave for downtown; she was relieved that the housekeeper did not intercept them, which was decent of her; an explanation could be embarrassing so soon after giving out the easy advice to ignore Daddy. It was not so much that Helen felt that she was giving in to him as that quite obviously a different sort of response was called for: a very cautious humouring.

Behind his wicket in the station, Mr. Rossdance looked a little guilty under his green eyeshade as he handed out the tickets to Daddy and accepted the cheque. Helen imagined that the agent had no intention of cashing the cheque, that the tickets had no more value than stage money. Daddy was quite satisfied, however, and insisted that they go into the Ladies and Escorts section of the Cascade Beer Parlour to celebrate the purchase.

When she got home there was an accounting to make to her mother, for Miss Tinsley had phoned the house.

"You didn't help Belva, you know."

"Oh, Mother – the tickets aren't real tickets – Mr. Rossdance won't present Daddy's cheque to the bank . . ."

"That isn't the point. It's encouraged him and made it harder for her. I don't understand why you – it's almost as though you – Daddy will take it as though you had approved . . ."

"I don't disapprove of his taking a trip – a short one south – that may be how it ends up and it would be good for him. This is the time of year when he's likely to have his old bronchial trouble. I felt it wasn't wise – right now – to interfere . . ."

"Sometimes it's our duty to interfere for the good of another person."

"I've never seen the time, Mother, that people didn't interfere without justifying it as being for someone else's own good."

"South Seas!"

"In a way," Helen said, "it's Belva Louise's own fault."

"How can you say that! She's done everything to stop him!"

"That's just it – now it's time to try something else. A little delicate substitution. It would never have happened if she hadn't been reading him those adventure magazines – all about diving for pearls in tropical lagoons . . ."

"That's all he'll let her read."

"She'd better go easy on *Astonishing Scientific Stories* . . ."

"It isn't funny, Helen."

"I think it is – a little."

"Well, it isn't. Not when he has to be protected against himself. Miss Tinsley and I are worried . . ."

"I am too, but I know when it's no use to resist him openly in something. Perhaps if no attention had been paid in the first place, he might not have considered it such a fine idea."

"Nothing whatever is gained," her mother said, "by not facing up to things."

The flood anecdote, of course, was Belva Louise Tinsley's, and it was from her that David got the rest of the story. Very soon after Daddy had got his tickets from Mr. Rossdance, the housekeeper had been able to forget her concern about the projected trip, for a cold had settled on the old chest, persisted stubbornly to become bronchitis. Now she had a fresh worry, but at least she knew the old man was through with his notion of traipsing south, sailing round the Horn, and kicking up his heels in the South Seas.

That spring the Spray threatened the town again and by the middle of May everyone was remembering other flood years when train service had been disrupted, the north–south highway under water, mail and food deliveries almost impossible. Remembrance of past disaster thrilled all together with a sort of shot in the community veins, at a time when feeling ran a little sluggishly through the civic body convalescent, after the fever of spring seeding had cooled and calving was over. The possibility of flood gave the town a fillip of excitement. It was actually a welcome one.

But as the river rose with turgid urgency, consternation lifted within the hearts of the townspeople. Business men removed stocks from basement storage; every evening concerned groups of people clustered at the CNR bridge to gauge the rise of the waterline on the cement pilings. Potato sacks had come to be at a premium. Town council held an emergency session, was addressed by a worried Mayor Fraser.

"It has been brought to our notice that the Spray – due to the recent heavy rains coinciding with the glacial run-off from the mountains – has risen dangerously high in the past four days. I'm afraid we've made a – we've underestimated the threat to our community this year. We seem to be in agreement that we ought to – ah – it's too bad we postponed for another year the fill and dyking we intended doing from the CNR bridge to a hundred yards above Daddy Sherry's house. No use crying over spilt milk. We can congratulate ourselves that we did set up our Emergency and Disaster Relief Committee to handle just such a situation as might arise in the coming week. I don't think it will. However, I do think it well that the Emergency and Disaster Relief Committee – ah – should – ah – begin functioning – that they make sure their machinery of – action – is ready – to act."

"Just what do you mean by that?" asked Ernie Fowler, who had been appointed head of the committee against his will the year before.

"Well, now, Ernie – it's your committee – flood is – can be considered an emergency – could be a disaster –"

"I know that," Ernie said, "but it still doesn't answer my question."

"Well – for one thing," Mayor Fraser said to him, "sand bags and sand – these should be at hand and ready for . . ."

"They are," said Ernie.

"And crews to work round the clock in shifts."

"They are," said Ernie.

"Millie Clocker at the telephone office quite clear about the difference between the blue alert and the red alert?"

"She is," said Ernie. "My point is . . ."

"You might try a few trial runs," Mayor Fraser suggested.

"On Millie! She touches off the town hall sireen – the Mounted Police patrol cars and Ollie's ambulance come screamin' through town – St. Aidan's church bell tollin'. Way nerves are in this town now, we'd have real panic on our hands!"

"All right," said Mayor Fraser. "All right. It was only a suggestion. If your key men are standing ready twenty-four hours a day – Tom Seeley in charge of shelter . . ."

"Tom Seeley's down with 'flu. Mr. Rossdance's at the coast on his vacation before the summer . . ."

"Well – whoever you've appointed to act in their places – Harry Richardson – first aid – Hickory Bob Smith – flat-bottom boats – it's your committee, Ernie!"

"It's my committee," Ernie said, "but it isn't my flood! And if you remember last year it was me that tried his damnedest to get some action on that breakwater project and it was me that said bein' Fire Marshal was enough responsibility in itself without bein' saddled with the Emergency and Disaster Relief Committee as well!"

"You were the natural man for the job," Mayor Fraser tried to soothe him. "We have every confidence in you and in your committee. Oh, there's one thing – the houses on the flats – those people – wouldn't it be a good idea if they were to . . . ?"

"They all been warned," Ernie said. "They're all ready to get out at a moment's notice – move in with friends or relatives – all except one."

"And who's that?"

"One that's in the most danger. Be under water first thing – right plock in the old river course – Daddy Sherry."

"Well, get him out."

"We've tried – suggested he move out now since he isn't – wouldn't be as spry as the others. He won't budge."

"All right," Mayor Fraser said. "You'll just have to make certain he's moved out – in good time – "

"But if he won't co-operate . . ."

"If you have to, use force – take as many of your shelter committee as you need. Actually, I don't think it will be necessary. I don't share your pessimism. If this rain eases up there won't be any flood at all."

But the rain had not stopped, and two days later with the water just a half-inch below the CNR bridge, the flats were evacuated; Mayor Fraser himself called on Daddy. He found the old man recovered from his bronchitis, rocking on the porch. Binoculars dangled from the strap round his neck.

"I ain't stirrin' from here," Daddy said. "Got a ringside seat right here on my porch."

Mayor Fraser returned to his store to check the flood reports there. He found Ernie Fowler waiting for him. "You just take two of your men," he told Ernie, "some time this afternoon or this evening at the latest – move him out and over to Cliffords'. I've told Mrs. Clifford and she expects him."

"All right," Ernie said. "The crest is expected through Broomhead some time between two and four – should hit us around midnight tonight. I need more trucks – more town sand – more bags . . ."

"You'll get them," Mayor Fraser promised. He looked at Ernie's haggard face; the sand-bagging shifts spelled each other off every eight hours, but he strongly suspected that Ernie had been going round the clock for the past two days. "Sorry about that dyke last year, Ernie."

At four o'clock, just as the crest of the flood reached Piney Dell, and only ten minutes after Headley McConkey had hooked the farmhand onto his tractor to ride out to the south end of his earth dam, Ernie Fowler and Hickory Bob Smith went up Daddy Sherry's front walk.

"We're taking him," Ernie said firmly to Belva Louise, "whether he likes it or not."

"Thank goodness," said Belva. "He's in the . . ."

Daddy stood in the doorway, his ten-gauge goose gun in his hands. Ernie Fowler saw that both hammers were back.

"You fellahs aren't takin' me anywhere," Daddy said. "An' you can get the hell outa here before I count ten."

It was eight when Ernie Fowler and Hickory Bob Smith reached the sidewalk, still not certain whether Daddy's ultimatum meant the porch, his yard, or the entire block on which he lived.

Out of effective shotgun range they turned and looked back; what they saw sent them running for higher ground. It was much too late now to rescue Daddy Sherry and Belva Louise Tinsley.

Three miles west of Shelby, Headley McConkey with the tractor had intended taking only a small bite out of his earth dam to drain the water flooding over his eighty acres of registered seed oats; within minutes the entire dam had crumbled and McConkey Lake rushed to reunion with the Spray just reaching its crest there. A quarter-mile above Shelby the CNR bridge, always a bottleneck during flood season, resisted the onrushing water for only minutes, then gave way. Accurate reports were understandably confused and contradictory later, but many were agreed the wave that swept down upon the Sherry cottage had been at least six feet high. Even before Millie Clocker had sounded the red alert, the cottage was snatched from its foundation and carried past the river's curve and out into centre stream, where it began a surprisingly steady and balanced but slowly spinning voyage south.

She had never been so terrified in her life, Belva Louise explained to David, as she clung to the porch post and watched the river-banks slip past. It was not true, she said, that she had stayed to save Daddy or to protect him or to go down with him. It had happened so fast that she had been unable to jump clear. She could not swim a stroke and her only hope was to stay with the ship. As shock faded slightly she saw that Daddy was in his rocker, must have gone into the house and come out again since they had embarked, for he was wearing the white, visored and gold-braided yachting cap he had bought earlier in preparation for his intended South Seas voyage.

"Jump to them mizzen sails there – throw out the sea anchor – let her roar . . ."

Bracing herself against the tilt of the porch floor she made her way to the rocker, grabbed at the high back for support. "We're going to be all right, Mr. Sherry – if we just don't panic!"

"Batten them hatches an' head for the squid-jiggin' ground – Mary Jane's got the bit in her teeth – runnin' with the wind an' as soon as we lay our han's on Blackbird Teach there'll be keel haulin' – then for the South Seas. . . ."

"We've got to get inside – inside!"

"You go on below – I'll take her round the Horn myself. . . ."

"But, Mr. Sherry – if we hit – if we tip – there's nothing to stop you sliding right off the . . ."

"Get the hell off my bridge!"

But she had stayed to hold the rocker, hoping that the flood current would carry them close to one bank or the other, hardly able to gather her wits while Daddy raised his cracked old voice in sea shanties, keeping time with his cane and returning always to "Rule Britannia!"

They were almost saved a mile north of Foxhole when the house went aground on a sandbar there, but the river had plucked them loose again before Hickory Bob Smith and his Flat-Bottom Boat Committee could launch a rescue. The entire Emergency and Disaster Relief Committee, with the RCMP detachment's four patrol cars, the Shelby Fire Department's engine and resuscitator, and Ollie Pringle's ambulance, followed their leisurely course downstream, halting wherever the highway or side roads touched the river. In this way the house was almost always in sight until darkness fell. The last glimpse had been at the rear of the Co-op Grain Elevator in Tiger Lily.

With nightfall Belva had managed to get the old man into the house and into bed, she told David. As she had tucked him in he had commented, "I always heard she was rough, Belva – but we made her round the Horn. You stay at the wheel now. Sing out if you need me – but only if you need me – smell that there sea air – nothin' like it to make a fellah sleep."

It was perhaps an hour before dawn that she sensed an extra steadiness under her. She had ventured out onto the porch only to find darkness. She went back inside. She was quite sure now that they were aground, for she could feel no movement, hear no creaking in the house – only the lapping of water, the pulsing shrillness of spring frogs. She had lain down on the chesterfield then, and, incredibly, fallen asleep.

She awoke to morning light streaming through the living-room window, went to it, looked out and up to see the Star-spangled Banner limp about a flagpole a few hundred feet from the house. At some time during the night they had crossed the border, without visas, illegally after border-crossing hours, and smuggling in under cover of darkness one undeclared Canadian house with all its contents.

Even as she turned away from the window there was a light and questioning knock at the front door. She opened it to the olive uniform of the American Immigration and Customs Service. Before she or the two border officials could say anything, Daddy, still nightshirted, spoke from his bedroom doorway.

"Take me," he said, "to your cannibal chief."

14

⊷∕ᴥ∖⊶

Hang Your Mink on a Hickory Limb

W. O. spent most of his summers as a child and adolescent at the family cottage on White Bear Lake, which at that time was called Carlyle Lake. As soon as school was out in late June, the Mitchell family, including Grandma McMurray, migrated eighty miles east over rough prairie roads to spend July and August at the lake. This piece was written in 1961 just as W. O. and Merna were exploring the northern Okanagan area for their summer cottage location. They bought a lot on Mable Lake on the Shuswap system and built their family summer cottage in the spring of 1961. Over the years it did become a "beautiful lure" and the most recent summer family gathering included six grandchildren and three great-grandchildren from as far away as New York, New Jersey, and Peterborough.

✑

Most of the summer cottages of my childhood would have been condemned outright by the most indulgent of slum inspectors. Check off
the black marks: no running water, since you walked half a mile for
it at the hotel pump; outside sanitation; no insulation; fifth-grade
shingles starred with sunlight. The cottage, of course, had no ceiling
at all, displaying its stud and rafter ribs to all within.

These cottages twinkled with not one single pane of glass, just
screens and their shutters. During a sudden rain or wind storm, the
shutters could be lowered by ropes, though sometimes they clattered
down automatically – generally after dark when you were playing
pinochle with your grandmother in the luke light of a lamp with its
body-odour smell of coal oil.

Today any public health officer would grade our cottage at Carlyle
Lake as unfit for human habitation. For my grandmother and me it
kindled a sort of inebriation that lasted all through July and August.
I hate to think what this black Scot in her mid-eighties would have
thought of today's summer cottages. A Presbyterian stoic crippled
with rheumatism, she would have disapproved of the sybaritic comfort
of not having to thread her way past the saw-horse and the woodpile
and through the birches to the convenience.

We drove to the lake in a great, yellow-wheeled, McLaughlin
monster and several miles before the actual revelation of water there
occurred what was a wonderful thing for a Saskatchewan prairie boy:
the live smell of it plain upon the July air. Then I appreciated how an
Arab with very dry nostrils feels when he approaches an oasis under
date palms with arrow-feather grace, the stone well surrounded quite
possibly by several ladies shouldering pregnant clay jugs the way they
always did on the front of our Sunday School paper. Soon we were
enclosed by the true forest, musky with the smell of leaf mould, loud
with the tapping of leaves.

My grandmother loved the cottage; she sat on its screened veran-
dah and watched the vacationing world go by – played more casino,

euchre, cribbage, and rummy during the two months at the lake than she did during the rest of the year. And she went down to the beach each Sunday afternoon to bathe, making it with my arm and her cane to the water's edge. She sat then in the lake, to her navel, and she bathed – literally with soap foam lapping about her middle as she went over her neck and face and arms and legs with washcloth. Children splashed and dog paddled around her. Several hundred people on the beach watched her. They were compelled to, for as well as her skirted cotton bathing suit, she wore her velvet neckband and the attached lace that hid her goitre. She was the only bather on the beach, wearing a black velvet neckband and a Queen Mary hat, a high black turbanish affair with a polished jet gadget like a miniature coach lamp fixed to the top rim.

After her bath, she would sit in the shade of the birches and give me a dime to buy two of those great monolithic suckers cast in the shape of a cob of corn. She was very fond of these suckers.

To buy these suckers my brother and I went into business, the frog business, selling them at a cent a piece. My brother was very good at selling so it was usually he who left the cottage with a large lard pail holding over a hundred frogs. Mail-sorting time, two o'clock, the front or post office part of the hotel was a good place for frog sales. Here, just as they came up from the beach, people in their bathing suits and bath robes, mostly bare-footed, waited before the mail wicket. Mostly they were young girls, anxious for departmental exam results, Normal School certificates, letters from some boy who had stayed forlornly behind in their home town. Among the proper ladies of the lake there were mutterings about the impropriety of all this feminine semi-nudity in the hotel at mail time. The beach was the place for it; a hotel was not. An August Saturday afternoon in 1928 my brother fixed that up for the balance of the summer.

Ordinarily he left the master frog pail down by the hotel dock, but for some reason he took it into the hotel with him that day. Between the grocery counter and the lattice covered with life-size pictures of bather girls with rubber roses and rubber butterflies on their rubber bathing caps, my brother stubbed his toe, or was tripped, and went flat on his face. The lard pail flew, and on impact with the floor, sprung its lid off, emptying four gallons of water and two hundred frogs amongst the bare feet and legs of seventy-odd mail-expectant girls.

The girls leaped; the frogs leaped, though silently. One of the Weyburn MacIntyre girls made it to the top of the grocery counter and then a pyramid display of Rogers Golden Syrup tins, but only momentarily. The beautiful Boswell twins from Brandon scaled the latticework partition, dropped lightly down on the ice-cream-parlour side, only to find more hopping frogs there; both jumped in unison to the top of a table where a honeymooning couple from Arcola were having a banana split. All this confusion did not help my brother, down on his hands and knees as he tried to recapture some of his frog merchandise.

The owner of the hotel, who had the restraint of Buster Keaton, told my mother that frogs dead and alive kept showing up in the dining room, the ice cream parlour, the grocery and post office sections, for two weeks after. He also said that the next time my brother or I turned over the canoe with its lateen sail and leeboards out in the middle of the lake, there would be a five-dollar towing charge for the hotel launch when it went out to retrieve us. Up till that time the hotel launch had come for us for nothing.

For many of our earlier years at the cottage, our neighbour was an English lady almost as old as my grandmother. She had a lark-happy laugh that slalomed down the scale and burst clear with the words: "how love-lah!" She was an interesting person to me, for she said that her father had been personal surgeon to Charles Dickens. She proved this conclusively by having a glass case in the middle of a table in her cottage, and in the case lay a wooden thing that looked like two hollowed-out potato mashers hinged at their mashing ends. It was Charles Dickens' personal lemon squeezer, and though he hadn't bothered to autograph it, I knew she was telling the truth when she said he had given it to her father.

She had a precise sense of property and one day firmly ordered my youngest brother and me to step back and away from her choke-cherries.

We did, though we resented it. We discussed it later, questioning whether we had been on her property at the time at all. Even Tarzan couldn't have been sure in all that tangle of bush and sapling and tree. For that matter none of us at the Lake *owned* the property our cottages stood on. This was an Indian Reserve and the land was simply leased for ninety-nine years. The berries – hers and ours – belonged to the Indians, didn't they?

I have realized in later years that she had no intention of being unfriendly or un-neighbourly. We may or may not have been on her property, but one thing was certain. We had been not ten feet away from what my mother called the convenience, my grandmother – the privy – and we boys – the backhouse. The impropriety of two boys so near had offended her delicate feelings.

My brother and I did not realize this as we sat on our back step and stared out towards her outhouse, a rather pretentious one for the lake, its shingled walls whitewashed to gleaming purity. Its door had what no other such door at the lake had – a square glazed window instead of the usual diamond or crescent cutout.

I heard the screen on the cottage next door slap at the drowsing August stillness; up the path, past the choke-cherry and saskatoon bushes she claimed for her own, she walked with bolt-upright dignity. The outhouse door opened and quickly closed. On demonic impulse I slipped into the cottage and returned with my Little Daisy air rifle. My brother and I then besieged her, taking deliberate turns, politely cocking the rifle before we handed it to each other. Such a satisfying ringing ping as the bee-bee hit the glass! She was truly held at bay; modesty would not permit her to come out and confront us with the enormity of what we were doing; yet the repetitive outrage was insupportable.

The door behind us opened; my grandmother held out her hand for the bee-bee gun; my brother, whose turn it happened to be, gave it to her. The outhouse door opened. As one my brother and I dived under our cottage, snaked our way through the sting of nettles and out to the shelter of a hazelnut bush, through which we would see my grandmother confronted – the bee-bee gun in her hand – by the angry Sassenach. I am quite sure that my grandmother did not squeal on us. I know this, because I was invited several times after the incident to look at Charles Dickens' lemon squeezer; also my grandmother was not ever again invited over for tea. Nor did I ever see the Little Daisy bee-bee gun again.

Perhaps the picture-windowed, insulated, electrified, central heated, air-conditioned, expensive summer cottage of today is a status symbol – but only for parents; nothing could make it so for children. And there is a hidden dividend in a summer cottage. Last summer in the Okanagan I visited a Canadian journalist crippled with rheumatism. He sat on his front porch, surrounded by innumerable creepers and crawlers and toddlers and tree climbers and dog paddlers and teenaged water-skiers. There is no new thing under the sun. The summer cottage persists as a beautiful lure. When your sons and daughters live out their life from yours, a cottage on the lake, with its cluster of satellite cabins, will draw them from anywhere on the continent with their babies and your grandchildren for the two summer months.

There's this lovely sailing lake northeast of Vernon with a beach of purest white sand; waterfront property is still only ten dollars a foot; clay and wattles are cheap in British Columbia, and for about six thousand dollars . . .

15

⌒⌒⌒

The Day I Caught Syphilis

This "fictive memoir" is truly in the oral tradition of story-telling. As far as we know, there is no written text for it and what follows is cobbled together from a recording of a performance W. O. gave on July 4, 1978, at the Banff Centre of Fine Arts (where for many years he taught a summer course in creative writing), some phrases from The Vanishing Point, *and a taped interview with W. O. on December 26, 1983.*

⌒⌒⌒

My father died when I was seven, very early in life. He was a druggist. I was able to read his anatomy books – just to the left behind the diamond panes of the bookshelf doors by the fireplace. They were beautiful with their marbled covers, maroon corners, and raised welts on the spines. You opened them and there was this guy standing like this – arms straight down at his sides and open palms held outwards.

And his balled eyes staring out blue. You peeled a page back and then he looked like an Italian brigand with criss-crossing cartridge belts on him – the pleated muscles, you know? And you would peel off another and another and another and you could get the circulatory system. Then the nervous system. I was mostly interested in the urogenital system. Of the opposite sex. And there were rows of the female parts, sort of like a graduation picture or a stamp album page.

My mother was an eminent Victorian. But I'm getting a little ahead of myself. I knew more at the age of eight about venereal disease than Dr. Eaglesham did. Oh – the name of this little fictive memoir is "The Day I Caught Syphilis at the Age of Twelve." My mother told us always to put paper on the toilet seat, though not in our own house for some reason. We went down to Los Angeles the winter I was twelve – on the Soo Line through Moose Jaw and on to the coast. My younger brothers, Dickie and Bobby, and I – we were pretty obedient kids. We put paper on the toilet seats. Jesus! We papered the foothills, we papered the Rockies, the Livingston range, the Monashee range, the Coastal range. If you went anywhere on the CPR there were lots of places festooned with our toilet paper.

We came back the next summer to a place called Carlyle Lake. And there was a thing that used to hit us – salmonella, intestinal infection – which we called Riel's Revenge. I got it. Suddenly. I was down at the beach and just made it up to the hotel public toilets. Anybody used them. Including chambermaids that – well, I heard things about them. I made it there, but not in time to lay out the toilet paper. Now, informed as I was, I was appalled at what happened next. It was after the exact incubation time for the primary symptoms of syphilis to appear that I formed loathsome lesions all over my crotch. Just like the picture of the strawberry-red chancre in my father's anatomy text.

We always changed our bathing suits in a tent on a platform right near the house and now my problem was my older brother – seven years older than I was. A number of times I was in there, about to take down my bathing suit, and he would come in and I would pull it up again. And it wasn't really funny at the time. I went up to Sandy Beach to Pringle's Point and looked down and considered jumping. I intended to destroy myself. I went back about eight years ago and looked at it. Huh! – what I would have got was a lot of nettle burns. It wasn't ninety feet high – maybe twelve at the most – and it went down at a forty-five-degree angle. Someone did the same thing to Pringle's Point that they did to our house – time did.

So finally, one day my brother says, "What the hell is wrong with you?" Now, you must understand I was twelve, I looked about eight. When I was eighteen, I looked about fourteen. I had big horn-rimmed glasses. But I was smarter than he was. I just dropped them down and said, "I got syphilis." To this day I don't know whether I then received the greatest compliment of my life or the worst insult. He said, "Who'd you get it off of?" I said something about the chambermaids – I think he said "Which one?" Oh, I won't stretch it any more. He didn't say "Which one?"

He took me to a young internist, the brother of the girl he was going with at Long Beach. He said, "This smart little bastard's picked up syphilis. Take a look at him." And Max looked and said what I had was what we called prairie itch – a scabies mite found in algae. It burrows under the skin and then it festers and then it blisters and then they suppurate and then they scab. *That's* what I had. And Mother had to boil the sheets and there was a Swedish or sulphur ointment you had to use. But it was too late. I had infected my Auntie Josie, my grandmother McMurray, my cousin Margaret, my cousin Jean, my brothers – the whole goddamned works! Except maybe Mother, who wouldn't let me know if she got it.

16

Grandmother MacMurray

In the early sections of Who Has Seen the Wind, *young Brian sees his grandmother MacMurray as a stern and meddling presence who continually crosses his wishes. But as he matures he develops a special bond with her – particularly in her last days. In the following sequence of scenes Brian, now eleven, pays daily visits to his grandmother's room to watch her knit his hockey socks and listen to stories about homesteading days with her husband John. The stories she tells Brian are stories which W. O.'s grandmother Maggie McMurray told him when he was a child.*

In her room on the second floor, Brian's grandmother sat by her window; it was open and she could see the yellowing leaves of the poplar outside, shot through with the blue of the fall sky. Her window stood usually open now, teasing her old nostrils with the softness of spring, the richness of summer, or the wild wine of fall.

The eighty-two years of her life had imperceptibly fallen, moment by moment piling upon her their careless weight; and now it seemed that her years were but as yesterday; the little time that was left to her seemed as much as she had lived. Her world now was that of her window.

She had tried to explain to Maggie, had tried to tell her not to pull the window down. It wasn't fair. The rippled pane had no right to distort the clouds, the leaves of the trembling poplar. When the world was completely through with her would be time enough to lose the sounds of the street below; the tack-hammer strokes of women's heels on the walk, hooves dropping quick cups of sound, children calling. Maggie could wait – draught or no draught.

The electric clock on the commode said five. Brian would be in to see her. He never failed to call when school was over. He would bring the wool – black and yellow. He had set his heart on long hockey stockings – wasp-striped. She would knit him his stockings.

As she rocked, she thought of other days, prairie days. In her mind she lived them over, picking crocuses if she willed it; freckle-throated tiger lilies, saskatoons, wild strawberries, pin-cherries – she picked them all as she once had. There was silver wolf willow from the bank of the river running by the homestead hut; the faint, honey smell of it remained long with her as she reminisced.

The yellow lace of the window's poplar stirred. Brian stood before her with his dark eyes steady upon her face. He held two balls of wool in his hand. When he had got her needles from the drawer of the dresser, she began to cast on stitches, her arthritic swollen knuckles making the once unconscious work difficult.

She told her grandson again the story of his Grandfather John and the bobcat with tassels on its ears.

"For about three weeks he hung around the sod hut," she went on. "He kept pretty well out of sight, and we used to hear him only at night. It was winter – oh six and seven – the year of the blue snow. Every morning we'd find his tracks in the snow all around the back, and the second week after we first saw his tracks, we saw him. John had gone out to saw up some birch chunks, and he looked up, and there was the bobcat spang in the middle of a branch of the poplar by the woodpile. John looked at him and he looked at John and ye should have seen his eyes. They were green and they were slitty-like; they didn't blink the while he stared at John. He kept right on setting there, staring like John oughtn't to be there. And John told me later, he thought to himself, 'There isn't any bobcat going to stare me down. No siree bob.' John kept looking right back up at him. It was the only time he ever stared a bobcat down. The only time."

The poplar moved. A wavering wedge of geese crossed the window.

"The bobcat finally gave up," said the grandmother. "He turned his head like he hadn't been trying to stare John down at all. When John came in the hut to bring me out, the bobcat was gone."

The old lady talked and knitted on. She told of how the bobcat had sneaked into their shack and stolen a tin of John's chewing tobacco. He had trailed it, she said, by following the tobacco-juice trail the cat had spit brown upon the snow. He had killed it.

"It was a fine hide, as nice a bobcat hide as ever I saw. I made a cushion out of it. Just left the tassels on the corners for decoration."

The bedroom door opened and Maggie O'Connal stood there.

"Mother."

The grandmother looked up from her knitting.

"Don't you think it's a little chilly to have your window up? It isn't good for –"

"I'm warm, Maggie."

"But – even I feel it cold now that I'm in here. Please let me put your window down. Oh – you're knitting."

The grandmother did not answer her. She continued to knit on the sock, her hands trembling noticeably. It worried Maggie O'Connal that her mother used her eyes for knitting; she wasn't sure that it was good for them now that cataracts were forming.

"Mother, I don't think it's good for you to be straining your eyes doing that –"

"I'm all right – leave me be, Maggie!"

"If you would only do a little at a time, Mother. But you go right on and – I'm going to have to put down that window. You'll catch your death of cold." She went to the window.

"Leave my window alone!"

"I'm sorry, Mother."

Although she had not intended it to, the window gave suddenly and came down with a bang. Maggie turned away. She picked up the wool and needles from her mother's lap. "Leave this for a while now, Mother." She went out, hoping that the old lady, given time, would forget about the knitting.

Mrs. MacMurray sat in her rocker, waiting for the blood to stop hammering in her ears and the calm to come back in her. Long after Brian had left the room, she got up laboriously and with difficulty opened her window. She sat down again, her hands half-closed over the arms of the rocking chair. Motionless she sat, watching the sun-chinked pattern the poplar's leaves made along the side of the window.

When Maggie brought in her supper, the old woman still sat by the open window. Her daughter set the tray down on the commode top and stood hesitantly looking at the window. She finally went to the bed and returned with an afghan which she threw over her mother's shoulders.

The grandmother continued to sit, leaving the tray untouched. For a long while, as the leaf pattern in the window dimmed, and the autumn sunlight thinned to the pale violet of dusk, she stared. When there was nothing in the window for her, other than the clear moon high over the dark trees across the street, and a careless wind now and again stirring among the dead leaves, she began to wonder.

She wondered as old people do, why she had been. A girl, a woman, and now an old woman. She did not find it frightening; just senseless. She sneezed twice. She got up from her rocker. She went to bed.

She'd make the boy his hockey stockings.

When Brian came to see her the next day, she sat in her rocker. He said nothing about the stockings nor did his grandmother. She told him about the tame coyote named Tom. Grey, its eyes had been, and it had belonged to a Cree, Little Johnny Whiskeyjack, who had a squaw named Sally Eagleribs. Little Johnny, she told Brian, trained Tom to howl tenor. It was very pretty to hear Tom carry the harmony when coyotes out on the prairie howled at night.

She looked at Brian. It was no use. He wanted hockey stockings.

Through the open window came the sound of a carpet being beaten. "Whap!" The sound bounced off the sides of the house outside and slapped at the still afternoon. They could hear the penny thunder of coal for winter, chuting into the cellar of Sherry's house.

"Do you know where your mother's put the knitting?"

Brian looked at her eagerly. "It's on the mantel," he said. "There's an armchair right beside."

"Make sure your feet are clean."

When he had come back, she began to knit again. She talked as she worked.

Telesphore Toutant was a man who shot a brown bear in the East; he raised her cub on a bottle. He brought the cub with him when he came West, and one day he played with the bear when it didn't want to play. The rest of his life Telesphore used a purple saskatoon berry for a glass eye. There was a tickling in the back of the grandmother's throat near the end of the story.

She had just stopped coughing when they heard Maggie's footsteps upon the stairs. Brian shoved the needles, wool, and knitting into the top drawer of the dresser; he was just closing it when his mother entered the room.

"You're coughing, Mother," said Maggie O'Connal anxiously and accusingly.

"Was I now?" said the grandmother.

"And no wonder!" Down went the window. *Her* window.

The grandmother did not get another opportunity to work on the stockings. Maggie made her go to bed just because she had been coughing a bit. She put a burning mustard plaster upon her mother's chest. Then she went downstairs and phoned Dr. Svarich, who promised that he would come over later.

Her chest had been aching that morning, and the flat, hard cough came oftener and with greater intensity. The evening before, Dr. Svarich had come with his stethoscope, thermometer, tapping fingers, and the bitter smell that doctors always have. After the examination, the grandmother had heard Maggie and the doctor talking out in the hall. The voices subsided, then she heard Svarich's footsteps going down the stairs. Maggie had come into the room and told her that she was to stay in bed. With the window down.

So she lay now, looking at the flat faces of four walls and a ceiling, at the log-cabin quilt that covered her over, at the commode by the head of the bed, at the spoon there and the beaded water glass and the bottle of dark medicine. The clock bothered her; it was an electric clock with a thin, gold thread of a hand to push time around its square face. Crazy, quivering, enamel box trying to tell all the time in all the world. It had measured out little of her past life, and now it thought it was going to dole out what was left.

Brian killed it for her; he pulled its plug and turned it around on the dresser. Then, at her request, he got the knitting from the dresser drawer. She told no story as she knitted the stocking; it required all her concentration to keep the needles going.

The next morning unpleasant things were happening to the pane of her window; the centre of it had crinkled. Harsh waves, spreading out like wrinkles from a pebble tossed into the centre of a pond, filled the window. She could taste them. Over the wallpaper they snarled and, rolling jagged up the quilt, broke over her face. All day they did. And the next, while the old woman's breath sounded impatiently short and roupy through the still room.

And then for a brief while the window glass was smooth; the wallpaper was calm; she lay in her bed, filled with inexplicable sadness.

Brian came in to see her. He seemed ill at ease as he stood by her bed.

"Have ye got the knitting?"

He said that it was in the dresser drawer.

"Do ye expect it to knit itself there?"

She was almost half through the first sock. She had done hardly one row when the window pane began to wrinkle. Over there part of the wallpaper's pattern had begun to sag.

"Open –" Her voice thinned. She tried again. "Open – my – window."

Brian went to the window. He lifted; it refused to move at first, then, as he struggled, it gave, only to stick again a few inches above the sill. He bent his knees and placed the heels of his hands on the bottom of the window. It slid the full length of his arms, and the warm room was suddenly filled with the mint freshness of the outside. Stray flakes of the winter's first snow floated out of the afternoon and into the room, to melt in mid-air.

As he turned around he saw that the knitting had fallen upon the quilt and that his grandmother's head lay back on the pillow. Her eyes were closed.

He tiptoed from the room.

The black branches of the trees along Sixth Street were edged with white, the staring white that belongs to a child's paint box. Feathering lazily, crazily down, loosed from the hazed softness of the sky, the snow came to rest in startling white bulbs on the dead leaves of the poplars, webbing in between the branches. Just outside the grandmother's room, where she lay quite still in her bed, the snow, falling soundlessly, flake by flake piled up its careless weight. Now and again a twig would break off suddenly, relieve itself of a white burden of snow, and drop to earth.

17

⌘

See the Pattern Forming

Visitors to the Mitchell household over the years have remarked on how accident- and crisis-prone W. O. is. After his first visit with the Mitchells in High River, the writer Bruce Hutchison announced that if a bull moose in northern Alberta started charging south, it would go right through W. O.'s front living room. In the following piece W. O. muses on the nature of the force which may account for his ability to attract and create chaos.

This piece was first published in Maclean's (May 1964).

⌘

Around our home more and more often there has sounded a refrain: see the pattern forming. I think the better word for it is gestalt, and I have known about gestalt almost all my life, not at first in a clearly conscious way but mystically ever since a Christmas morning very early in childhood.

133

The most magnificent gift I got that year was a gay little machine which had a hopper and a truck on wheels to run up and down a slant track, a vertical shaft with a weight suspended inside a great deal like an elevator cage. This machine stood primly still until a child filled the hopper with sand. The sand would then trickle from the mouth of the hopper, fill the little cart until the weight of cart and sand overcame the weight of the counterbalance. The cart would roll down the inclined track, thereby closing off the trickle of sand from the hopper, would trip at the bottom and dump the sand. Now feather-light, the little cart would run back up the inclined track to hit a lever that would release a new trickle of sand, to refill the truck until it had reached the counterbalancing point and was ready for another trip down. This went on busily until all the sand had been transferred from the hopper to the living-room floor.

While it seemed a lot of trouble to get sand from a hopper to the floor, it was magic to watch, as though one were looking at the naked soul of gravity or as though sand had suddenly become passionate to get from the hopper to the ground. But I think the real reason it entranced was that the pattern of movement never failed either in its dynamic parts nor in its inevitable outcome: all sand out of the hopper and onto the floor. Also this Presbyterian toy seemed to give a reassuring promise: keep your hopper filled with sand, your cart on the track, and you will be a successful human. Horatio Alger Jr. books used to tell us this, too.

I am afraid that life is not so beautifully predestined as that toy, nor does it follow the ground rules laid down by Presbyterianism or Horatio Alger Jr., for me at least. As long as I can remember, I have been harried by gestalt patterns which refuse to form properly.

I keep remembering from university days the two German gentlemen on the Canary Islands with their chimpanzees. In this colourful and startling psychological adventure, they spent their days hanging bunches of bananas just out of reach or jump of the apes. They placed a box in a far corner of the cage and each day moved it closer to the hanging bananas until finally proximity had dynamically changed its meaning; it ceased to be a box-by-itself-in-a-far-corner-of-the-cage and became instead a box-close-enough-to-be-used-to-stand-upon-so-that-I-can-reach-the-bananas. This new pattern had changed the box to a tool and the unattainable bananas to attainable ones, the ape from a hungry one to a sated one.

I can see myself as one of Dr. Wertheimer or Dr. Koffka's chimpanzees without difficulty at all, but life's gestalts never seem to form as they ought to. For instance – the box moves closer and closer till it has dynamically taken its new place in the Mitchell pattern. I stand on it. I reach up for the stalk of bananas and, as I do, any one of a million unpredictable things happens, not one of them a foreseeable closure to the new gestalt. The box collapses under me. The stalk parts and the cluster drops to brain or smother me – almost. The individual bananas take on life and leapfrog up the stalk keeping always out of reach. I take one off, peel it, and just as I put it to my mouth, it explodes. Always the pattern closure surprises, forms, if not in a malevolent fashion, then toward an unfriendly or ludicrously unkind goal which I cannot possibly foretell.

I remember particularly a morning in Toronto fourteen or more years ago when I set out to my work as a fiction editor. Little did I dream, as they say in *I Confess* magazine, that I would within three-quarters of an hour end up in the emergency ward of the Toronto General Hospital. Numb, I had driven the same route hundreds of mornings. I had always laid my tobacco pouch and pipe on the car seat beside me so that I could fill it at the several Danforth Street stoplights, then light it at the Wellesley and Yonge corner. How could I have known that a little elderly lady would be standing with her umbrella on that corner at that precise time? I could have anticipated the Orange Parade with sashed marchers, fife-and-drum bands, all the King Williams on white horses; who couldn't have; it was Toronto and it was the morning of July the twelfth whether I remembered it or not. Actually the parade had little to do with whether or not I ended up in the emergency ward. What happened to one of the King Williams on his white horse was not an integral part of the main gestalt, though if there hadn't been an Orange Parade the closure could have been truly tragic: loss of life. Mine.

It had been my custom every morning within moments of the same time, to pick up the filled pipe by my side. Then, with my eyes carefully on the lights, I would reach forward, snick open the glove compartment, take out the kitchen box of matches there, light one and put it to my pipe. As it happened this morning, the Orange Parade was passing, which in turn accounts for the elderly little lady with the umbrella on the corner. With others she was watching the parade. I was stopped on the one-way street in the second line from the left, five cars deep, as the tail of the parade came past. This gave me an unusually long time to complete the pipe routine, which went as it had always gone until I scratched the match against the side of the box. The pattern fizzed, buzzed, spun, and struck as the match ignited all the other matches left in the box. This converted the small aperture, slid open to extract one match, into a lethal sizzling muzzle, a blowtorch of acetylene force, trained upon my hand, my chest, and my face as I bobbled it about and then with quick-witted response lobbed it out of the opened driver's window and – quite unintentionally – through the opened window of the truck parked between me and the curb. The trucker's helper caught it and yelled, "Judas Priest!" He tossed it into the lap of his partner behind the wheel, at which time I noticed that the truck was loaded with gasoline, for it had INFLAMMABLE written across the side. The driver tossed the still sputtering and flaming matchbox out of his window, thus setting afire the elderly lady standing on the street. He jumped out and began to beat her helpfully with her umbrella.

Meanwhile back in the car, with the nape of my neck I sensed that something more was wrong. I turned to see that flying matches from the explosion had started hundreds of tiny fires on the nylon slipcovers of the back seat; also my hair was on fire. I slapped it out then leaned over to put out the backseat fires. This took my foot off the clutch, and the car leaped out and into the Twelfth of July Parade, stalling against one large dirty-white horse bearing a King William. The car barely touched him, but it did startle his horse with the rump-lowering, tense-legged panic that precedes bolting. King William slid down the horse's neck on the opposite side, rounded the steed's rear, and came at me. I saw the expression change on his face from anger to horror. "My God, man, you'd better get to a doctor quick!" I looked down to see that my tie was burnt through, my shirt front and vest black; I could only guess at the barbecued state of my face.

I drove straight to the emergency door of the General Hospital where the morning's quota of terribly hurt people waited in line for their turn at the desk. The recording-and-admitting nurse glanced up and the same look came over her face as had come over King William's. She beckoned me to the head of the line, took my name, address, *Maclean's* magazine group-health-and-accident-plan number, next of kin. Two interns took me by each arm, pranced me into the operation room and up onto a sheeted operating table, where two nurses began gently swabbing me while we waited for the doctor specializing in burnt patients to be summoned from the bowels of the hospital.

"Does this hurt?" they would murmur to me. "Does this pain you badly?" "Am I hurting too much?" Strangely they weren't hurting me at all as they went over me from the hairline to neck – to shoulders – elbows – fingertips. I assumed at first that I was so badly burned that the nerves had been fried beyond registering pain, but when the doctor had arrived, the nurses had finished every inch of swabbing and established that under all that cleaned-off flash-sooting the only burned area on my body was a disc the size of a dime on the ball of my right thumb.

"Where is he – where is he?" the doctor asked and the nurses pointed to me on the table. "What's his injury?"

I held out to him my self-explanatory thumb.

It has been so all my known life; I recall in France at the age of eighteen, climbing out of a silk puptent I'd put up the night before in pitch dark on what I had thought to be a grassy field. I found myself on a boulevard in the heart of Toulouse; I could tell from all the people in the sidewalk cafés that it was the aperitif hour. I had just climbed out of my sleeping bag naked. Most people restrict this sort of thing to their nightmares. I have been constantly threatened with decapitation. Now most people would accomplish this by sabre, scimitar, axe, or guillotine. I have come poltergeistically close to beheading with: a water ski, a car door, a Canada grey honker, a dumb waiter, a flying four-foot piece of galvanized pipe, numerous ladders I have known, and a seventy-five-foot length of scarlet ribbon bearing the name MAZO DE LA ROCHE, in gold. The latter I could almost have foreseen on the gala opening of the British Book Services Yonge Street shop when the storefront was covered with gay gift paper to be pulled away on signal by authors and Rank film stars, each clutching his ribbon attached to the paper two storeys up.

All this makes for novelty and perhaps I would have it no other way, but if our lives are formed and determined by dynamic gestalts, there is one sobering possibility: these in turn could be parts of a great pulsing life gestalt urgent towards one grand, climactic, twenty-fourth of May closure. In the words of a certain truck driver: "Judas Priest!"

18

Interlude at La Guardia

On the reading circuit W. O. has encountered a number of strange experiences in hotel and airport toilets. Once, for instance, he found himself cheek by jowl at a urinal beside John Diefenbaker. In the following piece, written in 1989, he recalls a particularly embarrassing gestalt moment at La Guardia airport in 1966. This incident became one of the family's favourite "W. O. stories" – that is, stories about W. O. – which over the years gathered mythic and prurient proportions. Some family members (like his wife, Merna, shown here) feel that he finally wrote it up 23 years later to put on record what actually happened in that airport bathroom.

༄༅

I believe I've had more than my fair share of embarrassing experiences. I have come to realize that they don't just happen; they have an inevitable event pattern with an early beginning leading to a humiliating climax.

My most embarrassing experience began thirty-five years before its conclusion, a seed planted when I graduated from St. Petersburg Senior High School during my Florida boyhood and adolescent years. My mother asked me what I would like for a graduation present. That was an easy one. A Cuban fellow senior, Tommy Jaipur, was a tap-dancer performing on every possible occasion in or out of St. Pete High, with malacca cane and tilted white Panama hat – or perhaps a straw boater. He had quite a staccato repertory: "East Side, West Side," "Chatanooga Choo Choo," "Shuffle off to Buffalo," "Tiptoe Through the Tulips." A devout springboard diver, I had no interest in tap-dancing, but I envied Tommy the white Palm Beach suit he wore when he performed.

"Yeah – white Palm Beach, double-breasted suit like Tommy Jaipur wears."

My mother's face showed a shade of concern. "Oh, Billie, this past year you've grown so fast, shot up." I hadn't. Just turned seventeen, I was a good head shorter than anybody else in my year, male or female. "It's a lot of money for something you could wear for maybe only half a year."

My older brother, who was by now smoking openly, said, "Even if it did still fit you, when you go to university you'd look pretty funny wearing a Palm Beach suit in Winnipeg in forty-below."

I can't remember what the hell she did give me for my graduation present, but again and again over the decades I have recalled my disappointment at not wearing a white Palm Beach, double-breasted suit up on the St. Pete High auditorium stage to receive my parchment roll behind a quarter-mile bank of blowtorching poinsettias.

That was the beginning of something that finally bloomed thirty-five years later in San Francisco, where I was involved in a documentary film. We finished shooting early in the day and I had a free afternoon before my flight to New York. I went into Frederick and Nelson's men's wear section, and there I saw a long row of suits. They were pure cotton and they were double-breasted, and I bought two of them. My mother had been right. They *were* expensive. One of them had a blue, the other a chocolate, pinstripe. Seersucker. I decided to wear the blue striper. Before checking out of the hotel, I changed and looked at myself in the mirror and felt a rush of catharsis such as I had never experienced before.

There would be a two-hour wait in the small hold-up room in La Guardia airport before my flight to Toronto, then on to Calgary, and half an hour before the boarding announcement I had to go to the washroom. I was alone in there when I stepped back from the urinal and went over to the pedestal sink to wash my hands. When I turned on the tap, I underestimated New York water pressure; the flow hit the basin with such force that it blew like an Alberta oil well.

Right on target: my crotch!

Seersucker is cotton and it truly does suck; instant absorption had left a dark trail down the inside of both my thighs, and there was no way I could walk out of the men's toilet to face all those people in that small hold-up room; every one of them could recognize urine stain when they saw it. I looked for the paper towel box. There wasn't one. I went into the single cubicle. Some guy had used up the last square on the roll. Then I saw the blow-dryer on the wall to the right of the pedestal sink. The snout could be rotated up or down. I turned it up, climbed up on the basin edge to balance on one knee with the other high and out like a dog at a fire hydrant, then directed the warm flow upwards to dry and erase the embarrassing shadows. It was going to take time, but it was working. I simply had to snap the dryer on again and again and again and again and . . .

Perhaps the fifteenth time, I heard the door open behind me. I looked back and up over my shoulder to see two fellows, both with attaché cases and their mouths open under their white cowboy hats.

"I'll be through in a moment," I said.

I was. It could have been worse; just before they'd entered, I had realized that my underwear shorts were quite damp and had decided not to bother with them. How much worse to have been caught with my pants at half-mast.

As I boarded my Toronto flight I had to pass the same two seated in first-class, and the one in the aisle seat nudged his partner and pointed to me with his thumb. He did so again when I boarded my Calgary flight. With their gabardine suits, string ties, high-heeled boots, and white cowboy hats, I'm pretty sure they were soft-thighed oil patch executives who had never forked a horse and had been in New York, mulleting for risk capital.

I was relieved that my wife, Merna, had not been with me on that trip. In time I told her about what had happened in that New York airport washroom. She laughed herself silly and kept bringing it up for the next ten years, mostly for the amusement of dinner guests. I think the last time she reminded me of it was when the secretary of the mayor of Weyburn, Saskatchewan, where I had been born and raised for the first twelve years of my life, wrote to say that they would like to erect a life-size bronze sculpture of my fictional characters, Jake and the Kid, on the south entrance to the city. That would be Government Road heading for the border and North Dakota. I said I would be honoured. Merna laughed.

Months went by before I heard from the mayor's office again. Evidently they had found out that foundry costs in Winnipeg were much higher than they had anticipated. They did not want to abandon the project, though; would it be all right with me if they did just the Kid in the spring and Jake a year or two further on down the road? This time she really laughed.

"Doesn't strike me as all that funny," I said.

"Oh no – it isn't."

"Then why the hell are you laughing so hard?"

"I just thought of something."

"What?"

"They got the wrong subject for their statue. Shouldn't be Jake and the Kid."

"What should it be?"

"You," she said.

"What, you mean – me?"

"I can just see you there at the south entrance to Weyburn – the white pedestal – up on one knee, balancing on that basin – with your right leg lifted up high."

I still have those seersucker suits hanging in an upstairs closet. I have worn neither of them since that afternoon in La Guardia airport twenty-three years ago.

19

The Napoleon Threat

Rory Napoleon is one of many Mitchell characters who is a manifestation of that mysterious force which W. O. considers in "See the Pattern Forming." In this episode, Rory comes out of exile, and the community of Shelby meets its Waterloo.

This story was originally read on CBC *Radio and published in a collection of short stories edited by Robert Weaver,* Ten for Saturday Night *(1961), under the title "Patterns." It had originally been a part of a 1950s novel,* Roses Are Difficult Here, *which was eventually published by McClelland & Stewart in 1990.*

Often on a Saturday night, when he found himself badly blocked in a sermon, Mr. Cameron found release in tying dry flies; it was a solitary and mesmerizing occupation which somehow freed his mind and imagination. The loose feathers lifted and slid over the desk top under his gentle breath; the completed flies increased one by one, resting high and light on their hackle tips at his elbow. With each fly the tension loosened more and he experienced a little of the satiety that attended the netting of a trout itself. Rings slowly widened and spread to grassy banks; sunlight disked and danced on green water; clear bubbles and foam were borne slowly circling; mosquitoes whined thin; grasshoppers leaped clicketing; and he had broken off for himself a warm and humming fragment of August.

Plato, he felt, would have approved of dry-fly tying; the feather filaments were so spirit-light they could lift and float the heavy dross of the material hook, ideal camouflage raying from the barbed and lethal matter. These were classical flies to ride bravely down summer streams, drifting like waterborne stars on their tantalizing course over slicks and riffles where hungry rainbow lay.

The minister leaned back in his chair and poured himself another cup of tea. Somehow tonight the fly-tying did not soothe – certainly not enough to rid his mind of the thought of a Rory Napoleon missing for three days. And why was it that he must always be so concerned for the Napoleons? He was too practical a man to imagine he could bring them spiritual nourishment. They were not members of his congregation, though that would have been impertinent if they had been in actual want. To his knowledge they never were; they were warm; they were fed; they were clothed; their goats and their eighty weed-infested acres and Rory's job as town garbage collector seemed to take care of their material needs. Their health was the continuing concern of Dr. Fotheringham, who made sure they got to the clinic once a month.

The minister could understand the doctor's interest in the Napoleons; he could also appreciate Mr. Oliver's concern. The police magistrate was the tidiest man in town. Proprietor of the Oliver Trading Company General Store, law was only an avocation with him but it was his first love, all the same. In the impeccability of the lawn about his house, store window displays, grocery shelves and counters, one could see that order was Mr. Oliver's passion. His interest, the minister felt, might simply be attraction to an opposite. Mr. Cameron could not so simply explain his own fascination, a disturbing one dating from the time that he had first come to his charge in Shelby ten years ago. Deliberately then he had set out to discover all he could about the Napoleons; Dr. Fotheringham had been a most fertile source of information.

In Rory Napoleon's veins, the doctor thought, flowed the blood of Brittany tinted with some Basque and mingling with one-quarter Peigan contributed by his maternal grandfather, Chief Baseball, who had signed the Blackfoot Crossing Treaty in 1878. These had been given Rory by the French half-breed mother, who had met and loved under lodge-pole pines a remittance cowhand in 1908, so that Rory as well boasted the proud blood of the line MacCrimmon, composers of pibroch and pipers to the chiefs of Scotland. Mame, his common-law wife, was ten years younger than Rory; like Ontario cheddar she was pure Canadian. Their offspring: Buster, Byron, Avalon, Evelyn, Ester, Elvira – living – and Violet, Herbert, Calvin, and Clarence, who had died at birth or in infanthood, carried the Breton-Basque-Peigan-Scots-Canadian blood.

Town legend had it that Byron had been born on Dominion Day and on top of a Ferris wheel at the thirty-ninth Annual Shelby Fair, Light Horse Show, and Rodeo. This was not precisely true, Henry Fotheringham had explained to the minister.

"Byron was born exactly nine months *after* Dominion Day," the Doctor said. "'I always been fussy about the Ferris wheel,' Mame told me. 'Fair was almost over an' I told Rory I'd like one more ride before we went home. Ferris wheel broke down. We never did get a good type of Ferris wheel at our fairs, you know. An' there was Rory an' me with the motor broke down an' our seats swingin' from the top of midnight for a good hour. What else was there for us to do. . . .'"

A slight, dark, and insouciant man with a rather wild eye, Rory could be seen daily in the Post Office just before mail time. He wore a faded blue jacket, its breast pockets lined with a battery of fountain pens and pencils. Usually he took up a position, leaning against the wall near the door and under the WANTED posters and the civil service examination notices. He had no mail box, so that when Mr. Fry lifted the frosted window and swung in the brass grill, Rory took his place in line with those lesser individuals whose mail came in a lump under the initial letter of their surnames in General Delivery.

Mr. Fry at the Post Office handed him out regularly: the Shelby *Chinook*, both the Calgary dailies, the Regina *Leader-Post*, the Winnipeg *Tribune*, Nor-west *Prairie Farm Review*, the *Country Gentleman*, *Maclean's*, *Star Weekly*, *Saturday Evening Post*, and Dr. Winesinger's Calendar Almanac. "I see by the papers today," was Rory's unfailing gangplank to conversation. He was unable to read or write.

With their herd of forty-seven goats the Napoleons lived just at the edge of town and next to the farm of Dan Sibbald. Year after year of goat trespass had thinned Mr. Sibbald's patience until an afternoon in the Maple Leaf Beer Parlour just three months before, when Rory had laid open Dan's head with a beer bottle. Mr. Cameron had talked it over with Mr. Oliver, the police magistrate, before he visited the Napoleons.

He found only Mame at home, accepted her invitation to a cup of tea, and came directly to the reason for his visit. "Mrs. Napoleon, I've called to see you about Rory."

"Uh-huh."

"And about Dan Sibbald."

"Did you?" There was little warmth in the red-rimmed eyes.

"Something has to be done, Mrs. Napoleon."

She turned away, took down a brown teapot from the wooden board that formed a shelf above the stove. As she began to shake tea into it she said, "What?"

"I've talked it over with Mr. Oliver . . ."

"Him!"

". . . and he's had a talk with Dan Sibbald . . ."

"Might have known Oliver'd get into it with his big flat English feet . . ."

"Mr. Oliver has been very just about . . ."

"Always had it in for the Napoleons – can't leave us alone!"

"Mr. Oliver! Oh, I don't think so . . ."

"Well, I do."

"But why would he have it in for . . ."

"I don't know why," Mrs. Napoleon said, "but he always has – always will – stubborn – he was to drown'd they'd find his body upstream!"

"But Mr. Oliver is willing to give Rory a chance. That doesn't sound as though he . . ."

"What kind of a chance?"

"He is willing to use his influence with Dan Sibbald – persuade him not to press charges against Rory either for trespass or for assault."

"Is that right?" Some of the coldness had vanished from Mrs. Napoleon's eyes. "Don't sound like Oliver."

"But it is."

"Don't sound like Dan Sibbald either," she said. "What's Rory got to do – apologize to Dan?"

"That would help, Mrs. Napoleon – to begin with."

"What else has he got to . . ."

"It's not Rory who has to do something else – it's you."

"Me? How?"

"I'd like you to have Rory interdicted – for his own good – for your own – for the children . . ."

"An' if I don't put Rory on the Indian List?"

"Then Mr. Oliver will have to let the law take its course."

"That sounds more like Oliver."

"There'll be a summons tomorrow."

"An' Rory'll have to go up before Oliver."

"Yes."

She tipped the boiling kettle over the teapot.

"I'm sorry, Mrs. Napoleon," Mr. Cameron said.

She set a cup before him. "I believe you."

"I wanted to talk it over with Mr. Napoleon but Mr. Oliver said it wouldn't be a good . . ."

"He's right. Wouldn't have a chance if Rory got tipped off first." She sat down in the backless wooden chair by the table. "If it's gotta be done – I'm the one's gotta do it."

"Will you do it for us?"

"I won't do it for Oliver."

"Will you do it for Rory?"

She shook her head. "Kids has it bad enough without Rory goin' down to Lethbridge jail for a couple months. I'll do it for them. Drink your tea while it's hot. And I'll do it for you."

Now, in his study, Mr. Cameron set aside his empty teacup, stared at the half-tied grey hackle held in the slant nose of the fly-tying vice. It had been so much easier than he had anticipated it would be – and persistently successful; to his knowledge and to Magistrate Oliver's. Rory had put in a sober three months; the goats had stayed in their pen on Napoleon land. Pangs of conscience had come more and more infrequently to the minister as he assured himself that the man's loss of drinking privileges had benefited his work for the town, his wife, his children. Of course there had never been any questioning the desirability of the end; it was the means that had disturbed Mr. Cameron. He would have felt so much better if he had talked it over with Rory first, given the man a chance to agree. It just wasn't right to push people about – even for their own good, for in a way then it stopped being their *own* good, nor was it such a satisfactory good. There was a comparable difference between a rainbow taken on bait and a rainbow taken fairly on a dry fly.

Obviously with the man missing for three days, it hadn't worked out so well after all. For three months he had deluded himself. Behind the casual façade the Napoleons presented to the world the minister had always sensed a faint threat, but exactly what was threatened or to whom it was threatened, he had never been sure. He knew only that the threat was there – vaguely ominous – persistent. Somehow – tonight – the minister told himself as he leaned forwards over the fly-vice – the Napoleon threat was the strongest it had ever been; in the heart of some dark place a hidden Rory waited – had always been waiting – but was now almost through waiting.

For three months Rory Napoleon had waited; for three months his tongue had stuck to the roof of his mouth and his throat had got stiff for the tickle of beer and the earth taste of beer. But Cameron and Oliver and the law had said God Save the Queen to it and that was all there was to it – he couldn't do a thing about it. Couldn't go in the place even. Well, send the law victorious – didn't know beer was glorious! Beer never hurt him – never hurt anybody. Let everyone suck beer down and not a drop for him!

At the end of three months he had called on Artie Buller, black-mailed the taxi man into selling him five jugs of wine improved by the addition of grain alcohol to the mother Catawba. Artie had resisted making the sale until Rory had threatened to inform Mr. Oliver that Artie had many customers among Napoleon relatives still resident on Paradise Valley Indian Reserve. Rory left Art's Taxi building with his five jugs of Artie's Own; among his cousins out at Paradise Reserve it was more familiarly known as Old Wolverine.

There was one thing to be said about being interdicted for over three months, Rory Napoleon decided: when a man did get hold of the stuff it had gained in muzzle velocity, increased its range, and improved penetration power. He had quite soon achieved a holiday state of total anaesthesia, reclining on sweet clover hay in a corner of the pole shed south of the goat pen. Three days and four-and-one-half jugs later he awoke chilled, in dusk musty with the smell of mould, aslant with dust-vibrant bars of late-afternoon sunlight.

He teetered out of the shed and across the yard to the goat pen. He made a place for himself by pulling aside the brush that Byron had piled on top to keep the goats from leaping to freedom and Dan Sibbald's land, then climbed up and hooked his heels on a lower pole. He stared down upon the forty-seven goats below. It might have been a matter only of common clues in eye and jaw and nostril; Rory was not interested in the perceptual why, he only knew that now he looked down upon citizens of Shelby, members of Shelby Rotary, the Activarians, Knights of the Loyal Order of Homesteaders, the town council, North Siders.

"You – Mrs. Fotherin'ham," he addressed the white nanny just beneath him, "can go spit up a rope, for I ain't emptyin' another can for you. I'm human same as anybody else, ain't I? Don't that mean somethin', Oliver?" He was speaking to the billy behind Mrs. Fotheringham, a one-horned roan with a glassy wall eye fixed upon him. "Don't it mean somethin' if a person's a human? Ain't it more important to be a human than to be a horse or a dog or a goat! It's a head start, Oliver!"

But Mr. Oliver had turned and was making his slow way through the herd to the opposite side of the pen. Rory was suddenly filled with uncontrollable anger against Mr. Oliver – all of them. He half-rose from his perch.

"I was born human!" he shouted after Mr. Oliver. "I'll die human! I eat human! I drink human! I am human! I'm me! I'm Rory Napoleon!"

All the assembly had turned their attention up to him, but they were just goats now. Forty-seven plain goats. "I am human," he explained carefully to them. "What's more I am the only human on this whole earth, which *is* Rory Napoleon."

He grabbed the butt end of willow brush by his thigh and wrenched it loose from the pile; he attacked the rest furiously, flushed with wine, elation, and exertion. It was only a moment till he had the top of the pen cleared of the brush that had been piled there to keep the goats inside.

"All right – all right now!" he yelled at them, "you can come up outa there – nothin' to stop you now! High-yuh!" he shrilled as they huddled together at the far side of the pen, blinking up at him in the astonishing sunlight.

"Get your lazy nose out of it, you shag-anappi-spring-heeled, china-eyed, English bastard, Oliver! Hough-hough-hah-hup-yaah, Mrs. Tregillis an' Revrund Cameron! Hell's about to go out for recess!"

In thirty seconds the goat eruption was complete.

Rory Napoleon had selected a Saturday night precisely right for the outrage which followed his release of the goats. It was the Saturday night of the month on which the Shelby and Greater Shelby Emergency and Disaster Relief and Civil Defence Committee met. It was also the night that the Cameo Theatre was exhibiting to its only packed house since the advent of television to Shelby, a vista-vision religious spectacular showing the slaughter of five thousand Christian extras and nine thousand animals in the Coliseum, as well as the Crucifixion and the sack of Rome. The Russians had just shocked the world with the announcement of another successful satellite; ten days ago a two-hundred-yard section of the TransCanada Pipeline had exploded twenty-nine miles east of Shelby; Northern Lights the night before had tented the entire sky with frightening brilliance. The day, the week, the month, the year were unique in a chain of chance fragile with coincidence which might have parted at any line short of the final anarchy.

As soon as Rory Napoleon had herded his forty-seven goats to the head of a brightly lighted and teeming Main Street, the Saturday-night traffic came to a halt and quickly bottled the street back in both directions to the ends of the block. The goats left the street itself and took to the sidewalk, trotting as far as Oliver's Trading Company General Store, where Mayor Fraser (goat) caught sight of the fresh vegetable display and led a splinter group of seven through the open door. Eleven others followed Mr. Oliver (goat) to the front of the Maple Leaf Beer Parlour, where one of the outgoing patrons obligingly held open the door. To any of the Napoleon goats a doorway was a familiar phenomenon and now in their frightened bewilderment they automatically sought the security of a confinement they'd known for three months.

Nettie Fotheringham (goat) took her diminished retinue of twenty-eight as far as the Cameo Theatre where the double doors stood wide for the changing of shows. They entered the darkened interior just as Alaric's Visigothic hordes breached the outer gates of Rome. Mr. Cameron (goat), a dissenter from Mr. Oliver's (goat) Maple Leaf Beer Parlour group, trotted to the corner, went up a side street and out of the business section entirely. Three blocks away he came to the shelter of a vague cluster of buildings and stopped to clip the dry grass there.

Within the Maple Leaf Beer Parlour the banter and laughter and friendly argument had changed to curses, grunts, shouts, and roars as beer-inflamed men and sober goats mixed together in bleating, butting, kicking, struggling nihilism over a floor awash with spilled beverage, broken glass, and chairs and overturned tables. The concussion of the fray vibrated the common wall the beer parlour shared with Totecole's Hardware next door, and Morton Totecole, looking after the store during his father's coffee break, took down the double-barrel ten-gauge from the shotgun rack and slipped in two number-four magnum shells.

Torches had been touched to the Palatine Hill; gladiator and Goth battled against the leaping Technicolor flames. Cameo Theatre patrons in outside seats were aware of numerous rustling, moving shapes tapping along the darkened aisles.

Unable to dislodge Mayor Fraser (goat) and his grazing council from the fresh vegetable and fruit counter, Mr. Oliver (human) admitted failure and phoned Millie Clocker, asking her breathlessly to ring for the police and as well have Fire Chief Alsop turn out a couple of available men. In his excitement he did not explain to Millie that there was no fire and that the men were needed for extraordinary duties. Millie set off the fire siren first, then plugged in for the Mounted Police.

Mr. Cameron (goat) had been grazing, minding his own business, when the fire siren on the fire hall beside him set up its scooping wail. He catapulted to the roof, picked his way along the ridge, at the end of which he could discern a towering skeletal structure; his hooves clanged as he soared upwards and came to brief rest before climbing to the top, high over the town buildings.

On hearing the fire siren Cross-cut Jack Brown (Rescue and First Aid), Malleable Jack Brown (Flat-Bottom Boats and Flood Control), Pipe-fitting Jack Brown (Shelter and Alarm) went to the Main Street window of the Ranchman's Club smoking-room where they were holding their meeting of the Shelby and Greater Shelby Emergency and Disaster Relief and Civil Defence Committee. They saw the Mounted Police cruiser wheel round the Royal Bank corner with red light flashing, sensed the confusion in the street below, and heard the rioting uproar from the Maple Leaf Beer Parlour. Pipe-fitting Jack Brown ran to the phone and gave Millie Clocker the blue alert. She signalled the red, however, which would sound the siren again, ring St. Aidan's Church bell, warn the hospital staff, summon Dr. Fotheringham with stretcher-bearers, and flush out Ollie Pringle – with ambulance and resuscitator.

Morton Totecole stood before the Maple Leaf Beer Parlour with the loaded ten-gauge in his hands. He had no intention of using it as he had seen sheriffs and their deputies do on CBC; he was simply waiting to hand it to someone older and much braver than he. The fury within the Maple Leaf had abated, for Taffy had gathered his waiters and some of the patrons at the bar end of the parlour, formed them into a slowly advancing line of men facing a slowly retreating line of goats. Taffy himself stood to one side of the door, ready to throw it open at the strategic moment that the goats were close enough to recognize the triangular gestalt of themselves – the door – freedom.

On the street before the Maple Leaf, Morton Totecole heard the sounds of two new sirens; the one on the fire engine racing south on First Street, the other on Ollie Pringle's ambulance racing north on First Street. St. Aidan's bell began to tongue the night. The fire siren gave three preparatory whoops before it took up the sustained ululation of the red alert.

The church bell penetrated the stirring darkness of the Cameo Theatre where skinned barbarians were garrotting fine old senators with their own togas and carrying shrieking Roman matrons through falling marble columns and burning rubble. The scrambling in the aisles and the elastic hysteria of three sirens instantly convinced all patrons that the theatre was ablaze.

As Cameo patrons erupted from the theatre they thought was burning, the herd burst out of the Maple Leaf. Ollie Pringle's ambulance reached Main and First Street at the same moment as the fire engine. Morton Totecole went down in a smother of goats. On the roof of the power plant Mr. Cameron (goat) put out a moist and inquisitive nose to the thing of gleaming glass and metal cable before him. Morton's hand convulsed on the triggers of the ten-gauge goose gun and discharged both barrels at a distance of eighteen inches from the twenty-six-foot plate window of his father's store. The shotgun blast coincided with the superb head-on collision of the ambulance and fire engine as well as with the crackling detonation that signalled the electrocution of Mr. Cameron (goat), who had grounded the power plant transformer with a Queen's Birthday fountain of sparks and a sheet of violet light that winked up the town and the district as far as the correction line. Citizens of Khartoum heard the explosion; those of Tiger Lily said they had.

In the pitch darkness of Main Street there were too many people and too many goats. Humans stampeded blindly towards the Royal Bank corner and brought up against the barricade formed by the fire engine and the ambulance. They swept back through the lightless night, driving the goats before them. Some sought safety in cars, others in stores. Those in cars and trucks turned on their headlights so that a grotesque magic-lantern show of goats and humans was projected against the flat faces of the stores; it was neither VistaVision nor Technicolor, but the sack of Rome had been pale by comparison.

Within the stores kerosene and mantle lamps, flashlights and candles were brought out, but they had hardly been lit before full light came on from the town's auxiliary power plant. Some order was reasserting itself, for many now knew that there had been no fire, invasion, earthquake, pipeline explosion, falling Russian satellite – just the Napoleon goats. Except for Maple Leaf cuts and bruises now being treated by Dr. Fotheringham there had miraculously been no serious injuries.

Right after he had turned the goats into the top of Main Street, Rory Napoleon had gone back through Hepner's lumber yards, retraced his steps over the CNR bridge, and made straight for home and the feed shed. There he fell upon the hay, reached down for the last of his jugs of wine. He finished it.

Slightly after midnight Constables Dove and Clarkson entered the shed. One took Rory by the legs, the other by the armpits. They carried him out, a snoring hammock between them to the cruiser, headed for the town and the barracks.

The Reverend Cameron finished whipping the head of the last grey hackle, touched it with a bead of black enamel, released it from the vice, and laid it down by the others. He had intended going to bed by eleven, but with the power break which had put out the lights it had taken him till now to tie the dozen flies he liked to complete at one sitting. He leaned back in his chair and as he sighed three flies drifted over the varnished surface of the desk. Fly patterns – Plato's patterns – God's patterns – man's patterns – oh, so terribly fragile! Always the Napoleons to destroy them; that was the Napoleon threat. That was it indeed.

20

Whites Herd Better

Carlyle Sinclair, the central character in The Vanishing Point, *is the agent and schoolteacher for the Paradise Valley Indian reserve. He is emotionally and psychologically "possessed" by the conditioning of a culture dominated by Old Kacky's rigid Presbyterianism and Aunt Pearl's anal-erotic puritanism and he has been living his life in retreat since the death, nine years earlier, of his wife. Archie Nicotine, a Coyote trickster who delights in disrupting the neat patterns of white civilization, plays a key role in freeing Carlyle from his demons. In the following scene from early on in the novel, Carlyle picks up Archie who is hitch-hiking into the city to buy parts for his truck. Old Esau is Victoria Rider's grandfather who is dying from* TB. *Victoria is Carlyle's star student on whom he has pinned all of his hopes for "saving" the Stoney Indians through education. Later, through Archie's machinations, Heally Richards will "take a run" at healing Old Esau at the Rally for Jesus.*

Archie Nicotine is an amalgam of a number of life models – a Blood and two Stoneys W. O. met while teaching on the Eden Valley Indian reserve in the early 1950s, a Hungarian ("who was not nearly so intelligible in his speech as Archie Nicotine"), and W. O.'s second son, Hugh. Archie first appeared under the name Raymond Shot-close in the 1961 CBC *Radio play "The White Christmas of Raymond Shot-close," became a major character in* The Vanishing Point, *and appeared again in* Since Daisy Creek (1984).

cᴀᴏ̃ᴏ̃ᴅ

He saw a figure up ahead with arm upraised, in time to slow down and stop beside it. Archie Nicotine climbed in, slammed the door.

"Thanks, Sinclair."

He shifted to second, to high. Damn it all!

"We got held up for the rings and for the carburetor. Moon underpaid me, but I still got enough for the rings and for the carburetor. Then we can get her rolling and I won't have to impose any more for a ride. On you."

Conversation with most of them was difficult, like trying to play catch with someone who wouldn't throw back the ball. Most of them. Not Archie, damn it!

". . . after he took out for the grub he said there was only forty-eight left . . ."

It was never a game of catch with Archie; it was a defensive and tiresome duel. He didn't want to fence this wonderful morning; he leaned over, pushed in the button on the radio.

". . . Moon always was a tight-ass and that's the whole situation."

". . . does not claim – has not ever claimed the healin' pahr. Heally Richards does not heal through the practice of medicine – chemotherapy – the surgical knife – spinal adjustment – high colonic irrigation – deep analysis – hypnosis . . ."

He had instantly recognized the recorded voice, American, soft with the South, glib and truculent.

". . . deep heat – leechin' – cuppin' – transfusion – organic diet – Asiatic herb – sonic vibration – radioactive clay . . ."

Choice that wasn't really a choice at all; endless flow of primitive oversimplification from either the faith-healing evangelist or from Archie Nicotine.

". . . astrology – phrenology – or tea-cup readin'. Like I say through none of these does Heally Richards – has Heally Richards – or will Heally Richards ever – lay claim to the healin' pahr."

The faith healer was a favourite with most of the Paradise Valley people, particularly Archie, for Archie was a religious joiner, had been in turn: original Methodist, Presbyterian, United, Baptist, Pentecost, Mormon. As nearly as Carlyle could tell, he was between dogmas now. When it came to a choice between Archie and Heally Richards, he preferred Archie. Which still didn't say a great deal for Archie. Carlyle reached over and shut off the radio.

"I generally listen to him," Archie said as Richards' voice paled to silence.

With fastidious tails held high, several white-faced and mahogany calves went rocking down the fence line.

"We have got a lot of sick people in our band – one way and another. I listen to him when I can," Archie said again.

The calves stopped. Springs unwound.

"I know, Archie."

"And he heals sick people."

"Not likely to do us much good."

"Why not?"

"Somewhere in the States, isn't he?"

"No."

"Yes, he is," Carlyle said. "That was just a recording – played all over."

"I know that. But if you listened to him regular you'd know."

"Know what?"

"That's alive."

"Is it?"

"Hey-up, he's here. Since all last week. Rally For Jesus."

"Oh."

"They announced it several times – for a month and he heals sick people. That's his business."

"It may be just a business."

"That's what I said. He heals them by faith. Through his hands."

"Does he."

"I never seen him do it, I just heard it over the radio. What I mean is, they wouldn't let him onto the radio if he couldn't do it."

"They might."

"Look at all this TB we got now. Whenever some kid gets his feet wet then he coughs and then he coughs some more and then he coughs some blood and then he coughs a lot of blood and then he dies out of it. All out of wet feet. That's the whole TB situation in Paradise Valley."

"Not quite."

"Esau coughed up a lot last night."

"He was sitting up this morning."

"Wasn't any TB in the olden days," Archie said.

"Maybe there wasn't but . . ."

"Before the white savage come," Archie said.

"That's right, Archie."

"Lots more wet feet then when we just had moccasins, before we had rubbers or boots – but all the same no TB then."

"There wasn't a single case of TB in Paradise Valley fifteen years ago!" Carlyle said angrily. "After Wallace Ear died and the unit came out – you're the one kept the others from getting X-rayed – you told them the machine was what *gave* people TB."

"Maybe I did."

"You *did* – no maybe about it."

"You think he could?"

"Could what?"

"Heal people."

"Who?"

"Heally Richards."

"Not so well as doctors and medicine."

"You figure they got a monopoly on it."

"All I figure is if I had trachoma like Susan Shot-close I'd take the doctor's advice. I wouldn't miss one single treatment if it went on through my whole life. If I had Mark Lefthand's hernia I'd go to the hospital and have it mended. All the faith healing there is won't cure Mary Roll-in-the-mud's diabetes."

"Like you said – he's sitting up this morning even though last night he let go half a slop-bucket of blood."

"Did somebody lay hands on him? Is that why . . ."

"No. Also there wasn't any doctor there or medicine, but all the same he did sit up this morning."

"He's a tough old man."

"Hey-up. But he wasn't tough enough to beat them TB germs. They won now."

"But he could have beat them five years ago if he'd gone to the San. He refused to. You people have absolute sovereignty – nobody can make you do one single damn thing you don't want to do – even to save your life."

"Most the time that's piss poor . . ."

"I agree."

". . . and a lot of people die anyway in hospitals."

"More out of them."

"You're wrong there – more in."

"Oh – come on, Archie."

"Hospitals specialize in dyin'."

"What you mean is – they're full of patients who have contracted disease or – injury – they're in there for treatment – surgery – so naturally more people in hospitals die than the well people outside hospitals."

"More Indians die in hospitals."

"Just because white people go there sooner – when there's still some hope of recovery. They don't die like Gatine, *after* his appendix burst. They don't wait for it to burst." Or pneumonia like Moses Rider – or eclampsia like Sarah MacLeod. All the deaths he'd died in nine years!

Each one leaving him older – sadder – more helpless! Oh Jesus – the three smoke threads still wisping upwards like reluctant souls from three little charred bundles in the fire-scabbed tangle of bed-metal standing in the ruins of the Ernie Wildman cabin! Stop it, Sinclair! Stop it!

"Us people don't like to go in hospitals."

"Neither do us people."

"Us people get sick easier than you people do."

"Maybe."

"Germs can dig in quicker and easier and worse into us."

"Maybe."

"So I think a hospital crawlin' with all those goddam white germs from all those goddam sick white people herded up is one hell of a place for us people to go into." Archie lit the cigarette he'd made. He exhaled. "Especially when we are sick."

"They protect against that, Archie."

"Them germs is pretty small and there's millions of them and they can miss some easy. They just got to miss one germ – just let one of them get into us – or maybe two. Have to be two – wouldn't it?"

"What do you mean?"

"Take more than one I guess – bull and cow for increase."

"No. There don't have to be."

"Wouldn't want one of my kids in there – in the hospital."

"You telling me – if Maureen or Maxine or Marion got sick and the doctor said she had to go into hospital to save her life you wouldn't . . ."

"I guess I would," Archie admitted, "to save her life."

He might, but Carlyle was no longer interested in the possibility. Somehow their conversation had gone past a hidden significance. Earlier Archie must have implied something important, which Carlyle had missed. "Damn sight more likely to save her than some evangelist laying on hands." But even as he said it he was trying to remember what it might have been that eluded him now. "Just what were you driving at, Archie?"

"You said if one of my own kids got sick . . ."

"No – before. Nothing *is* wrong with your family – is there?"

"They all had a cold. I had one."

"I see."

"And our bowels loose – two weeks ago I moved my own bowels many times. We're all over that now."

As usual Archie had succeeded, manoeuvred him into the distasteful role of explaining – advising – preaching. It demeaned both of them. No – just himself.

"One good way to find out," Archie was saying.

"Find out what?"

"Heally Richards. If he can heal."

"He's not getting into Paradise, Archie."

The corners of Archie's mouth pulled in slightly. "He can't get in even if he might make our whole band healthy."

"That's right."

"You say that."

"And I suspect Mr. Fyfe – the department would say that too."

"You – Fyfe – the department say who can come into Paradise and who can't come into Paradise." Archie was actually grinning now. "Then I guess we just have to use some of that stuff, Sinclair."

"What stuff?"

"Absolute sovereign you said we got – even if it was to save our poor life."

He saw that the grin had widened full from ear to ear. "You just let me know, Archie – whenever you want to talk sensibly!"

Without relaxing his grin one stitch, Archie slid down on the seat. He laid his head back and he closed his eyes. "Hey-up."

Which could be Stoney for "touché," Carlyle told himself sardonically.

He was just as annoyed with himself as he was with Archie now. Why could he not learn that impatience always delivered him into Archie's hands. If only he could discipline his irritation, Archie wouldn't be able to score again and again; the best defence was restraint of course, for counter-thrust only told Archie he'd been successful. Archie made sure he never let you know you'd pierced that smug certainty.

"Have you an objection if I listen to him anyway?"

"What?"

"Richards."

"Go ahead."

Archie turned on the radio.

"While he still has something left to . . ."

". . . everywhere – Jeeesuss Christ – EVERYWHERE!"

"Jesus, Archie – turn it down!"

". . . EVIDENCE – THESE SAME PEOPLE ARE the ones will tell you Jeeesuss did not exist – that He did not live – that He did – was not cruceeeefied – oh yes – they'll say – I have had them say it to me – and you have had them say it to you – oh yes – it is quite likely there may have been – ay – man – named Jeesuss – ay – ordinary – every-day – mortal – man and His name may have been Jeesussss – He may have hailed from Galilee – but He – was – not – thee son of God! Oh no. He was not born of virgin birth! Oh no. He was not risen from the dead and not ascended onto Heaven. Oh no – oh no – oh no. I have been told this on the very best authority – ministers of the gospel. Yes – I have! Presbyterian – Methodist – Congregational – Episcopalian – all theossified churches. No – not all – at least there hasn't been a Catholic priest tell me that yet – no – not yet – nor Baptist. But – just you give them time. They will – sooner or later they will – they'll all tell you. Ay man – just – ay – man. That's all. Now – I want you to do somethin' for me. I want you – please to do this for me; you tell me – just – what – was – this ordinary mortal man's full name. I know – I got his given name all right – but what was his last name. Jeeesuss Brown? Jeesuss J. Jones? Jeesuss Kelly? Jeesuss Kennedy? Oh – hallelujah! Jeesuss Lenin or Jeesuss Stalin maybe – or was it just Jeesuss Marx of Galilee! Hallelujah! Not one of these mortals was born in ay stable in Bethlehem – was he! Not one of them was found there in any manger in swaddlin' clo'es – was he! By the three wise men who followed a star? You want evidence – existence of Jeeesuss Christ.

Just you let me tell you where you can find it – everywhere – that's where. Why – in a little child's fairy tale – I can show you evidence – in "Snow White and the Seven Dwarfs" I can . . . show you evid . . ."

But Carlyle had snicked off the radio.

"How could he do that?" Archie said.

"Walt Disney helped him."

"Generally he can explain all right," Archie said.

"I'm sure he has an explanation for everything."

"One time he explained the whole situation with us people."

"Did he."

"We are the lost tribes out of Israel."

"Hey-up," Carlyle said heartily. "A long way from home."

"One way to find out."

"If the Stoneys are the lost tribes?"

"No – whether he can heal by laying on his hands."

"He's not coming out to Paradise, Archie." And, by God, he wasn't, though he possibly should not have said it again.

"I guess if he isn't a department civil servant then he can't get in even if he could make our whole band healthy."

The prick lay in the deliberate "civil servant," so he must at all costs be civil. "That's right, Archie. It might be difficult to convince them that Heally Richards could heal the entire Paradise band. Seventy-five families is a lot of heal . . ."

"What I mean was – one way to tell if he could heal or he couldn't heal – let him take a run at Esau."

"Oh – for God's sake, Archie – just leave Esau alone!"

"I'd like to find out if he could . . ."

"No healer's going to bother Esau!"

"If Esau requested him to heal him then . . ."

"Esau isn't likely to. It's the last thing Esau would want!"

"Maybe not."

"Look, Archie, let Esau alone – just let him die his own way – let him die Indian!"

"Us Indians didn't invent TB."

"Archie – no!"

"I just made a suggestion that might . . ."

"No!"

"Like a test – while there was time."

"There isn't time."

"Sure isn't. He hasn't time even to wait for his smart grand-daughter."

"What?"

"For her to finish and come back and heal him."

So that was it! That had been the hidden jab! Victoria. He knew he'd missed something earlier; and how dearly important it was! "For once you are right. She is smart. She's the smartest child . . ."

"No child."

"Smart enough not to drop out the way Maxine did last winter – or the way Marion will before summer." Father of such moon-faced truculence, Archie had every right to be envious. "Don't ever give her a break, Archie!" Or me – spoil it! Spoil her whole life – make her fail!

"Sinclair," Archie said.

"Yes, Archie."

"I been thinking about a conclusion."

"That's nice."

"Whites make it their own way – everything. That's the whole sit-uation with you people. Take cattle . . ."

"What about them?"

"Look at cattle."

"I am – I do – every day."

"Hereford out there."

"Yes?"

"All Hereford."

"Not all – there's Shorthorn and Galloway . . ."

"Few. Mostly the whole situation is Hereford. You people made it that way. Even cattle."

"What do you mean, Archie?"

"What I mean is white face – all white face – Hereford."

"That's right. That's one breed."

"Which you people made. You bred for that. It wasn't that way first at all. You know what I mean. You people want even your cattle to be white face too."

Carlyle felt a stir of his earlier annoyance. "I don't think that determined Hereford breeding at all."

"Sure."

"The breed came about . . ." Carlyle began to explain.

"It didn't come about," Archie corrected him. "You people made it."

"Possibly we did. Yes. I guess we did. Through careful selection, trying for the most beef for the least grass."

"Hey-up."

"Good foragers – tough – winter well."

". . . and that white face."

"All right – all right, Archie, but whether they have a white face – black face – spotted face – red face hasn't got anything to do . . ."

"But they haven't got it."

"Haven't what?"

"Got a red face or a black face."

"I know they haven't."

"Deliberate white face."

"I don't think so. Not deliberate."

"I do. Deliberate and that's the whole situation with white tits." Archie spit out the window. "Even if they snow-burn."

"Sort of silly if it were deliberate," Carlyle said.

"Hey-up."

Now he was truly annoyed with himself. "Nice we can agree on something, Archie."

"You don't. And they're lucky."

Always Archie started from the same conviction: white was lucky; red was not. He had a ready answer for his own envy of that luck; whites needed it.

Carlyle saw that one corner of Archie's mouth was caught up slightly with incipient amusement. In five more years and after fifty or seventy-five pounds more weight, the hairless cheeks would be glossed and plump; with the broad quirking mouth and the short neck Archie would no longer be subtly amused and cocky. Frog smug.

"Lucky they didn't make a white belly too," Archie was saying.

"Herefords generally are white underneath."

"Inside. You know what I mean. They got their stomach red inside."

"All stomachs are red inside."

"I didn't mean that. I meant a red stomach is superior to a white stomach. Herefords had a white stomach to go with their white face and their white belly outside then they'd be in trouble."

"Would they."

"Hey-up. Poor doers. You couldn't finish them off the grass then. Have to grain-finish all them delicate white stomachs."

"They already do – more cattle finished on grain than off range."

"I know. The whole situation is red stomachs are superior . . ."

". . . to white stomachs," Carlyle said, "inside."

"Deer – moose – antelope – they all got good red stomachs and Hereford still. I got a red stomach – but you got white. Your white stomach couldn't take what mine does – blue elk – bannock – them survival cookies for the kids with cocoa at the school or you take your bowels – you just try eating like us people eat – your white stomach – your white bowels, you couldn't make enough bismuth hydrate to cork all the white ass-holes all over the white world."

Carlyle laughed. "All right, Archie. I do cork a lot of red ones, but I agree with you." He quenched the unkindness of a comment on liquor and Archie's superior red stomach. "I guess you don't have too much use for anything white, Archie."

For a moment Archie considered. "Anything they make, I do. That's the whole situation."

"What is?"

"Anything you people make is superior. Houses – cars – bridges – everything you make. For instance glass. White luck is the whole situation."

"What's so lucky about glass?"

"Somebody decides to make something hard you can see through clear. You know what I mean. He comes up with glass."

"Does he."

"And concrete is another good example."

"Of white luck."

"Hey-up. Very lucky. Not so lucky as glass maybe, because glass was so stupid to start with."

"Why?"

"To take something hard and fix it to see through it anyway – some fellow had nothing better to do to think of trying for that, he's worse off than the one pounded up rock so he could mix with water and sand to make rock out of it again. Both of them were lucky but glass was luckier than concrete."

"Maybe it wasn't simply luck."

"Oh yes. But goddam lucky at that. And guns and television – soft ice cream . . ."

"And beer and rye and aftershave lotion and vanilla extract . . ."

". . . clocks and X-ray and medicines and steel . . ."

"But, Archie, behind all these there were hundreds of thousands of men. There was research . . ."

"Hey-up. That's the whole situation. Whites herd better."

"I suppose they do," Carlyle agreed. "We do."

21

Santa Comes to Shelby

In the 1970s W. O. met George MacClelland, former RCMP Commissioner and later the first Ombudsman for Alberta. They became close story-exchanging friends and for years W. O. urged MacClelland to write about his RCMP experiences in the north – and warned him that if he did not, he would plagiarize him! And he finally did. The following episode from Roses Are Difficult Here (1990) is based on one of the many stories W. O. heard from MacClelland. We again visit the small foothills town of Shelby, home of Willie MacCrimmon, Daddy Sherry, and that great orchestrator of chaos, Rory Napoleon.

Well into the dirty thirties Canon Midford had taken over his Shelby parish. These were the desert years, when mid-America thirsted. Hot and constant winds siphoned wells and creeks and sloughs and hold-up ponds, blistered and cracked the prairie and the foothills skin, smoked up topsoil to smudge the sky, blot the sun. Light the lamp at noon.

Okie time had come. Grain elevators paid ten cents a bushel for wheat, three for oats and barley, but only if farmers were able to harvest a crop. No price offered for tumbleweed or Russian thistle or wild oats. Never, since Shelby's frontier birth or throughout her rural career, had there been hard times like these, when drifted land and blind homes must be abandoned. Dust to dust; dust to dust. Head north for the parklands and just possible rain in the Peace River country.

Canon Midford had come by Pullman coach to the new Sahara; many others travelled by freight, human flies on boxcars and flatcars and tenders, rolling east and rolling west. Most were looking for a chance to make a living, but some of the young were not seeking work: the scenery hogs, who had left the East to see the West, or the West to see the East. There was of course an older group, bindlestiffs or lump bums, the hobo professionals who long before any depression had been non-paying railway passengers. These had their own jungle jargon for the people you encountered: the hard tails, johns, harness bulls, gazoonas, gazeenas, gazoots, and gazats, or the canned-heat, vanilla, and aftershave-lotion artists, winos or McGoof hounds, wolves and their young proosians. The dinos were those who went into cafés and ordered four-course meals, said they were broke, hadn't eaten for three days, and were willing to wash dishes to pay for the meal. This dangerous stratagem could land them in the bucket for thirty days on charges of vagrancy and obtaining food under false pretences, though odds against that were much better if the restaurant were Greek or Chinese. When the snow flew, it was the Winter Christians who hit for the nearest Sally Ann drum to promise the rest of their life to Jerusalem Slim so they could confess sin, sing hymns, and do Bible studies to get bed and three until the meadow lark would announce the spring. City downtown street corners had the dingbats, dinging passersby for the price of a cup of coffee or a night in the scratch-house.

In Shelby district as in most other Western rural communities Bennett buggies – cars pulled by real horsepower – showed up, plagiarizing the Hoover buggies south of the Forty-ninth, where teams were also being hitched up to car bumpers. On both sides of the border, Thanksgiving and Christmas were soon tainted with irony. Celebration by gift was difficult on a twenty-five-dollar-a-month relief cheque. His third Christmas in Shelby, Canon Midford decided to do something about that.

He approached Mayor Oliver and the town council with the suggestion that they have Santa Claus visit Shelby Christmas morning with presents for every child in the district. His Worship and a unanimous council approved. The thing took off like prairie fire. A "Santa Visits Shelby and Greater District Committee" was formed, to be chaired by Canon Midford. Since the RCMP handed out the monthly relief cheques and had a list of the vulnerable needy, Corporal Broadfoot was named vice-chairman. Nettie Fitzgerald would perform her usual committee role: chief shit-disturber.

First item on the agenda: toys. The *Chinook* would run request ads: volunteers would gather in the fire hall at the back of the community centre to accept and repair donated gifts that had been outgrown: sleds and wagons, skates and toboggans, dolls and teddy bears, doll houses and carriages, doctor and nurse uniforms, cowboy and Indian suits, hoops, tops and skipping-ropes, cap pistols, tricycles, and kiddy cars.

Second item: Santa Claus. The choice was obvious: Art Ulmer sober. He hadn't shaved for a decade, probably by Christmas wouldn't have had a hair trim for two months. With his rosy cheeks, cherry nose, and foot-and-a-half white beard he'd make a dandy Santa.

Item three: Santa's sleigh. Not too complicated. Rory Napoleon's bobsled dray could handle the great gift cargo; Hickory Brown could jigsaw plywood sides, paint them Christmas red and green, and line their high arcs with tinsel.

Item four: the reindeer. Not so simple. Rory Napoleon's dray team would not do, since your general run of reindeer were not *black* or the size of Rory's Percherons. This problem was solved when Rory explained that he had just acquired a pair of two-year-old bays, and was sure he could have them broken to harness in good time. Antlers for them would be the twin set hung on the wall behind the Arlington Arms reception counter. Elk. In his shoe and harness shop, Willie MacCrimmon would design and fashion special horn-holding bridles as well as harness so that the team could be hitched up tandem-style.

Item five: event location. No doubt about that: the town square, opposite the Shelby Community Centre, where a dignitary platform would be built, and a twenty-foot Christmas tree set up.

Very early in their meetings, Nettie Fitzgerald said they must have a full choir, in which she would sing lead soprano, up on the platform with the mayor and councillors, the school board chairmen, the head of the Western Stock Growers Association, and the two Mounties in Boy Scout hats and scarlet dress tunic. She was told that the platform would not be big enough, but the committee agreed they should not have left out the regent of the Crowfoot Chapter of the IODE.

As regent of the Crowfoot Chapter of the IODE, Nettie had accepted that, but insisted that they really must stage a nativity play, which she was quite willing to direct, with a real live donkey she had found out at the Bar P ranch. Charlie Bolton said it wasn't a donkey; it was a mule. She said it was practically the same thing. Charlie said the difference was considerable: a mule was half horse, had a mare for a mother, and, just like Nettie, was noted for its goddam stubbornness. Nettie persisted, proving Charlie's point; have it without the donkey then. Charlie said all right he'd vote for that, but only if Arlington Agnes were cast as Mother Mary and he as Joseph, and even though by the time Santa made it to Shelby there would have been at least fifteen nativity plays in church basements and schoolrooms. Put to a vote, the nativity play – with or without donkey or mule or Arlington Agnes or Charlie Bolton – lost decisively.

Corporal Broadfoot had plotted out the strategy for "Santa Visits Shelby and Greater Shelby District" in careful detail. From his position up on the town square platform he would be in charge of tactics.

Santa must make his entrance from the north, of course. In the sleigh loaded and hung with toys he and his driver helper must take off well before daybreak under cover of darkness, go up the hill slope north of town, over and down as far as McNally's cottonwood bluff at the bottom of the down slope, a distance of roughly half a mile. They would take cover there, but keep a sharp lookout at all times for wave signals to be given by Canon Midford, who would take his position on top of the hill, approximately halfway into town. It was a fitting coincidence that this very hill had been used by the first RCMP, under Colonel Macleod, as a lookout in the old Blackfoot Crossing days, when they had put the run on the whiskey traders in 1874, Corporal Broadfoot explained. Charlie Bolton said that sounded like bullshit to him, but Corporal Broadfoot said he could show it to him in a history-of-the-RCMP book. "Just proves it," Charlie said. "History books is bullshit too."

From his vantage point Midford would have a clear view of the Corporal on the platform, so he could receive and relay signals to alert Rory. At twenty-minute intervals, Walter Oliver, who had been cast as Santa's messenger, would come out of the depot across the square, in Boy Scout uniform with staff and blue knees, waving a yellow telegram he would then hand up to his father. The following year Walter at seventeen would make it to King Scout and attend the Jamboree in England, then in 1939, at nineteen, to Spitfire pilot in the RAF, and in 1941 to death in the Battle of Britain.

It turned out to be a very white Christmas. And cold. Twenty below. Rory had been over-optimistic about breaking the young team to tandem harness; even without the elk-antler bridles in place they were difficult. It took four hostellers to ear them down while Rory and Art in costume got up and into the bobsleigh. Santa crouched to the rear in a nest of his toys; Rory up front, with a firm grip on the lines, his feet braced against the buckboard and the team facing north, gave the signal. The hostellers released the horses' ears and jumped free. Belly to the ground, the whites of their eyeballs rolled up, the team lit out in the direction of the North Pole. Because both had got the bit clamped between their teeth, it took Rory almost two miles to cool them down and get control. Only then was he able to turn them round and head back for McNally's bluff. The three-foot fall into the barrow pit gave him some trouble, but finally they made it into the shelter of the cottonwoods, where they uncorked a jug of Rory's Undiluted Best Number One Hard to fortify themselves against the chill as they waited for Canon Midford to give them the signal.

In spite of the weather, the turnout was great. The town square soon filled with young and old, behind the wide alley roped off along the front of the platform. Trucks and cars and rigs were parked outside the square for two blocks in every direction. The dignitaries came out of the community centre and took their positions on the platform. Mayor Oliver gave his welcoming address. Walter Oliver came out of the depot and handed the first telegram up to his father, who read it out:

"Santa Claus left North Pole 12:06 A.M. Arctic Daylight Saving Time Stop With reindeer rig and sleighload of toys Stop Just crossed Arctic Circle and entered Yukon Stop Headed for Shelby Stop Making good time Stop."

Walter Oliver's next telegram read:

"Santa Claus again Stop Well into North-West Territories Stop Headed for Grand Prairie and Peace River Stop Merry Christmas Stop Ho Ho Ho Stop."

And the next one:

"Still coming with Edmonton next stop Stop Blizzard conditions up here so speed reduced Stop After Edmonton Red Deer Stop Then Shelby Stop."

And the next:

"Weather cleared Stop Red Deer behind Stop Shelby next stop Stop Coming fast Stop."

This would be the last telegram. Corporal Broadfoot waved to Canon Midford, who in turn signalled Rory, who began to fit the elk-horn bridles over the horses' heads. No problem; they were quite subdued by two hours of standing still in the biting cold. Rory climbed back up in the bobsleigh, loosed the lines, slapped them and yelled: "Hi-yahhhhh! Senator! Duke! Get your lazy arses out of it now!"

Both responded, and did well till they hit the barrow pit, where Senator, the lead horse, made a couple of rump bucks to get up and out onto the road. That caused the reindeer bridle Willie MacCrimmon had made for him to slide down and over Senator's nose to form an elk-horn necklace that bumped alarmingly against his chest. Duke's followed suit. That did it. Even Rory could not hold back the team urged on by the antlers rapping them into a full gallop. At least they were headed in the right direction, but much too fast for Canon Midford, who was to have hitched a ride to the edge of town, but who had to leap clear into a snowbank to get out of the way. Santa crouched, clinging to the sleigh side with both hands, his tasselled toque down over his rosy cheeks and cherry nose, his driver helper standing upright and leaning back with all his might against the lines to no avail, as they entered Shelby town limits.

Down Lafayette Avenue they flew, then Marmot Crescent, which would become Bison and in five blocks Main, which arrowed right through the town square. It was Rory's best option, if only he could keep the reindeer team on course. He succeeded. Never in his entire rodeo career had he ever faced a greater challenge. Wild-eyed, goitre antlers bouncing, manes and tails flying, harness bells ajingle, snort clouds of steam from their nostrils, bits welded between their teeth, they hit the town square of Shelby, Alberta, Canada. Not Pamplona;

no amateur toreadors waiting for them here. As they passed the platform, Santa, now with tinsel and a hoop round his neck, forgot to
deliver his ho-ho-ho lines, nor did his driver helper call out: "A merry,
merry Christmas morn to one and all!" Instead: "Hold up, goddamit!
Whoa, you bay bastards! Whoaaaa-hup!"

They cleared the square, crossed the railway tracks, and kept right
on out of town.

Back in the stunned square children were crying; parents were
comforting. One tearful voice was heard: "Jesus Murphy! It looks like
Santy ain't stoppin' in Shelby this Christmas!"

By following the toy spoor, Corporal Broadfoot and others were
able to track down Santa and his helper. Both were trapped in drunken
darkness beneath the upturned sleigh. The horses were gone. Three
days later they were found ten miles south of town in an abandoned
barn, where they had taken shelter from blizzard winds.

22

How Do Rabbits Get Started?

In these scenes from Who Has Seen the Wind, *eight-year-old Brian and his friends Fat and Ike are fascinated by the birth of baby rabbits. Curious about the mechanics of how they came about, Brian asks his father for an explanation. Bobbie is Brian's little brother.*

⚜

At first there had been only two rabbits in the pen by Hoffman's barn; now there were ten. The boys were elated at this something for nothing, and although they had considered the possibility of increase, they had not hoped for it so soon. The bulging Belgian hare was the mother; Brian and Fat had witnessed the actual appearance of the baby rabbits.

"Gee, Fat," Brian had said, "they look funny – they haven't got any hair!"

"They will," promised Fat. "They'll grow up and get it."

"Then they'll have rabbits," Brian predicted, "and they'll grow up."

"And have rabbits too," supplied Fat.

"And they'll grow up and have rabbits."

"We'll have lots of rabbits," concluded Fat.

"What'll we do with 'em, Fat?"

"Sell 'em," Fat told him. "Dad paid fifty cents a piece for these. We'll sell 'em."

And so for two weeks they waited with impatience; Ike had already called their attention to the interesting coincidence of bulge and new rabbits, a phenomenon they had not before associated with birth. At the end of a month when no new rabbits had put in an appearance, Brian went to his father.

"Dad?"

"Yes, Spalpeen?"

"How do rabbits get started?"

From his chair in the den, Gerald O'Connal stared at his son, the lamp at his elbow, glinting on his dark, red hair, the room silent except for the deliberate *bup-bup* of his pipe. For some two years now he had been expecting this. He must be frank and honest about the thing. "You know how a plant gets started?"

"How?"

"From a seed. You plant it in the ground, and it grows into a plant." He let his arm drop to scratch an ear of Jappy lying beside the chair.

"I know that."

"Know what?" asked Bobbie, who had entered the room.

"Something I'm explaining to Brian. With animals, it's the same."

"Is it?"

"What is?" asked Bobbie.

"Babies," said Brian. "He's telling me."

"You remember asking me about pigeons – a long time – about four years ago?"

"No," said Brian.

"I told you then that the pigeon grows inside the egg – inside – the egg is inside the mother pigeon until it hatches out. All the time that she is hatching the egg, the baby pigeon is growing there. When it has grown enough, it comes out."

"They don't with rabbits," said Bobbie. "Brian saw them come right out – he said he saw them –"

"Rabbits are different. They don't have eggs. They simply grow inside the mother, and when it's time, they grow – they come out."

"They come out," said Bobbie.

Gerald O'Connal looked down at Brian's thoughtful face. Jappy rose and stretched himself, with his head lined out and his hind legs oblique and tense. He trotted from the room. Evidently the explanation had been enough, Brian's father told himself. He picked up his *Regina Leader* again.

"Where does the seed come in?" asked Brian.

"That – oh – that's what the baby rabbit grows from inside the mother rabbit, Spalpeen."

"Is she full up with them?"

"Yes – she – in a way."

"You can't grow anything without seeds."

Gerald O'Connal laid down the paper. He looked at Bobbie with his chin in his fat hands bent back at the wrists, with their fingers curled against his plump cheeks, his blue eyes watching his father's face. "That's right. The father rabbit plants the seeds."

"Where'd *he* get them?"

"Why – they're in him."

"Why don't they grow up in him and come out of him then?" asked Brian relentlessly.

"Because they don't. They have to grow in the mother rabbit."

Brian was silent. He looked up thoughtfully to his father. "And like Ike says – that's what he's doing when –"

"Yes – that's what he's doing. He's – planting."

Brian's intense stare was disconcerting. "In a way," Mr. O'Connal finished up.

"Dad?" Bobbie lifted his chin from his hands. "Could he plant turnips into her?"

Brian looked at his little brother with disgust.

23

Aunt Pearl

In this selection from The Vanishing Point, Carlyle Sinclair is tolled back to his childhood when his father takes him to live with his Aunt Pearl for a few months. For this episode W. O. draws on his own experience as a child, when he stayed with an uncle and an aunt while his mother accompanied his father to the Mayo Clinic for what turned out to be an unsuccessful gall bladder operation. As with Old Kacky's class, Carlyle's recall of Aunt Pearl's house and little dead Willis's toy room are part of his recognition of how he has been damaged by the imprintings of his WASP culture, and how he has been perpetuating that damaging influence on the Stoneys.

He had not lived with Aunt Pearl more than four months – three before his mother's death – one after. Yet he could see her at will: long and thin as milkweed stalk, leaning on her broom and sighing her intransitive sighs. Her eyes were pale like his father's, but they bulged above the short down-arc of her nose; her cheeks suggested chicken wattle.

In the day-coach, which smelled of oranges and bananas and babies' diapers, his father told him that his mother was very sick, and this was why he would be staying at Aunt Pearl's, and he had asked for how long, but his father had called the pop-and-candy boy over and bought him a lemon crush. Warm. Then he got train-sick and threw the pop back up.

After the long train trip he liked the city with all its noise, the stopping and starting whine of streetcars, the iron grind from brewery drays, the cupping sound of bakery- and milk-wagon horses. He had never before seen telegraph boys like monkeys clever enough to wear uniforms and ride a bicycle, or raddle-faced old men with newspapers under their arms, on corners, cawing something over and over again. Green, red, blue, yellow, white, a lot of city people wore uniforms, and they were wise and they were wicked and they were strange and exciting – but not frightening. How could a fair that went on all the time be frightening?

Aunt Pearl's house was a high, narrow one – three storeys. White. She lived alone – until his father left him with her. Uncle Edgar had died; so had little cousin Willis in the flu epidemic of 1918. Carlyle couldn't remember Willis, of course, for he had not even been born in 1918, but he did remember a man with a great front that smelled of cigars and horses and something else. He remembered very large hands, which had once gripped the handles of a fresno scoop. Uncle Edgar had been a contractor, and Aunt Pearl several times pointed out to Carlyle sidewalk squares which had printed into them: E. J. ROONEY – 1910.

There wasn't so much to do at Aunt Pearl's. At first, just after his father had taken the train back home, it had been some fun in the toy room on the third floor. Except for a steamer trunk and a table, there was no furniture in there. It was a room bared for playing in, and the trunk and the closet were full of toys; he could play with all of them, Aunt Pearl said, but when he was finished for the day, he must put them all back into the trunk and neatly on the closet shelves.

All by himself he was able to figure out how to run the little steam-engine with its brass boiler and lovely fly-wheel that had scarlet enamelled spokes. Aunt Pearl hadn't said he couldn't play with it; he didn't say anything about the five matches he got out of the kitchen. He poured wood alcohol into the flat little tin dish, slid the blue flame under the boiler, and waited. You had to help it by giving the fly-wheel a push with your finger, and the piston couldn't make up its mind, and then all of a sudden it could, and it went so fast it blurred, and never slowed down unless you pushed up the handle so the whistle could squeal. It was ill-tempered; it sputtered when it got really busy, and the hot spit stung the back of your hands. It filled the whole room with the smell of oil and steam and fruity wood alcohol.

There was a tiny pulley-wheel where a person could put a string belt and run something off it. But there was no Tinkertoy or erector set or Meccano in the trunk or the closet, so he couldn't make anything for the steam-engine to run. The wick kept glowing with a couple of red sparks after the tin dish was empty; then the sparks went out too.

The wooden table held the magic lantern, a box of blued tin with a stubby chimney; when you plugged the cord in, the metal got so hot it smelled. The door swung out at the back and had clips for slipping in photographs and postcards and valentines. The magic lantern threw very large pictures on the plaster wall, blurry till you twisted the tin snout – in or out. He looked at Niagara Falls, the Leaning Tower of Pisa, the Great Pyramids, Eiffel Tower, and photographs of little Willis and his own father and mother.

The only time he got outside was when Aunt Pearl took him to visit Willis, and right in the middle of a city wasn't a proper place for a cemetery; it shouldn't really be where there were cars honking. He could see the dome of the Parliament buildings like half a copper cantaloupe, or like one of the St. Johns boys' black-and-yellow caps with their quartering creases running down from the button on top. There was the stamping impatience of a streetcar bell, and then the electric crackle, and he was a little ashamed that his attention had been called away from Uncle Edgar's tombstone and the white marble lamb with its front feet folded under it. "WILLIS SINCLAIR ROONEY b. Jan. 16, 1914 – d. Feb. 10, 1918." Little Willis was under the lamb frozen on its slant slab of marble, but his mind wouldn't stay with Willis because the little lamb sparkled in the sunlight, just like those fat calendars that had a cabin under pines and snow curling down and around the eaves. That snow sparkled. He didn't feel very sad either – thinking "Mary had a . . . ," while up above, Aunt Pearl was crying. She was holding a handkerchief over her mouth and nose, and the sound escaping was very regular, like steam hissing from under the train engine.

And now he was thinking about the one lost from the ninety-and-nine and the high stained-glass window in Knox at home and his feet didn't come to the floor when he sat with his mother and father and Christ in His white gown with His Black Beard and Dark, Sad Eyes and the lamb's long legs spilling from under His Elbow and the yellow cart-wheel tipped up at the Back of His Head. He held out three base-balls to Carlyle's father and said to take a try for the little boy and his voice was raw as a scraped knee and his face was sweating in the car-nival sun and he had his straw boater pushed back from his forehead. The feathers on the kewpie doll in the crook of his elbow were lovely pink, and there were little roses on the elastic arm-bands above the man's elbows.

Nobody had to tell him he shouldn't be thinking about kewpie dolls and a fair when he was with Aunt Pearl crying over top of dead little Willis and the marble lamb and the glass bell sheltering everlasting flowers. Now Aunt Pearl's head was turned down more and she was tucking the handkerchief into her opened purse. He saw that it was hardly rumpled at all, still in its folded square.

"All right, Willis."

One time when they had come back from visiting Willis he had to go to the toilet, and he didn't know she'd already gone in there and hadn't locked the door. He had opened it on her, quite erect with her dress bunched up in front, her pink bloomers hammocking between her spread knees. It made him think of yarn skein being held out between two hands. Her shanks were long and white. He had shut the door right away, and afterwards, when she came downstairs, it was just as though nothing had happened at all, until she turned away and presented him with her pink, padded bum. She had caught up the whole back of her skirt with the waist elastic. After, when he did go into the bathroom, it smelled charred. She had forgot to flush the toilet too. Little white dumplings.

She was always burning string in the bathroom or in the kitchen. Bad smells bothered her, or any smells that were not perfume smells; yet she was always asking him if he'd gone, the last thing at night when he went to bed under "MACKENZIE FIRST SIGHTING THE PACIFIC" in little Willis's room, first thing in the morning, before he went out into the yard, whenever he came in from the yard. As soon as he had sensed her interest, he was anxious to help her out. Maybe if he ate a lot of apples, or prunes, or rhubarb – drank a lot of water – milk. . . . Instead, he began to make up bowel movements and urinations for her.

"I did a lot this time, Aunt Pearl."

"That's nice, Carlyle."

"A lot."

"Good boy."

"Not just some, you know – a whole lot and it came right up – it nearly came over the top of the . . ."

"All right, Carlyle."

"It wasn't easy – I had to try and try – but when I got the plug out . . ."

"Carlyle!"

And then the telegraph boy had leaned his bike against the fence, and Aunt Pearl told Carlyle his mother had died. They took the train, and the funeral was held in Knox, and people put their arms around him and cried, but it was difficult to know what to do, except to stand still. It was as though his mother had been dead a long time. After his mother's funeral he had cried though, when his father told him he had to go back with Aunt Pearl; it wouldn't be a good thing for him just with his father in the big house. Carlyle said it would be better, though, than being with just Aunt Pearl in her big house, but his father said no. He was back again in little Willis's bedroom with Alexander Mackenzie peering through his spyglass from behind the rock, and beside him, crouching in a breech clout, the Indian with the Buster-Brown haircut – quite uninterested in the Pacific, for he was looking down into his lap. The Indian had seen the Pacific before. He had good muscles.

This time he really hated it, and he knew he would hate going to school at St. Johns even though he would have a black-and-yellow cap and sweater and knee-socks and English pants. When school started in three weeks, he was to be a day boy, and that didn't sound like his father meant it when he said it was to be only a temporary arrangement. He wished he were at home with his father's deep voice going evenly on and on through *Wind in the Willows* and *Midshipman Easy* and *Swiss Family Robinson*. When Aunt Pearl said she would read him *Uncle Tom's Cabin* or *Sowing Seeds in Danny* or *Black Beauty*, he said no thanks. He missed even the bitter smell from his father's surgery.

There was really no fun in Aunt Pearl's house, in the living room with curtains drawn; if he wiped his feet furiously on the rug and then touched the brass plate of the light switch, there was a sound like a tiny whip cracking, and lightning chained from his fingertip. It showed up well in the darkened room. But she didn't like him to be there when she wasn't there – or in her bedroom.

Her bedroom was nice, with its great brass bed and the dresser curved in and out and in like a bow, and the colour of pull toffee. There were little eyes all over it. Aunt Pearl said they were birds' eyes. Everything on the dresser was neat; the mirror between the harp arms didn't have a smudge, and the lamp-chimney was beautifully clear, with the curling-irons inside and their handles bent at right angles over the beaded rim. She didn't have to tell him he mustn't come in her bedroom; he knew he'd likely muss it. So – back up to Willis's toy room on the third floor.

But this time the steam-engine wasn't much fun or the hanging clown or the sand machine. The wind-up train just went round and round the track until it ran down and you had to wind up the key again. The magic lantern was still all right, though he had seen Niagara Falls and the Grand Canyon and the Great Pyramids and the Leaning Tower of Pisa a hundred times – and all the valentines.

Generally he did what he was told, so it was hard to explain why he began to go into Aunt Pearl's bedroom. It was just her bedroom; there was nothing for him to do in there. He could scowl and he could snarl and he could blow out his cheeks in front of the dresser mirror. He could push up the outer corners of his eyes so they were Chinese, and hook his little fingers in the corners of his mouth and pull them down, which was funny. For a while.

Everything was laid out neat on the dresser top, the silver brush, the comb, the nail file, the fat thing she rubbed her nails with. They were the same distance apart and they were the same distance from the back and they were the same distance from the front. The lamp with the curling-tongs was in one corner and the powder box balanced it in the other corner. The box had sea shells glued to it. The ones all around the edge just under the lid had two tiny teeth each and under them, in what would be the baby's gum, there was a faint, pink stain as though the teeth had bled a little. The oval lid resisted him; he held it against his chest so he could get a better pull at it. It came off with a pop like a cork and he saw that he had been very lucky; if there'd been much powder it would have sprayed all over her dresser top. He was careful to wipe off any spilled powder with his sleeve.

There was still the powder smell – very faint – and for a moment he felt he might cry, but he didn't. It told him he'd better get right out of there, but he took a last look and reversed the nail file so the silver handle pointed away from the mirror. He turned it around again so that it pointed the same way as all the other things. He pushed the end over so that it wasn't even with the nail buffer. He stepped back and you could see it was crooked. He reached out his fingertip and pushed it a little straighter. Maybe it wasn't crooked enough now. He'd wait and see.

The next day the nail file was precisely in place, parallel to the nail buffer. She'd noticed and she'd straightened it. But maybe she'd filed her nails and put it back even again without noticing it at all. He moved the comb over to the left – quite a bit. At noon the next day when she sent him up to wash his hands it was back even again. He slid both the file and the comb out of position. Every day for five days he moved the stuff about on her dresser, and each time he had a chance to look, he found them all straightened out again. Finally he twisted the hairbrush around upside down. That evening she told him gently that he must not ever touch anything again on her dresser. He'd won!

A couple of days after, high up and back in the corner of the shelf closet, he found the box; from the dove-tail design at the corners he recognized it as a chalk box. When he slid back the lid in its tight grooves, he found it filled with marbles and balloons. Red, yellow, blue, green, pink, orange, he dumped the contents out: round bag ones, long cow-tit ones – one blue one collapsed and wrinkled. He was suddenly not so delighted, and for a moment was going to return all the balloons and marbles to the box and close it and put it back up into its corner on the shelf. He didn't. For a whole afternoon he blew up balloons and twisted their necks round and round so they'd pull in and knot themselves. Then he undid them all and put them back into their box. He did it early in the afternoon because he had the feeling she wouldn't have liked it for him to blow them up and spoil their tight, smooth newness – like the wrinkled, blue one.

He'd better be playing with the magic lantern when she called him for supper. He cast pictures on the white plaster wall until he'd come to the photograph of his mother and father beside the waterfall. His father had a high collar with a large, knotted tie, and his mother's dress had puffy sleeves and she had a bird-wing on her hat tilted on her head, and he began to cry and he took the photograph out. That was when he noticed that the lantern threw a hand-shaped shadow on the wall. He twisted the snout in and then out, and suddenly there was a hand up there. His own! Fingers – nails – creases – ten times larger! He tried the other hand. He took off his shoe and stocking, but his foot wouldn't go in there. He got up on his knees on the table. He found he had to take his pants right off and be very careful of the hot metal and it was blurred so he had to reach ahead and fix the snout. It came clear: his pecker on the opposite wall, way larger than his father's. When he moved it . . .

"Carlyle!"

She was in the doorway and she was looking at the wall, but his pecker wasn't there any longer because she'd made him jump and burn the end of it!

The next day his father had come; he got in on the same train that he and Carlyle had taken before his mother died, and again after his mother had died. As soon as his bags were up in the spare room he told Carlyle he wanted to have a talk with him, and they sat down in the living room by the bookcases with the lion statue prowling across the top of it.

"Now, Son – Aunt Pearl is a little upset." He leaned forward and touched the ashtray with the end of his cigar. The ash came away, held together as it rolled, and Carlyle was thinking how it was a lot like the stuff wasps made their nests out of.

"Are you listening, Son?"

"Sure I am."

"You know you're – a week or so you'll be seven."

"Week Friday."

"Ah – she is upset – about you."

"Her nail file."

"Her nail file?"

"And her comb and her brush the way I kept moving them on her."

"No."

"I moved the file over a little so it wasn't straight and then she moved it back and I moved it back crooked and she moved it back and I moved her comb and her brush and I put her brush upside down. . . ."

"No – that isn't it. . . ."

"She didn't like it very much."

"I don't think it's a very important . . ."

"She does. It bothers her . . ." The bronze lion had caught his eye and he had made an exciting discovery the way he sat on the couch below it so he was at the rear end.

"She told me about the magic lantern, Son."

He'd always looked at it from the front.

"Son, the magic lantern."

"I didn't hurt it." Now he could see right up under the base of the tail – for the first time.

"What I'd like to understand – at least I'm trying to – with a little attention and help from you I may – what exactly happened with the magic lantern that's got Pearl so upset?"

For a moment he'd thought he'd been seeing wrong, but he wasn't. Tucked high up under its tail, the lion had a cluster of three balls. Not two. Three!

"Carlyle – you aren't listening to me!"

"Sure I am, Dad."

"All right then – what happened with the magic lantern?"

"She came into Willis's playroom when I was working the magic lantern – you know that's a real magic lantern, Dad – it'll show anything on the wall – not just postcards or pictures – anything! Anything you want to stick in there, it'll show it on the wall."

"Yes."

"Stick your hand in the back and it'll show your hand on the wall."

"This doesn't explain why she's so upset. . . ."

"When she came in I'd stuck my pecker in. When she opened the door it was right on the wall there."

"Your – pecker was."

"Yeah – only big – bigger than the leaning tower of . . ."

"Whatever made you do that?"

"I don't know. I just did it. Seemed like an idea and I wondered if it would work and it did. You know that lantern magnified about seventeen times!"

"Well, it isn't exactly what it was intended for."

"I know. That bulb gets it hot in there. I burnt it a little."

"All right."

"She doesn't know that. Maybe – is that why she's upset – because I burnt the end of my . . ."

"No. I don't think so."

"Why should she get . . ."

"Son – for Aunt Pearl it was a little shocking. You shouldn't display yourself. . . ."

"I didn't know she was coming in! She's always coming in on a person – in the bathroom . . ."

"All right – all right."

"You want me to tell her I'm sorry I . . ."

"No."

". . . she's the one walked in on me . . ."

"No – it won't be necessary."

"Oh – Dad – I want to go home with you – why can't I . . ."

"All right – all right."

"Please, Dad!"

"Hold on now. Look – I'm taking you back with me." When his father had calmed him, he realized suddenly that he had forgot about the lion. He pointed out the extra ball.

His father had hired a housekeeper to look after both of them. Her name was Olga, and she made him a birthday cake for his seventh birthday.

His father's present was a magic lantern, but it only worked with glass slides.

24

❧

Body Language

Colin Dobbs, who teaches creative writing at Livingstone University, has a daily swim and sauna as part of his physiotherapy routine. He was badly mauled by a grizzly bear four months earlier, leaving him crippled and terribly disfigured. Before his encounter with the bear up Daisy Creek, Colin had already been emotionally and psychologically damaged from a broken marriage and a ten-year failure of creative nerve as a writer. While he has made some recovery physically, his interior world is still fragile and vulnerable from the shock of his encounters with the "capsize" element of life. In this scene he experiences for the first time in a long while the stirrings of a desire to re-engage with others.

There was nobody in front of the counter when Colin picked up his towel and left his watch and wallet with the attendant. He had the locker room to himself, was just as lucky when he left the shower and went out to the pool. All lanes stayed empty while he willed himself to fifteen lengths, the last three languid and on his back. He had just climbed out when a young boy came out of the men's door and did a racing dive from the shallow end.

The sauna blessed him; as he worked his hotter and hotter way up, he could feel the ache diluting in his back and hip and shoulder and elbow. The nausea and headache were almost gone. If his luck held, he'd be finished in here and out and dressed, without curious eyes tracing scar tracks over his back and chest and stomach. There had always been annoyances when he had company in here, somebody trying to turn the place into a steam-bath by dippering water again and again on the lava rocks so that breath intake could almost sear, or faculty young in search of parents, popping in and holding the door open. Last year, some fellow had relieved himself on the hot rocks so that the place would be public-lavatory offensive for later occupants, and for days after, it smelled like a sour citrus grove in Hell.

He moved up another bench. Carefully. Years of contraction and expansion had levered nail heads out from the cedar planks so that a first-time or careless user had simply to touch hot metal to inflict an instant buttock brand. Or, if male, much worse. He could feel the sweat gathering on his forehead, then a run starting from his left eyebrow to tickle down his cheek. Probably the right one too, though the nerve the surgeon had imported from the back of his knee could not let him know about that. He looked over to both doors. God, he hoped no one came in! Of either sex! The bear had made him modest.

Seven years before, when Human Kinetics had got its pool, gymnasium, indoor track, and squash courts building, it had not been its intention that the sauna be used heterosexually. But with cost overruns and the provincial government's unwillingness to increase its contribution, a second room had become a casualty of necessary budget compromise. Since then the university had made a vital, extramural contribution to the sex education of neighbouring Livingstone Heights youngsters as they watched both sexes running and rolling in snowdrifts. Occasionally during a chinook in early spring, some daredevils broke the ice skin at the river edge to immerse themselves in the therapeutic interest of shocking the heart, contracting blood vessels and genitals, erecting nipples, and slamming shut academic pores. Now one heard hardly anyone suggest another facility be built; mixed sauna bathing had become a well-established Livingstone University tradition.

For almost the only time since he'd abandoned the novel, his first visit to the sauna had tempted him to try a short story, one that would happen in this promising setting. Naked, people said so much about themselves. Unwittingly. Body language became more articulate. Negligent towels were dropped over privates. A casual leg was thrown over a knee; men leaned forward on their elbows, heads down in the thinker pose; women kept their legs together, arms folded across their breasts, or if they had long enough hair, they let it fall over both shoulders and hang down in front. Not all that effective a curtain if the breasts were large; nipples that peeped stimulated. Comparative Literature had taken one look at Classics in Translation's magnificent knockers and found himself evidently excited. How did you forbid an erection? He had draped his towel over it but the tepee still told on him. He had never returned.

Head of Drama always leaned back against the second level, flung one leg out, foot on the floor, and drew his other up on the bench beside himself, to display all he had. Which was considerable. Tait generally lay flat out on his stomach so he could hog the top level. Herbie Stibbard often read the *New York Times Book Review* and left with print on his thighs. All the news that's fit to imprint. Just might do that short story some day.

Chill surprised his ankles. He looked over to the women's door on his wrong side, then quickly away, but not before he'd seen her soft, dark triangle and one breast. The gold and black towel over her right shoulder hid the other. Brown-eyed Susan. With great will-power he kept his gaze considerately ahead of himself. It had to be the first time since Daisy Creek he'd averted his face for someone else's sake.

Eye slide let him see that she had seated herself on the far corner of the lowest planks. She had a most articulate back, shoulders level and well squared. When she moved her arms a shoulder-blade declared itself, the other still under the towel. The high edge of her hip was distinctly young. Rodin's *Danaid*. Seated. She must have just left the pool or shower, for her hair was a black calotte. Cardinal Wolsey.

He was running with sweat now. He ought to move down a couple of notches, but that would bring him closer to her. If he slid further along to his left, she might interpret it unfortunately. Maybe not, if he were to move away and down at the same time. His chest and stomach scars were livid red and purple. God only knew how the eye and cheek were. He'd better just get out of here!

She'd turned towards him. The breast with its chocolate aureole was not adolescent. Champagne glass! Goodbye, Cardinal! A cold blast hit him.

"I forgot the combination!" The child was holding it wide open.

"Shut the door, Robin!"

The weather moderated.

"What's the right combin —"

"Four-eight-three."

Brief winter again.

"I'm sorry."

"That's all right." Now they'd spoken to each other it would be rude to leave.

"He always forgets the number."

"So do I," he lied again.

Blizzard!

"I tried that one and it doesn't work!'

Continuing cold!

"Try it again! Four-eight-three!"

"It won't work!"

"Try it anyway and shut the bloody door!"

He was not going to have to come down now to cool off, after all.

"We haven't met before."

Naked or otherwise. "Colin Dobbs. English."

"Helen Sweeney – Philosophy."

Just what the hell did he say to her now?

"You're new to Livingstone?"

"Three months. Exchange. Lausanne."

"Sweeney's a very Swiss name."

"My ex was Irish. Is. I've kept his name. Not for myself so much as for –"

And we shall have snow.

"Jeezus H., Robin!"

"I told you! Four-eight-one doesn't work –"

"Three! Four-eight – three!"

"You said four-eight-*one*!"

"I said four-eight-*three*!" She looked up to him. "Didn't I."

"Several times."

She said she was sorry again and he said it was all right again. Four-eight-three must have been the correct combination for her son's locker because he did not return to freeze them again. She explained that she was not a sauna frequenter; indeed this was her first time in one, and just how long should one spend in one? He said half an hour.

She moved up a level. He came down one. A drop of sweat had gathered and trembled from the tip of her nose. She wiped at it with the back of her wrist. Perspiration was usually well started in about five minutes, he told her; until then, it helped to capture it where it first appeared – the forehead – cheeks – and transfer it to drier and hotter skin areas.

"Guess I'll take your advice." She lifted her breast, put her hand under it and brought it out cupped to spread moisture over her left shoulder, then underneath the towel still hanging over her right side.

"I've just about had it. My half-hour." He lowered himself to the first level and his cane.

Her whole body gleamed now. Quite lovely!

He stood. Too quickly for heat-slackened muscles. His hip gave out underneath him. He fell back and down, but only onto the planks.

"You all right?" She came down to him. The towel had fallen from her shoulder.

"Okay. Okay." Now he understood the towel. She had only one breast.

"You're sure?'

"Yes." He had made it to his feet again. "I'm all right."

She handed him the cane. "I –" She looked down at herself, then up to him. "I thought I'd have it all to myself."

"So did I."

"If there had to be someone else, I'm rather glad it was you."

"Me too."

"My being here bothered you?"

"At first."

"Until?"

"At first."

"Do you mind if I ask you . . ."

"I was mauled by a bear."

"Oh, dear!"

"About four months ago."

"So – you're an Ursus."

"They left that one off the zodiac calendar." He started for the door.

"Not mine."

He turned back to her. She had not replaced the towel. "Nice meeting you." In all your naked candour. "And Robin." Glorified by sweat!

She was grinning, for God's sake. "We must see more of each other."

25

Stopping Smoking

W. O. never has succeeded in kicking the nicotine habit. He graduated from chewing cigarettes to chewing the real thing – plugs of Black Strap snoose. He never could get the hang of spitting it cleanly, let alone accurately, so it ended up on his chin, shirt front, and random places within a three-foot radius of his mouth. At Merna's insistence, he kept empty soup tins in every room of the house and in the car so he could dribble his discharge directly into them. His friends in High River also kept tins handy to protect their rugs, furniture, pets, and children.

After a time, he finally discovered snuff. First Mother Rumney's Eucalyptus, then Joseph and Henry Wilson's Finest Menthol snuff, which he still uses – in large quantities. He is very generous with it and often offers it to innocent children and interviewers. His snuff habit led to his passion for collecting snuff boxes. His snuff box and the act of taking a pinch of snuff became an integral part of his readings. At key moments in a performance (for example, when the Arbuckle screen door slaps the stillness and Melvin's

grandfather starts walking to the backhouse and stops to spit) he does not
just pause for emphasis or suspense – he stops, opens his snuff box, taps it
to loosen the snuff, takes out a pinch, inhales it, closes the box, and then
continues.

This piece was published in Maclean's *(May 1964).*

⌒⊙⌒

It's one year since I decided to stop smoking, a decision I had been
shaping for almost thirty years. I was a poly-addict, smoking almost
a pound of pipe tobacco a month and a package of cigarettes a day,
so that there could be no easy compromise by turning from cigarettes
to pipe. This is no solution at all when you inhale every pipe puff,
when you fill eleven pipes a night and lay them out in a row on your
desk so that you can chain-smoke them the next morning. If I had
wanted simply to improve my smoking situation, I would have
switched to cigarettes alone, thereby cutting down my lung-tar intake
by 80 per cent, and getting rid of all the awkward paraphernalia the
pipe smoker has to carry out with him: pipes, cleaners, tobacco pouch,
kitchen box of matches, dustpan and brush for picking up the dottle,
ashes and tobacco crumbs he spills on other people's rugs and carpets.
It had to be sudden death: one last fond look at my favourite goose-
necked pipe with its sterling-silver ferrule and amber mouthpiece, a
final smell of the pepper tang of Latakia, the fig scent of Perique –
then no more forever.

That was just a year ago and strangely it never occurred to me then
that gestalt would be lying in malevolent wait. My withdrawal symptoms began almost immediately: inability to focus attention, heightened sensitivity to noise, the return of an old neck-muscle twitch,
involuntary muscular spasms on dropping off to sleep, shortness of
temper and a compulsion to brush my teeth and gargle with hydrogen peroxide eighty times a day. These abated after three weeks, but
I began to have nightmares in which I dreamed I had inadvertently

smoked a haystack of tobacco without knowing it, and too late realized in panic that I now had to go all through the torture of stopping
again. The sharp and rhythmic pangs of tobacco hunger came further
and further apart, rather like labour pains in reverse, so that at the
end of three months I might go as long as an hour without wanting
a smoke. This torment seemed to identify itself in some way with
the hands and the mouth, and was now accompanied by a saddening
world-weariness that seemed faintly familiar, but escaped me until
I remembered the spring my feet grew and I had lost the key to my
roller skates.

I didn't shout; my family tell me that I seemed "whipped." I wasn't,
actually; I simply couldn't waste any energy now, must save it for
will-power fuel. About this time – the fourth month – I discovered I
was short of breath, saw stars when I bent over to do up my shoes, had
bulging eyes and a feeling of constriction about my belt band. I was
chewing eight packages of English toffee a day; instead of the 165
pounds I had weighed for twenty years, I was now 182.

The withdrawal symptoms for kicking the English-toffee habit are
much the same as those for stopping smoking: inability to focus
attention, heightened sensitivity to noise, a compulsion to gargle
with hydrogen peroxide eighty times a day, and nightmares in which
you inadvertently smoke a haystack of pipe tobacco sweetened with
English toffee. To fight the double temptation it seems natural to
chew gum, something you haven't done since the age of twelve,
except for utilitarian reasons such as unbunging your ears on airplane
flights and trips over the Rogers Pass. Too late you discover that the
sugar intake is comparable to that of English toffee and you now
weigh 189 pounds.

The withdrawal symptoms for kicking the gum-chewing habit are
almost the same as those for stopping smoking or eating English
toffee, except that now in your nightmares you smoke an English-
toffee-sweetened haystack of tobacco that comes in Chiclet form. I
had reached this new plateau about the sixth month, had not an

inkling where the dynamic and ever-changing pattern might take me next, certainly not where it *did*.

My Uncle Jim, who farmed six miles south of our town when I was a boy, had a demented roan horse; he was what was known as a manger chewer. Now that I no longer smoked, ate English toffee, or chewed gum, I felt strong empathy for that poor horse; for the first time in my life I appreciated the frustration that had caused him to eat fork handles, chew his stall, gnaw and shred his manger.

I can't remember who it was that offered me the cigarette that was a dynamic part of the pattern forming, but I recall that I was shaken with special anger as I felt the stir of an appetite that should have been long dead. I took the proffered cigarette; I bit the end off savagely, began to chew with actual rage the damned stuff that had given me so much discomfort over the years that *La belle nicotine sans merci* had me in thrall!

For almost a week I chewed only my wife's cigarettes, then in late July deliberately bought a package just for myself. By this time I had discovered that a certain brand of blends was my favourite: the package flap said they tasted good, and so they did, for they were flavoured with molasses and reminded me faintly of English toffee. By now people were asking me why I chewed cigarettes: why didn't I buy proper chewing tobacco or snoose? In the first place, I would explain, I bore these forms of tobacco no ill will: there wouldn't have been any revengeful satisfaction in biting pieces off them, in grinding, chomping, macerating, dicing, masticating and spitting them out. As well, I had never in my life known a cigarette chewer, so I was in no danger at all of taking up a lasting addiction.

It is six months now that I have been a cigarette chewer, and what was always an aesthetically distressing habit is twice as obscene now that the spittoon no longer graces living rooms, hotel lobbies, barber shops, or pool halls. I happened to possess a morning-glory spittoon and when I first began to take this with me when we visited, my wife objected, but she has restrained herself since it is preferable to the

Dixie Cups I had been using. I no longer have to answer solicitous inquiries about my health or acknowledge get-well cards.

The withdrawal symptoms for kicking the cigarette-chewing habit are almost the same as those for stopping smoking, or eating English toffee, or chewing gum . . .

26

❧

Willie's Contract with Old Cloutie

The Black Bonspiel of Willie Mac-Crimmon *is W. O.'s 1930s foothills version of the Faust legend. In the following scenes a mysterious "travelling man" visits the small foothills town of Shelby, ostensibly to have his curling boots repaired by the town cobbler, Willie MacCrimmon, but really to check out prospects for his retail business. Willie, who has a deep passion for curling and a staunch commitment to the Presbyterianism of his forebears, strikes a bargain with Old Cloutie which results in the salvation of his soul riding on the last rock in the last end of a "Black Bonspiel."*

One of the first radio plays W. O. wrote, The Black Bonspiel of Willie MacCrimmon *first aired on CBC's* Summer Theatre *in 1950. He subsequently reworked it as a television play, then as a novella, and finally as a stage play. The following version of these scenes is from McClelland & Stewart's 1993 illustrated edition of the novella.*

❦

On Main Street, the year's first soft snowflakes had begun to feather down as the man in a dark fall coat stepped out of: "Steve Hazzard – Licensed Embalmer and Funeral Director," to walk down the street toward: "Willie MacCrimmon – Saddle, Harness, and Shoe Repair," an elderly building brittle with age, its foundation crumbled at one corner, causing it to tilt alarmingly. Beside it stood a building with a fresh young face of shining black tile, over which a crimson signature angled: "Chez Sadie's – Snips and Gossip." Ironic was Willie's shop next to a beauty parlour, like an old man in the company of a sporting woman.

The man with the homburg and van dyke was obviously a travelling man, not a resident, for he carried a tan case of the type salesmen use for their advertising literature and their samples. Under his other arm he held a paper-wrapped bundle.

Behind the long counter that separated the work from the public side of his shoe and harness shop, Willie MacCrimmon sat at his last as he mended a boot. Far right on the public side was a pot-bellied Quebec heater with a mica umbilicus. A stovepipe angled and kinked up and across the ceiling and out the side wall. To Willie's left was the shoes-and-boots-to-be-repaired shelving on which were jumbled ticketed footwear.

The bell over the door tinkled. The Devil a.k.a. Old Cloutie entered. Willie looked up from his last, laid his hammer down, got up, and walked to the counter. His face had a full, pursed look. With his eyes on the customer he lifted a hand and spat into it a cargo of tacks, then placed them on the counter. Satan, who had laid his paper bundle down, began to open it.

"Aye?"

"My curling boots. I would like you to do a resole job on them for me."

Willie picked one of them up, turned it over, set it down, and looked at the other one. As he did Old Cloutie stepped over to the Quebec stove, set the coffee pot aside, lifted the round lid aside with a bare hand, then plunged both down and into the flame to subdue the winter chill. Still examining the boots, Willie failed to notice this astonishing hand-baking. Done to a turn, Cloutie pulled his hands out, replaced the lid and coffee pot, and returned to the counter.

"They need a resole job."

"I can see that," Willie said. His attention shifted to the hands splayed on the counter and he experienced an immediate shock, gentle yet distinct as the hard kiss of one granite curling rock against another. The stranger's hands were small and almost fleshless, their backs coarse with jet-black wiry hair growing almost to the base of claw nails.

Willie looked up, and the stranger's eyes were on a level with his own: the black brows were rakish, with an upward flare at their outer ends that was matched by the angle of the ears. He pointed to the boots. "Never seen a pair quite like these before. Odd toes to them . . . broad . . . round – not point –"

"Custom-made for a true fit."

"So – resole – and these creases on the upper . . ."

"They stay. Just the soles. You'll do them for me?"

"I will. What I'm here for past twenty-three years. When – ah – when would you wish them done?"

"My next trip through – two weeks."

"Where do you curl? Glencoe? Calgary?"

"No. Can I have them in two weeks' time?"

Willie shrugged his shoulder toward the shoes-to-be-repaired shelf. "I'm behind on my repairs." He picked up the boots and turned them over thoughtfully. "Afraid you'll have to resort to buckled overshoes for – uh – three weeks?"

There was a calculated pause as Mr. Cloutie looked at Willie. "Three weeks, then."

"Best I can do." Willie set the boots down again and looked at his visitor. "You're no' from around here."

"No."

"I've seen your face before, though."

"Quite likely."

"Foothills Bonspiel?"

"No."

"Little Britches Rodeo, Bull Show, Craft Fair?"

"Possibly. I'm a travelling man."

"Fooled me," Willie said. "I figured you for a professional man. More like – oh – a university professor?"

The Devil laughed. "Very perceptive of you. I do a lot of business in academe."

"I'm not familiar with that town. Politician, are you, then?"

"I do spend a lot of time in your capitals. Provincial and federal. Three weeks, then?"

"I've got it! Bible salesman!"

"Oh Willie, did you ever hog that rock!" He turned away to the door. "Three weeks."

As the bell tinkled, Willie picked up the tacks from the counter and replaced them in his mouth. He turned away, seated himself at the last, and began the crooked rhythm of his hammer. But shortly he was back to the counter again, staring at the shoes, picking them up.

"Warm . . . warmer than they would be if he'd just taken them off. And he must have carried them a distance through cold outside air."

He moved toward the shoes-to-be-repaired shelf and tossed the boots into the tumbled and ticketed contents: labourer's felt boots, formless and somehow pathetic child's boots, Matt Stanley's newspaperman's brogues, flat farm boots, rancher's high-heeled boots, Dr. Fitzgerald's fancy riding boots, all lying there with Mame Harris's disgracefully run-over heels nudging the bunion bulges of Aunt Lill's sensible English shoes. There was shocking democracy in his shoes-to-be-repaired shelf, for he had thrown the footgear there with fine and deliberate disregard for their owners' social, economic, and moral position.

He moved back to his last. The cobbling hammer took up its impatient crooked rhythm in the dim stillness rich with the soft smell of new harness, bitter with the tang of leather dye. Now and again his hammer fell silent as he refilled his mouth with tacks.

He took a break, went over with a cup to the coffee pot on the Quebec stove, and as he returned to the last he saw the white card on the counter corner. He picked it up:

Mr. O. Cloutie
Wholesale Souls – Retail Sins
Business & Home Address: 1313 Sulphur Blvd. S.S.
Hell

"Hell!"
Just as he said it the bell over the door tinkled . . .

. . . Pipe-fitting came in, stomping his feet. "Who'd a thought it. Couple of days she'll be froze up tighter'n a bull's ass in fly time!" He headed for the heater, taking a cup off the corner of the counter. "Colder than the tip of a polar bear's –"

"Aye. Pour one for me too, Pipe . . ."

"Looks like Old King Winter has quit draggin' his ass an' covered alla Shelby district with a pure an' snowy blanket."

"You sure do keep your eye peeled, Pipe. Three sugar." He knocked off cutting Dr. Fitzgerald's riding boot uppers for a diamond inlay of white kid and sat down in one of the kitchen chairs next to the Quebec heater. As he handed Willie his coffee, Pipe-fitting said, "How many years I been curlin' third for you?"

"Twenty-two. You're a fine one, Pipe-fittin'."

"We're all good, Wullie. You're skippin' one hell of a rink."

"Aye."

"This year we're gonna be better'n we ever bin. We'll be hotter'n a firecracker. I bet Doc Fitzgerald won't stand no chance agin us. No more'n a gopher through a thirty-six-inch threshin' machine."

"Let's hope so."

"Ner McConkey either. We'll take him too."

"We'll see."

"Yeah!" Pipe-fitting tipped his cup, sighed. He got up to pour himself another. "I had a dream last night, Wullie. Curlin' dream. That Dominion Finals we seen thirty years back!"

"Thirty-two."

"I know . . . I know. That was sure some match in the Glenmore Club."

"Glencoe," Willie corrected.

"The rock that won it . . . extra ends . . . eleventh –"

"Twelfth."

"Yeah, yeah. Straight and sweet and true as a Baptist fart through a brass curtain rod for a double take-out and stay. What a shot!"

"Aye." A remembering smile grew over Willie's face as he leaned his head back in the comforting warmth and closed his eyes.

"The Canadian Brier Play-offs of Provincial Champions for the Championship of Canada and the whole world!"

Willie was no longer hearing Pipe-fitting's dry voice droning on and on. Within himself he was hearing a band playing "O Canada." He was seeing a man dressed in dinner jacket march smartly over the ice to the centre. . . .

"Thee winner – grand Champeens of thee Canadian Brier Play-offs – champeens by one rock . . . of thee Dominyun of Canada . . . and . . . therefore . . . of thee World . . ." There was a long pause by the announcer for effect. "Skip Willie MacCRIMMON and his rink made up of . . . Lead: Cross-cut Charlie Brown . . . Second: Malleable Charlie Brown . . . Third: Pipe-fitting Charlie Brown . . . all of Shelby, Alberta."

The Governor General came rushing down the ice, slipping and sliding with precarious and undignified balance, followed by the aides, and in the rear, the Prime Minister of Canada. "Here . . . here . . . I must meet him. Where is . . . who is this man?" the Governor General was demanding excitedly.

"Willie MacCrimmon, Your Governor Generalship."

"Yes . . . yes . . . I must shake the hand that curled that last rock . . . the winning take-out rock. The finest rock ever curled in the . . ."

Hard on his heels came the Prime Minister. "After you . . . I must speak with this man. Never have I seen such curling. He must come to Ottawa and curl there for my ministers who were unable to see this . . . who were in special session of Cabinet. I certainly must not disappoint them."

There was the Governor General, throwing his arm over the Prime Minister's shoulder in comradely fashion – or perhaps the better to preserve his balance on the curling ice. "By all means do this. Let them see it in Ottawa . . . let them see for themselves what we have seen today. This . . . this Willie MacCrimmon and his men from Shelby. I will have them come up and curl in Rideau Hall's private rink."

The Prime Minister broke in: "They shall have a ten-course meal in the Senate restaurant. Free of charge. . . . There will be the presentation of the cup and as well souvenirs for each and every one of them. They shall be given fourteen-carat-gold spittoons from the Senate chambers, engraved with their names, so that every time they spit they shall remember this great occasion."

There was Willie, kilted in his MacCrimmon tartan and his best Scottish bonnet, and his men standing at attention with their tams and brooms as the Governor General handed each his spittoon and shook hands. The Prime Minister embraced them. Only Cross-cut curtsied. The skirl of the pipes died away on the last notes of "O Canada."

Willie opened his eyes and shook himself a bit as he realized he had been dreaming. It was his one self-indulgence, this daydream that had started years ago as a sort of mental lay-me-down. It had grown more and more vivid with time, returning him fresh and exhilarated to his dark shop. From dream to dream, minor details might change: sometimes a silk-hatted Prime Minister doffed his morning coat, and in snowy shirtsleeves and white-piped vest, curled a true, slow rock down the ice! But always there was the sound of the pibroch; while Malleable, Cross-cut, and Pipe-fitting stood proudly by, the gleaming Brier Cup was received into the trembling hands of Skip Willie MacCrimmon.

"Pipe-fitting," said Willie in a low and fervent voice, "I would gi'e anything . . . utterly anything . . . for to skip the winning rink in the Brier!"

The bell above the shop door had not tinkled.

He stood next to the stitching horse, tan sample case and all, over-coat opened, one hand nonchalant in a side pant pocket so that his jacket was pulled back to reveal the miniature cloven goat's hoof charm that swung from his watch chain. "That's a bargain, Willie MacCrimmon."

"Huh!" said Pipe-fitting, his mouth dropping open.

"That is a bargain . . . Willie MacCrimmon."

There was a long, long pause. "Would you mind . . . giving a bit of a twist to yon damper on the stovepipe?" asked Willie. "Wee bit close in here."

Pipe-fitting moved to the Quebec stove and twisted the protesting damper, keeping his eyes on the stranger all the while.

"Pipe-fitting, meet Old Cloutie."

"Old Cloutie?"

"Beezalie Bub . . . Satan . . . Old Scratch . . . Old Nick . . . The Devil . . . Old Cloutie."

"Oh, him." Pipe-fitting straightened politely. "Pleasure."

"All mine," said Cloutie.

"Take a seat, Mr. Cloutie," Willie said. "You're early."

"Came through on an unscheduled trip involving an ungraded substitute schoolteacher and a Royal Bank cashier, lifting beer together in the Ladies and Escorts of the Arlington Arms Hotel."

"That'd be Maggie Sparrow an' Ron Shepherd," Pipe-fitting said.

"That's right." The Devil had rounded the counter to sit in the chair next to Willie.

"What's wrong with havin' beer?" Pipe-fitting said.

"A wee unimportant matter, isn't it?" Willie said. "For an unscheduled visit?"

"At first glance, yes. But Mrs. Sadie Burbidge saw them go in together. She told Annie Brown, who in turn got on the party line for the greater part of yesterday. Mrs. Brown looks quite promising to me."

"I'll say she does!" Pipe-fitting said. "Poor Cross-cut."

"Just argy-bargy, isn't it?"

"In itself, yes. But with this woman it's the accretion that counts. Nothing really flashy in the way of sin goes on in Shelby. My regular calls are the Bluebird Café – penny ante in the little back room. Mame Harris's little brown cottages by the CPR Depot is a routine call of mine. Then there's the pool hall."

"Aye."

"But there's a brisk trade in the small novelty line. Petty intolerance, lust for teapot power, self-indulgence, sins of omission, snobbery, within-the-family tyranny – that sort of thing. Quick turnover. But . . ." He sighed.

"But what?" asked Willie. "Can I take it – all's not well – in Hell?"

"All *is* well in Hell. It's up here. Sometimes I ask myself – just what am I doing – up on the territory again, century after century, selling sin. After millennia of calls and eons of detail work, all my lines are well established – but it's the same old inventory. You think it's a challenge to sell gluttony today? Avarice? Sloth? Lust? Lust just sells itself. And the quality of sinner. They simply do not make sinners the way they used to."

"I was wondering," Pipe-fitting said. "About the War, and Hitler . . . and further back. Did the thirties' depression reach down there?"

The Devil shook his head.

"No missions? No scratch-house pogies? Folks on relief with nothin' to eat but saltcod? No jobs?"

"No idle hands."

"Hmh. First thing good I ever heard about . . . uh . . . it," Pipe-fitting said.

"In a few regards you might find it pleasant."

"Aw, come on. Hell's gotta be hell."

"We curl."

"You do?! I don't believe it!"

"You will, Mr. Brown. When your time comes."

"Tell me. Just for curiosity's sake, how . . . in Hell can you possibly have ice?"

"Artificial," the Devil said.

"Hey. Beginnin' to sound all right. But . . . how artificial?" Pipe-fitting said.

"Basaltic sheets. Volcanic deposit. Highly polished, which gives us a fast knock-out game."

"Shirtsleeve bonspiels!" Pipe-fitting leaned over to pick up his toolbox and bag. "Nice to hear Hell ain't all that bad."

"Don't misunderstand. As you said, Hell is hell. It has one renewable resource economy."

"Sin," said Willie.

"Yes. Sin is an infinitely renewable resource and our economy's soundly based on it. We have as well a non-renewable natural resource."

"What might that be?" Willie said.

"Energy. I do have a threatening problem with that. You see, you people with your wasteful ways are going to run out of oil and gas and you're going to have to look elsewhere for your fuel and heat." He paused, lifted a dramatic finger, and pointed it straight down. "Deep thermal energy. Mine. All mine! Hell was given to me when I was cast out of Heaven! Hell, including all its thermal energy and mineral rights, is *my* province! When your time of energy need comes, I will grant no leases and release no territorial rights or powers of decision over my single *non*-renewable resource. Because when that brimstone runs out, I do not see how – in Hell – we can salvage our economy. And when the brimstone runs out – since we could not diversify – I don't know what – in Hell – we can do."

The Devil got a grip on his emotions. He lifted his attaché case to his lap, opened it, and brought out a cluster of what looked like foolscap-length legal sheets. He looked over to Willie and Pipe-fitting; he laughed.

"We have an expression we use often down there: 'Let those upper bastards freeze in the dark.'"

"Don't sound so neighbourly to me," Pipe-fitting said.

"In my situation you might just change your mind about that."

"You say so." Pipe-fitting had picked up his toolbox, slung his bag over his shoulder. "Judgin' from them papers of yours, looks like you two got private business to . . . I'll be goin'. Nice meetin' you."

"All mine."

"Never did get round to finishin' Mrs. Harrison's waste-an'-overflow. Plugged up agin. I gotta skin over there," he said over his shoulder.

As the door slammed behind him, Willie said, "I take it that your visit is about the bargain. You caught me unawares."

"I frequently do it that way." He got up from his chair and carried the papers over to the counter. Willie joined him there.

"These are some kind of contract?"

"You are correct. Look it over."

"My soul for the Canadian Brier championship."

"Right again. It's my usual Faust contract. It's much the same one I used decades ago with a ludicrous little one-balled paperhanger named Adolf. It now includes three items not even listed in the top deadly seven: bigotry, fanaticism, and hypocrisy. Never sell them short, especially the last one, which peaked in Victorian England and seems to be on the rise once more. Anyway, Mr. MacCrimmon, this is my standard soul-for-fair-recompense agreement that has stood the test of time."

Willie was finding it tough going, trying to find his way through the obfuscating fog of legalese.

"It does not bog down in hair-splitting detail obscuring the intent of the agreement. Nor does it oversimplify. I trust you will find no ambiguity."

Willie left off reading to look up at him. "I might, if you'd leave off yammering on and on and on whilst I try to read this thing."

"I shall try to get a laconic grip on myself."

"Whatever that means." Willie went back to work on the contract, and the Devil said no more till he had finished the last page.

"Well now. Near as I can make out, it's my soul for the Canadian Brier championship."

"That's our deal, Willie, and it's a good one, I assure you. For both of us."

"So you say. I do have one wee concern."

"Yes?"

"You do have an expanded list of the seven deadly sins, right enough, but what about a balancing one?"

"What are you driving at?"

"Well . . . how about one of moral principles? If you made a list, I'm sure trust would be the top one. And, well, I'm not so sure I can trust you."

"I see your point. I have to trust you too."

"Aye. Tell me. What makes you so fussy about *my* soul?"

"I might as well be frank with you . . . I need a good third for my rink."

"*You do?*"

"You've always dreamed of winning the *Canadian Brier*. Since long before the Ice Age I've wanted to win *our* championship bonspiel –

the Celestial Brier Play-offs. I can win it – with you curling third for me."

"I see."

"Does that ease your concern?"

"A wee bit. Would you entertain a sort of counter-proposition, Cloutie? You might call it a condition to this first offer."

The Devil got down with his elbows on the counter. "Shoot."

"I have a fair rink of my own. I canna say I'd care to curl third on a rink that couldn't beat the one I now skip. I'd be willing to curl for you in Hell only on the condition that your rink is a better one than mine – the one made up of Cross-cut Charlie Brown, Malleable Charlie Brown, and Pipe-fitting Charlie Brown, and me."

"And your proposition?"

"You curl us a match. If we lose, then I curl third for you at no price – when my time comes."

"At no price?!" The Devil looked incredulous.

"Aye. You need *not* deliver me the Canadian Brier championship."

"Well now." The Devil straightened up. "Do you really mean this? Your soul for nothing?! I've never before –"

"That's just one side of it, mind," Willie said. "The other: if *we* win then you must deliver according to the terms of your first offer. I will skip a winning rink in the Canadian Brier Play-offs, but again, at *no* cost to me."

Head down, hands behind his back, and the forked tail coiled to rest in his hip pocket, the Devil turned and walked toward the Quebec heater. He spent contemplative moments there, then came back to the counter.

"You really mean that?"

"I do," Willie said.

"Well then." He slid the contract papers over and turned them round. From his vest pocket he took out a pen, bent over, and began to write. "Party of the second part shall retain his soul."

"Intact," Willie said.

"Intact," the Devil added.

"Retains his MacCrimmon soul intact," Willie dictated. "MacCrimmon continuing Presbyterian soul intact should he and his rink skunk the Devil's rink."

Old Cloutie finished the amendment and looked up to Willie.

"The match to be curled on our own ice, of course."

"All right with me."

"And not to be binding on any other member of my rink, you understand."

"Of course."

"Well, get it down there."

The Devil did that.

"And it'll have to be curled on a Sabbath evening!"

"I curl *only* on the Sabbath," the Devil said.

"It's agin the bylaw here in Shelby, thanks to Reverend Pringle and others. But I'm sure we can arrange it."

"There." The Devil shoved the papers over to Willie. "I've initialled all the changes and signed." He handed Willie his pen, warm as his curling boots had been. "Please do the same."

Willie examined the papers intently, then initialled and signed and slid them back to Cloutie, who began separating them into two clusters. He handed one of them to Willie. "Original for you. Carbon for me."

"That figgers," said Willie.

"My boots?"

"I'll get to them immediately. Done by Sabbath next."

"They must be. Next Sabbath it is. You've exchanged a good bargain for a bad one, Willie MacCrimmon."

"We'll see. In four days."

27

Dear Mr. Manning . . .

On January 13, 1965, W. O. (looking very much as he does in the accompanying photo) appeared on CBC Television's "Across Canada" and read the following open letter to Premier Ernest Manning. It had come to the attention of two Social Credit cabinet ministers, A. J. Hooke and R. H. McKinnon, that the University of Alberta curriculum included Ferlinghetti's A Coney Island of the Mind and Salinger's The Catcher in the Rye. Hooke and McKinnon attempted to have the books banned. W. O. subsequently often "shared these passionate thoughts on book censorship" with his audiences.

This letter became particularly appropriate in the 1970s and 1980s when Who Has Seen the Wind was banned by various school boards in British Columbia and New Brunswick. His final line, preceded by a long pause and sweet grin, is especially popular.

꿍

High River, Alberta
January 13, 1965

Mr. Ernest C. Manning
Premier of Alberta
Edmonton, Alberta

Dear Mr. Manning,

I am a playwright and novelist and I am concerned about two of your cabinet ministers. Just two. The honourable R. H. McKinnon, Minister of Education, and the honourable A. J. Hooke, Minister of Municipal Affairs. They've been attacking literature, specifically J. D. Salinger's book, *The Catcher in the Rye*. They've called this book "trash literature," "filth," "junk," "literary garbage."

Perhaps you may know about this. But you may not know that I am a genuine Albertan and novelist, living in the foothills south of Calgary. And I have tried to create an illusion of life in my art so that my novels have included, of necessity, elements and expressions that your ministers, Mr. Hooke and Mr. McKinnon, should have called immoral. They should have called my work trash, filth, junk, literary garbage. Well, they haven't. And I want to bring it to your attention. It's unfair that they should show such arrant favouritism towards Mr. Salinger who isn't even a Canadian – let alone an Albertan. I feel quite slighted that Mr. McKinnon and Mr. Hooke haven't lashed out at my work and expressed some horror at the immoral elements in it. My books are in our schools and I think that if literary filth is to have official governmental recognition it should come first to our own Canadian trash before that imported from other countries or provinces.

I'm sure there has been simply an oversight. Mr. McKinnon and Mr. Hooke are busy men conducting the complex and extremely difficult tasks of their cabinet posts. So they haven't a great deal of time for reading books – as well as *Reader's Digest*. I don't see why they picked on Mr. Salinger, Mr. Manning. He's made no mention whatsoever of Social Credit in *The Catcher in the Rye*. This has hurt me. A writer is known by the enemies he makes as well as by the friends he keeps. And as a serious artist I don't want any sensitive or discerning reader to make the assumption that my work would, or could, appeal to Mr. Hooke or Mr. McKinnon.

I hope you can set this right so these two ministers of yours may take aim on the filth and garbage and junk in my books, next. Soon.

Love,

W. O. Mitchell

A month later W. O. was moved to write Premier Manning another love-letter – this time about some of his government's discriminatory attitudes and policies. The Social Credit government had used its Communal Properties Act to prohibit a number of Hutterite colonies from buying land.

High River

February 22, 1965

Mr. Ernest C. Manning
Premier of Alberta
Edmonton, Alberta

Dear Mr. Manning:

I saw you on television last week and simply had to write – though I'm afraid you may get the idea that I'm a compulsive writer. I am a *writer* – a novelist living in the foothills south of Calgary and I would like to commend the way in which you answered your critics on the matter of electoral distribution in our province – by saying you didn't consider it your responsibility – and that Alberta takes a back seat to not one other province in having an unbalanced distribution of her voting representation. I liked your quiet patience and charity towards all the news media who attribute anti-Semitism to you, who accuse you of saying that an opposition is unnecessary to the democratic way of government. The picture came through clearly and sincerely of the most misquoted public figure on the North American continent today.

It was not fair of you, however, to say that your minister Mr. Hooke couldn't possibly have summed up the Hutterite situation by saying, "some people say that it would be like letting a pack of starving dogs off their leashes." If a man can come up with a startling and provocative simile like this, he should receive credit for it. This is so much more vivid than the expression used in the deep south – of our Province – when people say, "Them Hooterites is swarmin' again." It is so generous of Mr. Hooke to contradict the canard that Hooterites are a form of *insect* life; how much better to grant that they are vertebrates.

While I am writing you I would like to comment on your earlier statement that you have "grave" doubts about the value of anti-discrimination legislation. I hope that this is not a misquotation. I liked your forthright answer to these charges – the way you threw the gauntlet at their feet when you said, "I challenge any person who implies that people in Alberta suffer from discrimination."

I keep thinking of the Hutterites whom Mr. Hooke compares so aptly to starving dogs. Some might feel that there is a case for discrimination here, but as you point out – this law was put in effect for their *own* good – to protect them from the hard feeling and passions of people at war. How foresighted to keep it in force for twenty years after the war is over – in preparation for any *new* war that might break out. And as you have said yourself – they are not *suffering* from it. They've had four and a half centuries of persecution by experts – so that actually they *love* discrimination. I am sure that the Communal Properties Act must be a great spiritual comfort to them, and the prohibitive decisions of your Cabinet must be a source of healing assurance, convincing them of our good will and good fellowship towards a minority group. It must soothe their inner tumult to read your statement: "There is nothing that prevents Hutterites from pursuing their way of life. I would fight for their rights to the very last ditch."

Love,
W. O. Mitchell

28

ↄⱺↄ

King Motherwell

In this sequence of scenes from How I Spent My Summer Holidays (1981), *Hugh, the central character, has returned to his home town after a long absence. His walk out onto the prairie to visit the old swimming hole triggers memories from over fifty years before about King Motherwell, his childhood hero. King is a kind of adult Holden Caulfield, a "catcher in the rye" who attempts to protect children from falling into the world of adult experience. He is particularly suspicious of would-be adult guardians whose lies betray the vulnerable young.*

ↄⱺↄ

It was almost twenty years since I had been back there when I returned for my town's fiftieth birthday in August of 1962. It was shocking to find that it had grown so, well beyond Sadie Rossdance's and right out to the edge of the Mental Hospital grounds. Yet so much had been

224

condensed – our own house, the distance from it to downtown, the Little Souris River. I walked out Government Road, now surprisingly paved, as far as the Mental Hospital. Those red-brick buildings seemed as large as I remembered them and the ground plantings of poplar saplings, which had resembled slender binder whips when I was a boy, had actually grown into tall bluffs of trees.

I climbed under the barbed-wire fence and walked across what had once been Muhlbier land. It was unchanged, for whoever farmed it now kept it as pasture.

Even as I began to walk towards the river, I realized that I was on a time return. It was the same wind as the wind of my boyhood, still careless in the prairie grass, like the braided whisper that sighed restlessly through our classrooms. Maybe it wasn't the wind but the grasshoppers, stirred by my feet to leap ahead of me and drift sideways on the wind, that carried me with them in a memory loop back to Sir Raleigh School. And Mr. Mackey.

For a moment it was difficult to find any relationship at all between our principal and grasshoppers, and then I remembered; *consequences*. I did not like the word as a boy. Mr. Mackey did.

"Any boy found carving his initials on the desks – any boy found on the school grounds in possession of a slingshot – any boy caught using the tin fire-escape as a plaything – will have to suffer the consequences." There it was: consequences were something to be *suffered*; our lives had been mined with them so that all pleasures must be followed by an explosion of unpleasant consequences.

At the beginning of each school year Mr. Mackey would line us up in the hallway, both sexes from Grade One to Grade Eight, to listen to his ant-and-grasshopper speech. After the grasshopper had wasted his summer in sloth and fun to die of starvation, Mr. Mackey went on to tell us of the ant society with its queen and warriors and workers and males and slaves, each caste with its own duty to perform. Each one of us too, he said, had his own obligation to the others.

Eight times I heard him explain that obligation formed a great ladder in our own society. Boys and girls were on the bottom rung. We had obligation to each other at work and at play; we owed it next to our family and parents, to our teachers and our school, then to our Province and its Premier, our country and its Prime Minister, William Lyon Mackenzie King, and the whole scarlet British Empire and our monarch. God stood on the top rung. Ascending this Aristotelian obligation ladder purified us, by refining us of all child matter. Mr. Mackey was there to see that we did not miss a single rung. Or else.

In the summer of 1924, we got a different slant on the ant and the grasshopper from King Motherwell, who owned the Royal Pool Hall. King had taken a swim with Lobbidy and Angus and Musgrave and Peter and me. We had come out to dry off in the early June sun and Lobbidy didn't realize till it was too late that he was sitting on an ant colony and got stung on both cheeks and the backs of his legs. When we had helped him brush the last ant off and he had dived in and come out again and picked another place to sit down and we had quit laughing, King said, "Which side are you fellows on, anyway? The grasshopper or the ant?"

That was an easy one for me to answer, because even when Mr. Mackey was giving his ant-and-grasshopper speech, I had secretly been pulling for the grasshopper. "Grasshopper."

"Ant," Musgrave said.

"Yeah," King said. "Most ants are Baptist or Methodist." That shut Musgrave up.

"Grasshoppers don't bite you," Lobbidy said.

"Which one are you going to be when you grow up, Hughie?" King asked me.

That was harder for me to answer. I always got a lovely lift when a grasshopper bunged and planed and clicketed ahead of me, and there was something quite friendly about an insect that would let you gently squeeze its abdomen and would obligingly spit tobacco juice on the back of your hand. But at the same time a grasshopper had no sense of consequences or obligation. "I wouldn't want to freeze or starve to death in winter."

"So you're willing to bust your ass working – lugging and pushing and rolling and pulling loads ten thousand times heavier than you are – every day of your life?"

"Better than starving to death when winter comes, isn't it?"

"If you're a worker ant you figure you'll live to see that winter?"

"Well – sure . . ."

"You won't. What's the life expectancy of an ant – except for the queen?"

"Search me."

"Three months. They're asking you to spend your entire life with no fun at all because of a promise that you will live through a winter you will not see because you're going to die of old age before first snow-fall – anyway."

That wasn't the end of it, because we argued about how long a working day the average ant put in and whether or not an ant even slept.

King Motherwell just about cancelled Mr. Mackey out.

Excepting my father and mother, I suppose that King Motherwell and William S. Hart were the two people who marked me most in boyhood. And Peter Deane-Cooper. But of the three, King's print on me has faded least. Quite uninvited the memory of him has returned to me again and again.

I can still summon him easily. At first I cannot see him, but I can feel his hands making a steady stirrup under my right foot. I am facing him, my own hands at his shoulders, in towards the column of his neck. The cords tighten; his hands lift me up with a powerful upward thrust and I am arching into a back dive or balling up in a backward somersault into the muddy Little Souris. Then there comes to me the escargot taste and smell of the river in the back of my throat and nostrils.

Still I cannot see him, but I can see his left hand, fingers fanned with just their tips touching the green felt, the thumb veeing out from the first knuckle while the cue slides forward to stop a fraction of an inch short of the white ball, then again, the butt of the cue held so delicately between thumb and forefinger, back and forth like a child's toe dragged under an idling swing.

No one could beat him at snooker or billiards or fluke or pea pool or the golf game they played a lot. No one could beat him at anything, in his pool hall, in the trenches in France, where he won all his medals, or on the ice at the Arena rink, where he played goal for the Trojans. I can see him quite clearly, goal skates clumping on wood down the narrow chute to the ice, with an awkward shoulder swagger because of the wide leg-pads with their coal-scuttle tops. I can see him reach over and down to unlatch the gate, step down onto the ice, and shove himself out of all awkwardness and into a slow and metronomic rock around the rink, the fat goal-stick held over his shoulder like a rifle. All the others follow him past the advertisements on the boards: McConkey's Drugs with its mortar and pestle, Crozier's Men's Wear, Nightingale's Funeral Home, Firmstone's Department Store, Riddle's Shoe and Harness, R. W. Cavanaugh's Livery Stables, Marshall's Garage, Co-op Creamery, Isbister Sash and Door. The Trojan colours were the same as the Boston Bruins': chocolate-and-gold socks and sweaters and toques; King doesn't wear a toque, instead he has a khaki wool Balaclava. God, how the dirty-playing Melville Millionaires and the city-arrogant Regina Aces and the Weyburn Beavers of the Saskatchewan Senior Hockey League must have hated the very sight of that old Balaclava.

If we didn't see King on the Arena ice in winter we saw him in the Royal Pool Hall. It was his. Pool halls were not considered the place for children; indeed I believe there was some sort of law that said it was criminal to enter one if you were under sixteen. But it was all right with King if we came into his pool hall between McConkey's Drugs and Riddle's Shoe and Harness; most of us went in there a lot, almost as often as we did into Chan Kai's Bluebird Café, next to my father's print shop where he published *The Gleaner*. In both King's and Chan's we could cash in empty pop bottles or use them as money. King didn't have ice-cream cones or cent candy the way Chan did, but he did have ginger ale and Coca-Cola and lemon and lime and Orange Crush, and Sweet Marie and Oh Henry! chocolate bars. He would also accept gopher tails in payment.

Entering King's pool hall was a lot like diving under water, dim and cool. "They built it before they invented plate glass," King said. The windows were just like ordinary house windows with square, small panes; as well, King had the blinds pulled to keep summer out; the only inside illumination came from the overhead lights and bounced off the green felt of four tables down the long, low, submarine cave. The whole place smelled of Wild Root hair tonic and Tiger Balm, cigarette and cigar smoke, and was ripe with the chewing-tobacco smell trumpeted from all the brass spittoons. Fig and molasses.

Once your eyes had adjusted, the first person you saw was usually Leon, working on a customer in one of the chairs to the right, or bent over the sink, or turning away from it with a steaming towel hammocked between his hands. If business were slow he would be sitting in one of his own barber chairs and reading. Usually the Bible. Leon was Holy Roller. He was doctor-pure in the white jacket he wore; he also wore an incredibly black wig that parted right down the middle and arced over his forehead like the wings of a gliding crow. I did not think that a wig, or having to wear one, was very funny; but in Leon's case it did seem ironic, for, being a barber, he should have been able to buy the best wig going. Wholesale. He should also have been able to get decent clippers that could trim your sides and neck less painfully than an attack of fire ants. I was spared them until I was eight, when my father took me in for my first professional haircut; if my mother had had her way I suppose I would have had Buster Brown haircuts and worn a middy until I was seventeen. Eight had been unforgivably late.

Unless he was in the rummy room at the back or on one of his runs over the border into Montana, King sat on a high stool with twisted wire criss-crossing between its legs; it was set behind the glass counter where he collected from the players for games or cigarettes or plugs, and now and again a cigar out of the boxes with dark Latin ladies on their lids. There were things below the counter-top that a child could buy: staghorn jackknives, mouth organs, and clay pipes that cost only a cent and were good for blowing bubbles, though their stems robbed your lips and tongue, your whole mouth, of all saliva. Unpleasantly. They could be smoked, once charged with dried Virginia-creeper leaves or corn tassels or tea, when you were young – Macdonald fine-cut or Old Chum when you were older. Except for their shorter stems these clay pipes were like the one being smoked in the Old Chum poster by the jolly old English squire in his white wig and square glasses, sitting with his plump, buttoned belly on his spread knees in the sun before an English pub. The stem on his clay pipe was grace-fully curved and at least four feet long. On the wall above and behind King there was a constellation of lacrosse and baseball and hockey team pictures, with fellows in their uniforms kneeling and sitting and standing. You could find King in every one of them. Also Eddie Crozier. But not in uniform; he was just the manager of the Trojans.

Just under the ceiling of pressed-tin squares with acanthus leaves and rosettes, a shelf ran almost the whole length of that side of the pool hall. King had probably put it up there himself with angled metal brackets for the life-size ducks and geese with their necks bolt upright or snaked out in the feeding position. King had carved them all.

He seemed to carve them mostly during the winter months, finding them again in blocks of pine after they'd flown south. Cedar wouldn't do, he said, because it wouldn't take and hold the detail the way pine would, and besides, pine was nicer to work with, more satisfying, the way it seemed to declare itself when carved.

When he carved he wore a celluloid visor so that the upper half of his face was shaded green and when he started out he would have his carving arm at full length out from himself, the block down at his thighs as he began to impose the rough beginnings of form. At the last he would have it clutched up to his chest, the knife handle almost swallowed in his hand, its tip digging and etching the feather detail.

"Pintail, this one." He held it out over the counter towards Lobbidy and me one time. "Pointy ass – wings set so far back on them compared to a mallard. Almost like they got no ass at all. Easy to tell pintails in the air. Out of the bigger ones. Any idiot can tell a teal or a butterball because they're so small."

He carved all the ducks there were: canvasbacks, spoonbills, buffleheads, mergansers, and even wood ducks, though there weren't any of those ever in our part of the world. He once showed me a dear little bluewinged teal he had just painted. "Just your size, Hughie. I'll carve you one some day." I would have preferred a harlequin or a Canada honker. I also coveted the pictures of well-bred dogs playing poker, the gentlemanly collie, the pert, card-cheating terrier, the cynical pit bull. The sad but dignified Saint Bernard, with pince-nez glasses, looked exactly like Judge Hannah. For that matter, the terrier looked a lot like Eddie Crozier.

I cannot recall ever hearing King truly blasphemous or obscene. Once when Peter and I were in the pool hall, Hilton Fraser missed an easy eight ball on the third table and started cursing. Among other things, he said there was no way he could get those "cock-suckers" into pockets that were "mean, skinny little cunts!" King didn't even go round the end of the counter. He bunged up off his high stool and over, grabbed Hilton by the seat of his pants and the back of his neck, and pranced him down the hall and out the front door. He told Peter and me to just finish up our pop and get out.

Out on the street after, Peter said the pockets on all four tables were micrometer-measured to professional size and that Hilton Fraser was a foul-mouthed prick anyway. It was ironic that King should be so careful of his own language and that of his players in front of kids when most of us talked dirty all the time. In his own way Austin Musgrave was the worst; he could talk dirty without using any dirty words – just ones out of the Bible.

We also saw King a lot out at the Mental hole, for like most heroes he was a magnificent swimmer; from the twenty-fourth of May to late fall he joined us often out at the Mental hole, driving his seven-passenger McLaughlin right over the bald prairie to the Little Souris. The Judge Hannahs had a seven-passenger McLaughlin too, but it wasn't maroon with yellow-spoked wheels, nor did it have the bullet-shaped little vases always filled with wildflowers King picked: crocuses in early spring, buffalo beans, brown-eyed susans, bluebells, and tiger lilies and goldenrod later on. On the two front doors he had his monogram in gold: K. S. M.

Out at the Mental hole, King went through the same ritual every time: took off his coat and sleeveless sweater and shirt, stepped out of his bell-bottom trousers and underwear, folded them and placed them on the front seat of his car, then threw himself off the bank into a long and thrusting dive to duck and roll and make the moon rise. He would come up facing most of us, lower his head so the water line reached just under his nose, then expel his breath in short, bubbling blasts – silly sounds just like angry elephant squeals. Right away he would start to swim upstream, doing the side-stroke, his left arm pulling down and along his side, the other thrown high and forward over-arm again and again with the wrist and hand loose and sloppy, yet synchronized with a scissors kick that drove him ahead in powerful surges. From the side of his face a small wave veed right out to either bank; you knew he could keep it up forever; it was as though he intended swimming all the way to the Souris and all the way to the Red and all the way to the Saskatchewan and Hudson Bay and maybe across the Atlantic to England. He could have swum the Hellespont. Easily. But only if he felt like it.

At one time or another most of us tried to follow him upstream – unsuccessfully. We all ran out of steam, the way the side-stroke took it out of you and you had to roll over onto your back to rest your arms and legs and get your wind back, and then each time you turned over,

King would be further away until you couldn't even see him any more and you climbed out onto the bank and your legs and your whole body felt just like lead.

After three or four tries that summer, I did make it, in early August when the river was low and the current almost dead. I simply stayed on my back, mainly shoving with my hands at my sides and kicking just enough to keep my body level. I didn't even know where I was till I finally rolled over to discover I was just downstream from the CPR bridge, a good mile above the Mental hole. It wasn't really a river here but a wide and shallow slough, its edges speared with bulrushes. I lowered my feet and instead of just touching with the tips of my toes, I could stand, the muddy bottom squelching up between my toes. I looked upstream and there was King under the CPR bridge. He was all covered with white foam.

I was a little worried; he hadn't invited me to follow him. He was lathering up his hair and then under his arms and then his crotch. He turned and he saw me.

"Hi."

"King."

"Wondered when you'd make it."

I didn't know he'd known I had swum after him those other times.

He reached out and tucked a bar of yellow laundry soap up into the corner where the last trestle support was, and I knew then that he always kept a bar of soap up there and when this one had thinned down he'd replace it with a fresh one. I also knew that this must be what he did every time he came swimming, which would make him just about the cleanest person in our district. In spring and summer and fall anyway.

"Easier going back – downstream."

He dived in and I could see the wide circle he swam under water to rinse himself off, suds and bubbles rising and betraying him. When he came up, his hair was parted right down the middle and hung down in two black wings, the tips at the corners of his jaw.

"Hey! You look just like Colleen Moore!"

He got me right in the chest; I should have noticed his cheeks ballooned out before he squirted me. He threw his head back and his wet hair flopped and he smoothed it down with his hands and he didn't look like Colleen Moore with her Dutch bob, but like Rudolph Valentino with his plastered pompadour and long sideburns.

He came out of the water and for a moment he was turned away from me while he reached up to the trestle again; his head tilted and held, and then he put the brown bottle back up with the soap. I guess he replaced that, too, whenever it ran out.

We went up on the bridge and sat with our legs hung over to dry off and the smell that came from him in the hot sun was both caustic and sweet: laundry soap and whiskey. Now I could get a good look at the serpent. Vein-blue and faint rust-pink and green it came out of the black bush of his pubic hair; scaled and about half as thick as my wrist, it coiled around his belly button and then up under his left nipple and across his chest to loop round his right nipple. The flat head with its almond eyes and forked tongue was cradled in the hollow of his throat just over his sternum.

"Don't you ever be stupid enough to get yourself tattooed."

I didn't realize it had been obvious to him that I was staring at his snake there.

"Understand!"

I said sure I did and I promised him I wouldn't. He didn't have to warn me. The Liar maybe. The Liar was already tattooing himself all the time by licking the end of his indelible pencil and then drawing on the backs of his hands and his forearms. The Liar could hardly wait to grow up and get to a tattoo parlour.

"I got drunk one leave."

"Did it hurt much?"

"Of course. Punch and prick you with a needle – blue dye and green and yellow – red and orange, but when that's all mixed with your own blood it doesn't show – scab forms over the whole thing – I had to sleep on my back over a week. Then the scab sloughs off and there it is."

He stood up.

"Rest of your life. Don't ever do anything you can't undo."

"Better tell the Liar that."

"Seemed like a good idea at the time." He laughed. "Another serpent crawling out of the buffalo-berry bush in the Garden of Eden." Then right away his face got serious. "Let's go." He started down off the bridge. "Not just tattoos either."

Swimming back he must have slowed down deliberately for me because we stayed side by side halfway to the Mental hole, then he suggested we get out and rest for a few minutes. We did, but as soon as we sat down on the bank, he got up and walked over to a big clump of rosebush and bent over it. When he came back the fruity smell of the whiskey was much stronger.

We didn't say anything for a while, just sat, King with his elbows on his knees and his arms hanging loose. The smell of sage was strong and there must have been mint nearby; it was too early yet for wolf willow.

"You know – there aren't just ten commandments," King said. "They must have over a hundred of them by now. Thou shalt not smoke. Thou shalt not drink. Thou shalt not wear rouge or lipstick or open galoshes or yellow slicker raincoats. Thou shalt not have a cootie-catcher hairdo. Thou shalt not fart. Hell – more like a thousand, and the funny thing is they didn't even need them – all they needed was the one commandment."

"What one?"

"Thou shalt not have fun. Covers nearly everything, doesn't it? Not official – doesn't say in the Bible Moses went up on that mountain and there was a bolt of lightning and he found *eleven* graven tablets and there it was on that eleventh one – in Hebrew – ancient Hebrew – thou shalt not have fun! I had my way he would have found a twelfth tablet up there while he was at it!"

"What twelfth?"

"My commandment! My own! There has been too much thou-shalt-notting going on all through all the centuries of man and all of this thou-shalt-notting has got to stop. Kingsley Spurgeon Motherwell's commandment is: 'Thou shalt not – shalt not.' *I* shalt not – that's all right – but no more of this 'Thou shalt not. Thou shalt not – *thou* shalt not.'"

I have never known anyone who made me laugh as much as King did – not clown laugh-making or boob laugh-making the way the Liar always tried to do. Unsuccessfully. King would tell you that something was enough to give a gopher's ass the heartburn, that H. B. Critchley, who managed the Home Bank, was tighter than a cow's ass in fly time and wouldn't pay a dime to see a piss ant eat a bale of hay. King did not seem to approve of too many adults.

But this time in the car he wasn't talking all that funny; it was one of the few times I ever heard him talk about the war.

"You believe what they said Cecil Rhodes said – on his deathbed?"

"I got no idea what they said he said."

"'So much to do – so little time.' He rared up on his deathbed and those were his last words. 'So much to do – so little time.' You believe he said that?"

"If they said he said it – maybe he said it."

"He didn't."

"How do you know he didn't?"

"I been there."

"Cecil Rhodes' deathbed!"

"Other ones. My partner, Merv, when he got it – I was right beside him. Shell hole, trench mortar – right in the belly. You could see his intestines just like a ball of garter-snakes all wove together in the spring. You think he lifted up onto his elbow and he said, 'So much to do – so little time'? Famous last words said by Corporal Mervin Herbig, lineman for Saskatchewan Telephone Company out of Moose Jaw. You believe that's what he said with his last dying breath? Nope. Oh, sure, he did *try* to lift up on one elbow, but he didn't have the strength left to do that and keep his guts in. I heard him – plain as day – he said, 'Aw horse shit!'"

I believed that.

"When people are dying they haven't time to get off good last words – unless maybe they decided ahead of time what they were going to say for their famous last words. They should. They owe it to the rest of the world. When famous people are dying there's always a lot of people hanging around waiting to hear what their famous last words will be – pencil and paper all ready to take it down – or make it up. Of all people you'd think Queen Victoria would have been ready, but she wasn't. She didn't look up to all those ladies-in-waiting round her bed and say, 'We are not amused.' Oh, she tried to all right but her teeth were in a glass on the night-stand by the bed, so she just had to settle for a fart – one last long whispery old-age royal fart."

"You decided what yours are going to be?"

"Mmm-hmh."

"What?"

"I get the chance – I'll say: 'Time to piss on the fire and call the dog.'"

He started up the McLaughlin. "Ought to do it."

He let me out at home.

29

Never Settle for Anything Less

In this closing episode of The Kite, Shelby and district gather at the community centre to honour Daddy Sherry on his one-hundred-and-eleventh birthday. David Lang, the Toronto journalist who has now spent a few weeks in Shelby researching his article on Daddy, has been boarding with Helen Maclean and her mother, Mrs. Clifford. David has befriended Keith, Helen's young son, and shown him how to make a kite for his birthday gift for Daddy, his great-great-grandfather. The town has selected a special gift for Daddy which, with great difficulty, has been kept a secret – Daddy's shameless attempts to wheedle or bribe it out of various people, including Keith, have failed. Not too far under the comic picaresque surface of The Kite lies W. O.'s very serious existentialist vision of human mortality and how to be.

Keith had given a delighted Daddy the kite at noon; the old man had been for flying it right away, but Belva Louise Tinsley had been successful in persuading him to postpone it till after the official ceremony, which was to start at three o'clock. When David, with Helen and Keith and Mrs. Clifford, arrived at the community centre a half hour early, they found the streets lined with trucks and cars for blocks in every direction; only the Activarians' five-card bingo the spring before had drawn more people. Town and country had turned out in full force to honour Daddy Sherry; in the ante-room filled with people waiting to go into the main body of the hall, men stood, tight of collar, with weight on one foot and hands in pockets, beside hair-slicked sons with weight on one foot and hands in pockets; mothers vaguely distracted in their best, tried to keep an eye on children playing informal tag through the forest of adult legs; older daughters in tartan skirts, nylons, woollen sweaters, now and again touched fingers tenderly to deliberately casual curls from Chez Sadie's or home permanent kits.

As David walked down a side aisle with Helen and Keith and Mrs. Clifford through the lemon pungency of sweeping compound, the bitterness of countless shoes polished for just this occasion, he saw that a long row of chairs stood on the stage; the table waiting in their centre held a glass and water-pitcher. They formed a half-circle about Daddy's shrouded birthday gift rearing up with all the salience of a prairie grain elevator. The gestalt of chairs and sheeted monolith suggested solemn ceremony to come; something profound would be acted out here – not a declaration of war, not a coronation, not the passing of a death sentence, the granting of a charter, or the conferring of a degree, not marriage or baptism; something of great import would be placed before the consciousness of all gathered in the hall; a higher reality than that normally sensed without ritual was to be revealed.

Florence Allerdyce had risen from her seat near the steps up to the stage; she went to the piano. As she spun the stool it shrieked; there came a preparatory shuffling of feet, a coughing and clearing of throats. She raised her hands in high warning over the keys; the hall filled with the concerted creak and scrape and knock of people rising. Mrs. Allerdyce's hands fell unerringly on the opening chords of "O Canada."

. The audience had hardly settled back in their seats when Mayor Fraser strode out of the wings. Behind him, supported by Mr. Spicer and Harry Richardson, came a bent and shuffling Daddy Sherry, elbows up and out, cane dangling free. Though the barber and the doctor eased him towards the chair intended for him, he took Mayor Fraser's, who was forced to pre-empt the one meant for Dr. Richardson; this in turn caused some shuffling, rather like an abortive game of musical chairs, among the other Druids: Canon Wilton-Breigh, Father O'Halloran, the Reverend Finlay, Urban Coldtart, President of the Farmers' Union, Mr. Oliver, school board chairman, and the provincial Minister of Economic Activity and Cultural Affairs.

Mayor Fraser opened the ceremony by welcoming all those from near and far who had come to do honour to Daddy Sherry. He called first upon the Minister of Economic Activity and Cultural Affairs to speak. The gentleman did so for half an hour, using Daddy as a spring-board opportunity to mention the great material advance made in the last twenty-five years of Daddy's life, those years being the length of time his party had been in power in the province. He came back to Daddy Sherry at the end of his talk by announcing the govern-ment's selection of Shelby as the site for a hundred-and-twenty-thousand-dollar old folks' residence to be known as the John Felix Sherry Twilight Lodge. He sat down amid enthusiastic applause, and was followed by Canon Wilton-Breigh. The Canon's address was beautifully balanced, and the biographic detail of Daddy's life, accu-rate; he had checked his dates and facts with Helen Maclean the week before; yet what was intended as a tribute had the sad flavour of eulogy. When the Canon's precise British voice had finished, Mayor Fraser rose to speak.

This, David was sure, must be the finest Fraser vintage, a rolling style of platform oratory with the sonorous rise and fall of short, deliberate periods. He established first that Daddy was a living symbol; he was older indeed than Canada itself; he joined the present and the future of his country; he reminded them of the hopes and the prides and the ideals Canadians had shared since Confederation, through war and peace and rebellion, through drought and adversity and prosperity.

David's attention was drawn to a dark-banged little girl who had materialized in the aisle beside him. Perhaps four years old, she stared up to him. He smiled at her; she turned and ran towards the stage, her starched skirt holding out stiffly from bare legs. At the front, just under the stage, she stopped, stood hesitant with the tie ribbons dangling from her bonnet, discovered the audience and, with face stricken, fled back down the aisle. David returned his attention to Mayor Fraser, now thanking those people whose generous and unselfish co-operation had made this day possible: committee members, presidents, vice-presidents, secretaries, delegates of Shelby Rotary, the Activarians, the Eastern Star, the Knights of the Loyal Order of Homesteaders, the Chief Poundmaker Chapter of the IODE, Mothers of the Maple Leaf . . .

David could tell that Mayor Fraser was coming to the end of his address, that after the presentation was made, the ceremony would be over. Already he could see that Merton Spicer was holding a watch on his upturned hand, had quite likely synchronized it with the shrouded grandfather clock, would give a prearranged signal to Mayor Fraser so that he could trim the end of his talk to coincide with the time the clock would be striking the hour. And now that the end was so near, David was disappointed; there was going to be no insight into the puzzle of Daddy's individuality this afternoon.

Mr. Spicer's right hand jerked up. Mayor Fraser paused. Urban Coldtart rose from his chair and stepped over beside the sheeted clock, encircling its waist with an arm.

". . . and now," Mayor Fraser was saying, "we come to the most important part of this afternoon's celebration." He nodded to the barber, who leaned over to Harry Richardson. Both men rose and stepped to either side of Daddy. David had never seen the old man rise from a chair as quickly as he did now. Between the doctor and the barber he walked in almost sprightly fashion across the stage to stop before the clock and Urban Coldtart.

". . . the senior citizen of our Province – of our nation – of the whole world – we deem it a privilege and an honour to make this presentation to him – material testimony of the high spiritual regard in which we hold him. . . ."

An event of great import throbbed here, David knew; and all the waiting people round him knew what it was to be. Daddy did not know; the inspiring secret to be disclosed when Urban pulled the string was not Daddy's any more than it was that of the lamb or the maid or the youth. All took part together in the propitiation of the god of mortality. Never in his hundred and eleven years of life had Daddy propitiated this particular god, nor did he now, passive in this display.

Watch in hand, the barber signalled Urban Coldtart. Urban snapped the string that held the sheet. The sheet fell away. The clock, sweetly and deliberately, struck four. As the last note died away the audience released its pent breath in unison and burst into applause.

For a moment it looked as though Daddy was overcome by the gift; he sagged against Doctor Richardson, but had straightened again before the applause was over.

High and wild the old man's scream shrilled through the hall. "Eye-yigh-eeeeeeeeeeeee! Graaaaan-dad-dy clock! Why in hell did you do that to me for!"

As the cane came up it caught Merton Spicer under the chin, then whipped through the air to smash the glass face; the clock teetered visibly for long seconds, and Urban Coldtart might have saved it if Daddy had not launched himself upon it; the weight of his body behind his shoulder knocked it toppling free of Urban's grasp. It might yet have been saved had the Minister of Economic Activity and Cultural Affairs been a shade quicker of wit and less concerned for his own safety; the parliamentary shoulder arrested the clock's descent for just a moment as the minister leaped aside. The age-dry case burst apart with the multiple, cracking explosion of an entire package of firecrackers ignited all together.

And with unsporting fury Daddy had leaped forward, to stamp it and beat it again and again with his cane as though it were a deadly snake coiled and reluctantly dying on the community centre stage. No one stepped forward to stay him; he did not stop his swinging and knee-high destruction until the clock was junk dead.

"Bad day – I say – one of his bad days," Mr. Spicer was heard to mutter with sad charity just as the stage curtains began to close.

"Good day," Daddy was saying as he and Keith and David walked over to the empty field behind the power house. "Had a real good day the way I oughta on my birthday. Except for that goddam clock. . . ."

"I figured you were having a bad day," Keith said. He held the kite high, its tail gathered up in his other hand.

"I have whatever I want," Daddy said. "Why'd I have a bad day on my birthday party?"

"Smashing that grandfather clock . . ."

"I hate clocks," Daddy said with intensity. "They'd told me ahead of time then I'd told them. Leakin', nasty, bullyin' things!"

"What do you mean – leakin'?" David said.

"Leak the seconds an' hours an' days," Daddy said.

"But you have a clock in your house," David said.

"I don't. Belvah has – 'lectric one over the stove in the kitchen. I never look at it. I ignored 'em for the past thirty years. Oh – an' she's got her alarm clock in her room. Me – I ain't got no – I don't want no loud tickin' clock – tricklin' away my time for me! I hate clocks an' watches – cuckoo clocks – wag-on-the-wall clocks – anniversary clocks – fryin'-pan clocks. I don't even like sundials or egg timers."

He picked his way over the grass, leaning heavily on David's arm. "Served 'em right! Hold up a bit – not so fast. We got lots of time left yet to fly her."

They rested for a few minutes, until Daddy's breath came more evenly, then continued towards a rock in the centre of the open field. "Aaaaaah – I love kites though."

They stopped by the rock. "All right," David said to Keith, "you hold it up." He took the string stick from the boy. "I'll pay out the string while you hold it up and run with it – after we've unwound quite a bit of it. You'll have to run some distance – light breeze like this . . ."

"I know." The shortness with which Keith answered him caused David to look quickly down to him; he surprised a look of ill-concealed impatience on the boy's face. There was no attempt to hide it, for it was an excluding impatience, the only way in which the very young could let the very adult know that they were interfering selfishly.

"Sorry," he said. "Of course you know – here . . ." He handed Keith the ball of kite string. "Let me have the kite and you take the string – just shout when you start to run and I can let go. . . ."

"Who the hell's kite is it?"

Daddy's simian face was thrusting raw annoyance at David. "Sorry," David said again and handed the kite over to Daddy.

The old man held it up and out before himself, waited for Keith to back up a hundred feet or more, the string stick spinning under his thumbs as it unwound. Keith turned away, held the stick up over his head. "All right, Daddy – let her go!" He charged upwind.

The kite left Daddy's hand, tail snaking along the ground beneath it, weaving softly as though to feel out the indecisive wind. Quite obviously it did not have life of its own, was kept up only by the running boy. The wind was not quite strong enough for the big kite, David thought; he felt as though he were watching artificial respiration without much hope.

Keith flagged; the kite sank closer to the earth that would catch it and still it; looking back over his shoulder, he put on a spurt of speed;

the kite lifted only to sink still lower, its tip clearing the sod just by inches. It could be, David thought, that the tail was too long and heavy for it, but even as he wondered, weight seemed to melt from the kite. Almost immediately David felt the breeze cooling against his cheek. Smoothly the kite lifted, hesitated, shaking impatiently, then climbed again.

"Quit your runnin', boy!" Daddy called. "She's sailin' good now!"

Keith turned and stood with eyes uplifted to the kite hanging almost straight over him. Even as he walked back to Daddy and David it gave no indication of sinking.

"Gimme your arm."

David helped Daddy as he lowered himself to the ground, leaned his back against the great rounded side of the rock embedded in the earth there.

"Here you are, Daddy." Keith held out the stick to the old man.

For several moments the three sat silently on the grass, staring up to the kite. "Let out more string, Daddy," Keith said. "I only unwound a couple hundred feet of it."

Daddy released the pressure on his thumbs and the stick began to twirl. The kite sagged, began to fall. Daddy clamped down his thumbs; the kite took heart, soared upwards once more. Alternately the old man held and released the string thinning from the stick. Before half the string was out the kite had found the higher, stronger wind so that Daddy could unwind without stopping, the kite climbing persistently with no altitude loss whatever, yearning ever upwards, shrinking with distance till finally the stick was bare, the kite a high stamp pasted against the cloudless sky.

"That there," Daddy said, "outa all the birthdays I ever had – an' outa all the presents I ever got on 'em – is the nicest one of all. Thanks."

"Okay," Keith said.

"Look at her up there – hangin' steady – pullin' real strong on this string. . . ."

"I made it myself," Keith said, "mainly – Mr. Lang showed me how."

"I know – I know. She's a nice balanced kite – steady." He gave a long pull at the string. "See that –"

"What?" Keith said.

"Never even dodged." He pulled on the string again. "Strong – she's a strong one. Before we put her up again we got to take at least a foot off of that tail – then she'll be strong an' she'll be steady an' she'll be acerobatic too." He pulled on the string. "When I do that she oughta loop the loop an' she don't. Aaaaaah – she's a lovely kite – maybe not even a foot off – half a foot might do it. . . ."

David was only half-listening to the old man, for suddenly his attention had turned inwards. Now he knew what it was that Daddy had for him – the astonishingly simple thing the old man had to say – and had said through the hundred and eleven years of his life – between the personal deeds of his birth and his death, knowing always that the string was thin – that it could be dropped – that it could be snapped. He had lived always with the awareness of his own mortality.

There were thousands of ways of holding the string, David realized: gently, tenderly, fearfully, bravely, stubbornly, carelessly, foolishly. Some dropped it without warning; others were given terrible vision ahead to the time that they must drop it soon. With some it was knocked from their grasp by another; through the ages many men had engaged in contests to knock it from each other's grasp; states broke it regularly with rope or poison gas or knife or bullet. With dance and chant and taboo and ritual, with fairy tale and song and picture and statue, with pattern of word and note and colour and conduct, they tried to insist that they did not hang on simply for the blind sake of hanging on. It was for such a short time that the string was held by anyone. For most of his hundred and eleven years Daddy had known that, and knowing it, with his own mortality for a touchstone, he had refused to settle for less. Quite simple after all. Time and death and Daddy Sherry insisted: never settle for anything less.

David saw Helen then, coming over the field to them; with a thrill of excitement he knew that he must tell her, not now but before he left, or perhaps when he had come back to Shelby again.

Neither Keith nor Daddy took their eyes from the kite as Helen reached them, sat down on the grass beside David. He put his arm round the shoulder of the woman he knew had never settled for less.

"Out of limbo," he said to himself, "for both of us."

"Aaaah – some day – some day." The old man's head lay back against the rock so that the raddled face thrust upwards. Wind stirred the white gossamer hair but the face beneath was rigidly stilled; nose and chin and the domed lids of the closed eyes in their raccoon dark wells, possessed coffin prominence. "Some day – let her go – let her go. . . ."

The great knuckled hands held the string in a talon clutch as they rested on Daddy's knees; they had simply to relax and the kite would sag and faint and bewildered fall to earth.

Daddy's eyes opened; he yanked on the string violently. "Loop-the-loop you weavin' son of a hunyack! Here." He held out the stick to Keith. "Keep her up there. Keep her up there forever." He laid his head back against the rock again and closed his eyes.

"Aaaaaaaaaaaaaaaah . . ."

30

⌒⌒

The Wind Wings On

In this closing section of Who Has Seen the Wind, *Brian has just visited his grandmother's room. She had died a few days earlier. He recalls the day of his father's funeral, how he had been unable to cry and had walked out to the prairie where, finally, his grief found release when a meadow lark's song "splintered the stillness." When W. O. reads this piece, his phrasing, pauses, and pace accentuate the rhythms and repetition of the model he used when he was writing it, Ecclesiastes.*

⌒⌒

Outside the door of his grandmother's room, he remembered the meadow lark that had sung the day he had been unable to cry. He remembered it with an aching nostalgia that he strained to keep within himself as he went down the stairs and as he took his coat and scarf and toque from a peg in the hallway.

The freshly fallen snow protested under his feet. Why did people die? Why did they finish up? What was the good in being a human? It was awful to be a human. It wasn't any good.

Goose-grey above him, the prairie sky had a depthless softness undetermined by its usual pencil edge, melting invisibly into the spread and staring white of the land. He walked over the prairie, his ankles turning to the frozen crust of hummocking summer fallow and stubble fields. No living thing moved; and he saw only the domino tracks of jackrabbits, the sidling wells of a trotting coyote's trail, the exquisitely stamped tracks of prairie chicken. These things filled his mind against his will. Sun, glinting from a wild rosebush branch, caught his eye; looking more closely he saw that it was crowded with crystals, each one pointed and veined, all of them growing away from him. He kicked at the branch and watched the frost drop in a white shower. He looked out over the prairie again.

All kinds of people had died. They were dead and they were gone. The swarming hum of telephone wires came to him, barely perceptible in the stillness, hardly a sound heard so much as a pulsing of power felt. He looked up at rime-white wires, following them from pole to pole to the prairie's rim. From each person stretched back a long line – hundreds and hundreds of years – each person stuck up.

It had something to do with dying; it had something to do with being born. Loving something and being hungry were with it too. He knew that much now. There was the prairie; there was a meadow lark, a baby pigeon, and a calf with two heads. In some haunting way the Ben was part of it. So was Mr. Digby.

As he turned back toward the town he saw the moon pale in the afternoon sky, a grey ghost half-dissolved. And the town was dim – grey and low upon the horizon, it lay, not real, swathed in bodiless mist – quite sunless in the rest of the dazzling prairie.

Some day, he thought, perhaps when he was older than he was now, he would know; he would find out completely and for good. He would be satisfied. From the weeds tall along the barrow pit twinkling light appeared and disappeared as the sun glinted from bowed stalks and frost-blackened leaves.

Some day. The thing could not hide from him forever.

A startled jackrabbit leaped suddenly into the air ahead of him. Ears ridiculously erect, in seeking spurts now to one side, now to the other, it went bounding idiotically out over the prairie.

The day greys, its light withdrawing from the winter sky till just the prairie's edge is luminous. At one side of the night a farm dog barks; another answers him. A coyote lifts his howl, his throat line long to the dog nose pointing out the moon. A train whoops to the night, the sound dissolving slowly.

High above the prairie, platter flat, the wind wings on, bereft and wild its lonely song. It ridges drifts and licks their ripples off; it smoothens crests, piles snow against the fences. The tinting green of Northern Lights slowly shades and fades against the prairie nights, dying here, imperceptibly reborn over there. Light glows each evening where the town lies; a hiving sound is there with now and then some sound distinct and separate in the night, a shout, a woman's laugh. Clear – truant sound.

As clouds' slow shadows melt across the prairie's face more nights slip darkness over. Light, then dark, then light again. Day, then night, then day again. A meadow lark sings and it is spring. And summer comes.

A year is done.

Another comes and it is done.

Where spindling poplars lift their dusty leaves and wild sunflowers stare, the gravestones stand among the prairie grasses. Over them a rapt and endless silence lies. This soil is rich.

Here to the west a small dog's skeleton lies, its rib bones clutching emptiness. Crawling in and out of the jaw-bone's teeth an ant casts about; it disappears into an eye-socket, reappears to begin a long pilgrimage down the backbone spools.

The wind turns in silent frenzy upon itself, whirling into a smoking funnel, breathing up topsoil and tumbleweed skeletons to carry them on its spinning way over the prairie, out and out to the far line of the sky.

31

❧

"The Poetry of Life"

Since about 1960 W. O. has travelled all over Canada, the U.S.A., and Europe performing his stories in banquet halls, school rooms and gymnasiums, libraries, university auditoriums, professional theatres and concert halls. These performances were an integral part of his creative life, for audiences have always galvanized him and recharged his creative batteries. His delight in scoring with a shared laugh or a moment of emotion or of insight is obvious when he reads.

There is no better example of this than the occasion of the last piece in this collection, "The Poetry of Life" – an occasion that is partly responsible for An Evening with W. O. Mitchell. He read this piece, from a wheelchair, for the Margaret Laurence Memorial Lecture at the Writers' Union AGM in Winnipeg in June 1996. Working on this talk and delivering it, his first public performance in some time, gave him a tremendous boost.

*And what an event it was. When they wheeled W. O. onto the Winnipeg Art Gallery stage the packed auditorium immediately rose and gave him a long standing ovation. W. O. grinned and gave a clenched-fist victory gesture. He started off with an ad lib: "My father was a turn-of-the-century elocutionist, what today is called a stand-up comedian. [*LONG PAUSE AS HE TAKES A PINCH OF SNUFF.*] I'm afraid that tonight I'll have to be a sit-down comedian." And then he worked his magic.*

⁂

We writers are travellers – all travelling through time from the time that we were born till the time we reach a common destination that all mortals have. As a boy on the prairies I was filled with a feeling of sad loneliness in the fall when long wavering skeins of geese drifted high over our town, their two-note plaint floating down as I stood with face upturned to sky. I was being left behind, passed by. That same feeling visited me as I stood on the Weyburn depot platform and the porters lifted their steps to put them back into their Pullman coaches and the train released a sigh from beneath itself, then pulled away for such exotic places as Minneapolis – St. Paul – Duluth. Then finally Florida. For at the age of twelve I had contracted TB from drinking the raw milk from my Uncle Jim's farm south of Weyburn. For this reason, on a doctor's advice, my mother was taking me down to St. Petersburg where I spent four years of my adolescence.

In writing there is an element of search – not pursuing anything quite so tangible as gas or oil or their by-products – but the search is an intense and continuing one and it takes a writer through many strata of human nature. Oil and the artist's truth are where you find them. Perhaps the writer's work is more closely allied to the work of the refiner. He separates and he combines until he has what he seeks. Any artist, but particularly a writer, uses the raw material of people – feelings delicate and passion vivid – wishes and fears – hopes and disappointments – sadnesses and happinesses – nobilities and intolerances. A writer looks for and finds bits of people and experience – a nose, an ear lobe, fragments of youth and age, the way people walk or talk, eat, sleep, make love or make hate. And from these autobiographical bits of truth the writer creates his story. Every single bit is the truth, but the whole thing is a more meaningful and dramatic lie – a magic lie. Many people who are not writers do this simply for the fun of it. They're called gossips. It makes up the sort of occupation that would attract any curious, undisciplined, and lazy man – or woman. I suppose we're all three. But writing is a search which involves a selection, a separation, and then a combining again into a poem or story or novel or play which explores larger universal truths.

Like many Canadians I have had a foot in both cultures north and south of the forty-ninth parallel. Between the ages of thirteen and seventeen, south – very far south – on the Gulf of Mexico. During those years my sense of being Canadian became incandescent. Yet my sense of similarity was also vivid. Both nations belong in the same cultural bag, for both are New World societies. Because of this, both of us have to pay a higher loneliness price than Old World humans do. White Canadians and Americans, relatively speaking, have a shallow and recent past; for us our part of the earth's skin is really – still – both wild and tame. A New World child has no medieval cathedrals with soaring Gothic arches to awe and to comfort him with ancestor echo. We do not unearth Roman baths and walls and roads. Because it was Western, my generation north or south of the border was the newest of all. American or Canadian, we were the first whites to be born and stained in childhood by the prairie or the foothill or the mountain or the seashore West. It is difficult to be much newer than that – and therefore historically lonelier.

However, Minnesota or North Dakota or Montana or Manitoba or Saskatchewan or Alberta grass is older than Roman cobblestone. Our grasshoppers probably go back to John the Baptist's locusts. The peaks of the Three Sisters in the Rockies are older than the Egyptian pyramids.

I am not sure what culture is, but I do know that it has a geographic dimension and that during the early litmus years of childhood, it stains. When I was twelve I developed a tubercular wrist and was taken out of school for almost a year. It was as though – every day between nine and four – some great blackboard eraser had wiped all the kids off all the streets but missed me. In our town of Weyburn – or the Province of Saskatchewan, or Canada, or the world – I was the only kid left alive. Nobody kicking a road apple down the street. No little girls playing hopscotch or jacks. No lisping hiss of a skipping rope. All streets – wiped bare.

I would walk to the end of the street and out over the prairie with the clickety grasshoppers bunging in arcs ahead of me and I could hear the hum and twang of the wind in the great prairie harp of telephone wires. I remember looking down at the dried husk of a dead gopher crawling with ants and flies and undertaker beetles. Standing there with the total thrust of prairie sun on my vulnerable head, I guess I learned – at a very young age – that I was mortal. I *could* die – end of Billie Mitchell. And the humming, living prairie whole did not give one good god-damn about it. But my mother did, my grandmother, my brothers. And Fin, Ike, Hodder, and Fat – quite likely they did.

I guess the time you learn you're going to die is the time you really understand you are human. So – I must have learned that too at the same time.

Unfortunately, ever since the industrial revolution only those things which can be weighed, measured, calibrated, and priced are valued. Forget silly things – the song of a meadow lark, the great harp of telephone wires in a Western wind, the faint mucous trail of a snail on a leaf, the hiccoughing sound of a diving board, the pale honey scent of wolf willow by an August river-bank – all the things savoured and valued in childhood. Let's not take the arts too seriously. When I attended university here I did not. I had acted lead in the senior play at St. Petersburg Senior High. My dear mentor in Public Speaking and Drama, Miss Emily Murray, wanted me to go on to the Yale Drama

School; my mother, a nurse who worshipped doctors, did *not*. I enrolled in Medicine. The TB which had metastasized to put my right wrist in an aluminum crate with leather straps till Florida sun healed it up, exploded again in my second year. I lost all my labs; end of medical career.

I switched to arts, became a Lodge boy majoring in Philosophy. Rupert Lodge was an internationally celebrated Socratic Scholar, who made us all Platonists. My aborted medical career had been a wonderful disaster for it led to my discovery that as well as logic logic there is artistic logic, the logic which is the thematic foundation for play, poem, and novel structure. This logic, which causes a work's final meaning destination, is not limited by the logic of this and next this.

I must apologize to Rupert wherever he is now, for about thirty years ago I realized that I was no longer a Platonist dedicated to the world of the one. Actually my older son, home from his first year in university, smartened me up. He said, "Dad, you aren't a Platonist."

"Oh . . . what am I?"

"Existentialist."

"What the hell is that?"

"Absolutes balanced with the world of the many."

Till he brought it up I had never heard of existentialism. He sold me on this new school of fluid philosophy which melds both materialism and idealism, the worlds of the one and the many. So too do the illusions of art. Not for Rupert Lodge, though; he would have labelled existentialism a euphemism for pragmatic dualism. In his book on Socrates he had compared a pragmatist to a frog that hopped off the river-bank, from which he had clear and true vision of the whole, to immerse himself in the obscurity of the water. Up and down, out and in again and again. In time, I suspect I would have made the philosophical switch without my son's nudging me.

The practice of all the arts is acrobatic, not much different from being a high-wire walker, a trapeze artist. No guarantee each time that you won't lose your balance and fall. And like most artists I have had spotters. Several. My first had been in high school: Miss Emily. Then Rupert Lodge here at the University of Manitoba. And years later at the University of Alberta, Professor F. M. Salter. During the first two years of writing *Who Has Seen the Wind* he was there to catch me. I owe them all.

It was during those years with Salter that I accidentally made my greatest discovery. At some point I stopped typing and leaned back to remember – not to write. Unbidden, my father, who had died when I was seven, came back to me. I remembered his reciting "In Flanders Fields" – "The Flag" – "Mr. Dooley Says" – "When Father Rode the Goat." I also remember standing with him in front of the upstairs toilet. We called it "crossing streams" – of course Mother never knew about it.

Each spring the McLaughlin seven-passenger car would come down off the blocks. Mother would take me and my brothers out to the cemetery just south of town, where we would play tag, making sure we cleared the graves, not setting a foot down on the earth mound over mortal remains. On our second or third first spring Sunday visit, there was a gopher hole right in front of the gravestone that hadn't been there the fall before. I was outraged. The gopher popped up and squeaked. He had no damn right to trespass on my dad's grave! I looked up to my mother, saw the prairie wind had laid a long dark lock of her hair across the side of her face, where tears were streaming down her cheeks.

More and more often I found myself travelling back into my stored past to find someone I had loved or hated, dramatic incidents, sights, sounds, feelings, smells. I wrote them down in detail. It wasn't writing; it was finding. When I would touch base with Salter almost weekly I would give them to him to read. In a way it was an imposition, for I was not enrolled in his creative writing class. We often met in his backyard after he had put aside the lawn mower or the hoe – or in his living room or his office at the university. At the end of almost six months in one of our meetings he said, "Bill, this stuff you've been showing me is autobiographical chaos. You've got to start behaving. I've been going over all of it to see if there's any possible literary order suggested."

He pulled the great pile of papers across his desk. With Scotch tape tabs he had singled out page parts. "Let's consider these." We went through them all one by one. The first had been the time Ike Parsons and Jack Andrews and I had discovered the pigeon nest in the loft of an abandoned barn out on the prairie. One of the eggs had just hatched out. I took the baby chick home with me, cuddled it in a handkerchief on my bedside table. Three days later it was dead. Next came the time my mother let me have a fox terrier puppy I named Tom – her suggestion because she had always regretted she had not named one of her four sons Tom. He existed just two years till the day that Snelgrove's Bakery wagon rolled over him. Then there was the two-headed calf in Stinchcombe's Livery Stable and veterinary build-ing. I saw it the same day Mackenzie King visited our town and spoke to all the Haig School students. I ran home and shouted the exciting news to my mother and Grandma and Aunt Josie: "I've seen every-thing! The Prime Minister of Canada and a two-headed calf!" Next came the day of my father's funeral in our living room with the open casket in front of our fireplace. There was the birth of my youngest brother, Dickie, when I was four. The death of my grandmother.

Salter shoved the papers aside. "Do you notice anything promis-ing in the way of a novel?"

"I don't know."

"Consider. First there's the just-born baby pigeon . . . then its death. Then there's the puppy, then he dies. Your father's funeral, the two-headed calf, your brother's birth, your grandmother's death. Get it?"

"No."

"Birth, then death, then birth, then death?"

"I don't know."

"It's a clear pattern. Could suggest a possible novel."

"Still don't get it. No plot."

"Forget plot. Think symphony."

"Whaaat?!"

"Alternating high and low notes."

"Sheeyit! I was born tone-deaf!"

"There are notes of vulgarity too. Look Bill, all art is one and indivisible." Whatever that meant. "Take a run at it."

I did. The result five years later was my first published novel: *Who Has Seen the Wind*. How I owe that man and the others – but especially him. In time I came to understand what he meant when he said, "All art is one and indivisible." He persuaded me to forget law study and become a teacher. After I got my certificate I taught officially as a high school principal for only two years. But ever since then I have helped writing protégés as a teacher and as an artist in residence in five different universities and at the Banff School of Fine Arts. I had no choice – I had to discharge my gratitude debt to Miss Emily and Lodge and Salter. It had been one hell of a creative breakthrough Salter had given me. Many of us in what Margaret Laurence referred to as "the tribe" have been helping first writers. Is any experience more satisfying than seeing their success?

Death and solitude justify art, which draws human aliens together in the mortal family, uniting them against the heart of darkness. Humans must comfort each other, defend each other against the terror of being human. Thus the dictum of Conrad (another existentialist), "We exist only in so far as we hang together – woe to the stragglers." Humans must comfort one another, defend each other against the terror of being human. There is a civilized accountability to others. The coyote, the jackrabbit, the badger, the killdeer, the weasel, the undertaker beetle, do not have that accountability. As a child I never did run across an artistic gopher or weasel or badger – though I'm not so certain about dragonflies or meadow larks. Coyotes and ants are quite political. The wolf is very much aware of territorial imperative.

The novelist Wallace Stegner, who was a prairie boy till he was fourteen in Eastend, Saskatchewan, has said in his book *Wolf Willow* that the prairie creates poets. I agree – all that land and all that sky do make poets. Prairie certainly teaches early that to be human means to be conscious of self – and separation from the rest of the living whole. "Human" therefore equals "lonely." Stegner used the word, poet, in the sense of its Greek origin – "maker." All artists make or create and the result is an important ingredient in the recipe for culture, for those bridges and patterns which connect us, which create human "solidarity." Humans are the only animals who make poems, plays, novels; the only animals who paint, dance, sing, sculpt, compose. Artists, philosophers, historians know that man is a finite, warm sack of vulnerability. And because of this knowledge they do have an unfair advantage over politicians – generals – and quarterbacks – and CEOs. Art is the only thing that man does for its own sake, that does not involve an adversary relationship. There are no winners over losers, no victors over vanquished, no toreador over bull. Readers are creative partners. As they read they have explosions of recognition from their own experience – somebody they have loved or hated, sensuous fragments, insights. Instead of relying entirely on what is written, they contribute from their own unique past, thereby making the fictional illusion all the more vivid and meaningful. Creative partners to artists, who look and wonder at a painting or a play or a ballet, who listen to a symphony – or even an opera – do not take anything from the artist. The book is not taken from the author. Both partner and artist win – through shared pity and terror, compassion and empathy, laughter and tears.

The writer explores and reveals bridges and patterns to the human community. They are fragile and they can be destroyed. They are only man-made. They are not divine, or absolute; they are life patterns, which grow like life and which change in a living manner. Man has grown them out of his generation after generation flow to defeat the heart of darkness. Exploring these patterns and bridges is of particular importance to our young. Our vulnerable young.

Many years ago Socrates said that the unexamined life was not worth living. Now, there's an old prairie expression that says much

the same thing: "Don't you eat that there stuff, Elmer. It's bull shit."
But humans do not live by reason and common sense alone – neither
the simply intellectual life nor the purely utilitarian life is the whole
answer. We must have *artistic* life as well. Over a hundred and seventy
years ago, Shelley wrote, "We have more moral, political, and historical wisdom than we know how to reduce into practice. There is no
want of knowledge respecting what is wise and best in morals, government, and political economy. We want the poetry of life. Poets are
the unacknowledged legislators of the world."

Shelley's warning – that our utilitarian culture has eaten more
than it can digest – is even more relevant today. Which means that
our culture is in even more need of the shared gift of the writer, the
"poetry of life."

OTHER TITLES FROM
DOUGLAS GIBSON BOOKS

PUBLISHED BY MCCLELLAND & STEWART INC.

THE CANADA TRIP *by* Charles Gordon
Author of *At the Cottage* Charles Gordon and his wife took the family car from
Ottawa to St. John's to Victoria and back. They are still married. The book is
a delight that will set readers planning their own trip.

Travel/Humour, 6 × 9, 364 pages, 22 maps, hardcover

TEN LOST YEARS: Memories of Canadians Who Survived the Depression *by*
Barry Broadfoot
Filled with unforgettable true stories, this uplifting classic of oral history, first
published in 1973, is "a moving chronicle of human tragedy and moral triumph
during the hardest of times." *Time*

Non-fiction, 5⅞ × 9, 442 pages, 24 pages of photographs, trade paperback

WHO HAS SEEN THE WIND *by* W.O. Mitchell *illustrated by* William Kurelek
For the first time since 1947, this well-loved Canadian classic of childhood on
the prairies is presented in its full, unexpurgated edition, and is "gorgeously illustrated." *Calgary Herald*

Fiction, 8½ × 10, 320 pages, numerous colour and black-and-white
illustrations, hardcover

THE BLACK BONSPIEL OF WILLIE MACCRIMMON *by* W.O. Mitchell
illustrated by Wesley W. Bates
A devil of a good tale about curling – W.O. Mitchell's most successful comic play
now appears as a story, fully illustrated, for the first time, and it is "a true Canadian
classic." *Western Report*

Fiction, 4⅝ × 7½, 144 pages with 10 wood engravings, hardcover

ACCORDING TO JAKE AND THE KID: A Collection of New Stories *by*
W.O. Mitchell
"This one's classic Mitchell. Humorous, gentle, wistful, it's 16 new short stories
about life through the eyes of Jake, a farmhand, and the kid, whose mom owns
the farm." *Saskatoon Star-Phoenix*

Fiction, 5 × 7¾, 280 pages, trade paperback

ROSES ARE DIFFICULT HERE *by* W.O. Mitchell
"Mitchell's newest novel is a classic, capturing the richness of the small town,
and delving into moments that really count in the lives of its people . . ."
Windsor Star   *Fiction, 6 × 9, 328 pages, hardcover*